i

THE COLLAPSE

Brian Pearman

Table of Contents

Chapter 1 - The Three

The lapping of waves upon the rocky shore filled the ears of the two adventurers. To their backs spread the endless expanse of the Atlantic Ocean. Their front faced an abyssal blackness of a newly formed cave. This was their destination on that cold, autumn night.

Douglas was a skilled rock climber and explored caves like this one in his free time. The headlamp atop his head had seen many, wonderful things in his various explorations. The ropes and climbing tools hanging off his belt had seen their share of rock faces and long drops.

His girlfriend, Susan, was not so adventurous. She fumbled with her head lamp in a frustrated frenzy. As much as she loved the man kneeling down in front of her, she did not want to come on this short journey outside of their hometown. "How do you turn this damn thing on, Dougie?"

Douglas used the light on his head to check out the formations of the rock before him. Marks crisscrossed the rock and soil all around the tunnel-like cave. It was unlike anything he had seen before with any naturally made cave. It looked as if it had been dug out.

"You listening to me?" Susan said.

Douglas stood back up and said, "Yeah, sorry hun," before he reached up to his girlfriend's head and flicked on the headlamp.

"Why're we out here anyways? It's freezing," said Susan, wrapping her hands around her chest.

"We've walked out here how many times over the last few years," said Douglas, "And have you ever seen this cave?"

Susan shrugged, "Maybe we just missed it."

Douglas shook his head and said, "I don't think so. Look at the size of it. I can barely touch the top."

He turned back into the mouth of the cave. He had no idea how far into the earth it descended, but he was ready to find out. He motioned for Susan to follow him and said, "Let's see how deep this thing goes."

"Can't we come back during the day?" Susan said.

Douglas replied, "Wouldn't matter. Walk around one corner or go far enough and there's no light anyways. I want to blog about this before anyone else can. That reminds me, you got the camera?"

Susan tapped on a camera hanging around her neck and gave

him the thumbs up. She then followed him into the darkness that awaited them.

The tunnel around the couple was smooth and damp. It twisted at a slight, downward angle, taking them ever deeper. Every so often, Susan would take a photograph of the walls, exposed roots or markings. The flash of the camera gave them a split second of complete illumination before being consumed by darkness again.

After several minutes of careful progress, the couple found a fork in the tunnel. Douglas said, "What is this place?"

"I dunno, but it's creepy. Can we please go back?" complained Susan.

Douglas flopped his arms at his side and said, "C'mon, we just got here. Where's your sense of adven-"

He was cut off by a scraping sound deep into the tunnel. It sounded like multiple knives cutting into the rock. Whatever it was, it sounded like it was coming closer.

"What's that sound?" asked Douglas, squinting to see anything with his headlamp.

Susan was slowly backing up as her fight or flight instincts started to take hold of her senses. She said, "D-Dougie, I want t-to go home."

"Yeah, let's get out of here. Might be a bear or something," said Douglas.

Behind him appeared two blue orbs. The azure light cast an eerie glow on the couple.

Douglas turned upon noticing the blue glow, but before he could get the orbs into the light of his headlamp, they were gone. The scraping sound echoed as whatever it was descended down the right-most path.

"What was that light?" Douglas asked.

Susan was already hiking towards the entrance and said, without turning, "Don't know, don't care. I'm gettin' outta here."

Her walk turned into a jog as she left her boyfriend behind. She had apparently forgotten how slippery the ground was closer to the cavern's mouth because her shoe skidded forward. She fell on her back. The tumble sent her headlamp off her head and into the darkness. She heard glass break as her camera hit the hard rock.

Susan said, "Dammit all. Dougie, I need your light. I lost my head thingy and can't see anything."

Her answer was the faint sound of the ocean's lapping waves beyond the cave.

"D-Dougie?"

As the night gobbled up her words, Susan began to panic. She could barely see the twinkling stars in the night sky above her. Seeing the way out made her find her feet and she began sprinting. She slipped but did not fall again.

As she met the salty, open air, she stopped to take a breath. She looked back down into the cave and shouted, "Douglas!"

Her boyfriend's name reverberated down into the pitch, but the words would not be answered by their intended receiver. Instead

4

she seen the blue orbs flash down below.

"Stay back!" Susan shouted, fumbling with her pack, "I have pepper spray!"

The blue orbs began hovering towards her. Slowly at first, but speeding up the closer they got to the frightened woman.

Susan froze as the orbs flashed from blue to red for the smallest of moments. The only thing she could get her body to do in response was press the shutter button on her camera. Its lens was broken from her fall, but she thought that the flash might give her an idea of what was chasing her. The bright flash of the bulb gave her a look at what was attached to those odd, illuminated balls.

She would have no time to ponder on it, however, as she soon met the same fate that fell upon her boyfriend.

As the tide of the ocean before the cave rose, so did the onslaught of the things that dwelled under rock and foundation. Humanity was not ready for the threat that came from below. The world would bleed as civilization collapsed.

Many miles away from the East Coast, in the Ozarks of northern Arkansas, three individuals were about to learn of this horror. It was coming like a tidal wave, and they were far from their home of Arborsville, Illinois.

Mundane lives led to boredom and resulted in their ambitious vacation. They wanted to clear their heads before continuing down life's path. The peacefulness of the outdoors refreshed their internal clocks and gave them pause before they would return home.

The adventurers had been friends for most of their adult lives. Jon Kilroy and Eve Parker were longtime sweethearts and were engaged, planning on a spring wedding the following year. They had been together ever since Eve had moved to Arborsville when she was twenty years old. Here, during their journey, they had aged ten years and were still just as passionate as they had always been.

Jon had been friends with Logan Foster, the third member of their troop, since he was a child. Because of their friendship, Logan had grown to see Eve as something of a sister.

Trails crisscrossed large expanses of forest and hills. The trees had mostly lost their leaves, but at some vantage points the travelers could see red and yellow hills that expanded out into the distance. No trail was wrong, as long as they headed north.

They were walking in a line up and down the twisting trails. Jon led them, always ready to be first, and Logan followed from behind. After a few hours they decided to stop and take a break, as they would not make it to their next campsite until nightfall. They unpacked foodstuffs out of their backpacks to make sandwiches and sat upon a fallen tree on the side of the overgrown trail.

"I love it out here," said Jon, "No stress, no worryin' about what's goin' on back home."

"I'm just glad there's no bugs," said Eve with a shiver.

"Don't be a wuss," said Jon with a smirk.

"Jerk," Eve said with a backhand onto his shoulder. She smiled all the same.

Logan was sitting apart from the couple. He had been silent for this first leg of their adventure, which his friends were accustomed to. He spoke little but observed much. They had noticed he would look longingly on the horizon, like he was looking for an answer to a silent question.

"What about you, man?" said Jon between biting down on his turkey and cheese sandwich, "Why'd you really wanna come with us?"

Logan replied while keeping his eyes on the cloudless sky, "I suppose I'm running from something."

"What're you running from?" asked Eve.

Logan looked at her. He noticed her soft, beautiful face but did not see her as a romantic attraction. Instead he seen a confidant. A friend. A friend he could not quite find the words as to what had been bothering him.

"Maybe when we get back I'll tell you," said Logan, returning to his own sandwich.

Jon rolled his eyes and said, "Always with the secrets."

Logan, wanting to shift the spotlight to anything else but himself, said, "So, Jon, what are you going to do now that you've left the prison?"

"I have a few interviews when we get back. I may work in

security somewhere else since I have a few years experience under my belt," said Jon, "You ever decide to go back to college? You're only a semester away aren't ya?"

Logan shook his head, "Yeah, but I don't think I'll go back."

"Ugh. Can we not talk about work while we're out here?" groaned Eve, "I gotta work three twelves in a row at the hospital when we get back home."

"I guess that officially makes Eve the breadwinner," joked Logan with a forced, weak smile.

Jon looked sidelong at Logan and said, "Hey, just right now. I'll get a job before our wedding."

"You better," said Eve with a mocking look of defiance, "Or I'll find someone who does have a job."

"Oh, stop," said Jon with a laugh.

They finished their quick lunch and continued onwards. Their hike was initially planned to last a little over two weeks. They would wade through the Ozarks of Missouri before crossing into Illinois' Shawnee National Forest. They were off the grid save for when they needed supplies or launder clothes.

After hiking for a few more hours they came to a bend in the trail. What they found in their path shocked the peaceful setting. It was a dead body, mangled and barely recognizable as human. Freshly killed, organs were strewn around what was left of the body. The putrid smell of death filled the three's senses.

"What the..." said Jon, unable to take his eyes off the

8

grotesque scene.

Eve's eyes were wide and she felt like she was going to throw up. Even with all of the accidents and disfigurements she had seen while being a registered nurse at the hospital, she had never seen anything like this. "What could have done this?"

"A bear?" said Jon, covering his nose.

"Doubtful," said Logan, "Bears are rare out here and attacks are even rarer. The slashes in his torso were from something larger."

"Either way, this is messed up," said Jon, "Anyone have any service?"

Eve already had her smartphone out to call 911, but she had no service. Neither did Jon or Logan, who checked theirs as well.

Eve said, "We have to do something."

"Our campsite is closer than any town, we'll have to wait until then to report it," said Logan.

"We should get goin' then. Wanna make sure we get there before nightfall," said Jon.

They walked around the body, giving it a wide berth as if it would jump up and grab them. The three kept silent as they walked, not knowing exactly what to say. It was the first time for any of them seeing a human body in such a state. Not knowing who it was softened the blow, but it affected them anyhow.

As the sun was about to lay down into the hilly horizon, they seen a crooked sign labelled CAMP DICKSON 1 MILE. They were

9

tired from walking so briskly after they found the body, hoping to find some kind of closure after telling someone about it. They continued onwards as the light began to fade. Half-leaved trees stretched up around them, like hands clawing towards the sky.

They eventually seen another sign before it was too dark to read. WELCOME TO CAMP DICKSON. Beyond this sign, posted on a tree, the forest opened up into a clearing with multiple campsites. Various tents of different sizes sat at the different sites, which numbered about ten. The dirt trail they were walking on became gravel as they walked into the campground. On the other side of the clearing there was a gravel road leading from a main road with a small wooden building on it. It was an office and the only permanent structure at Camp Dickson. A beat up, red jeep was parked outside of the office.

Most sites had a fire built already. Country music reverberated around the campground as Jon, Eve and Logan walked down the gravel trail towards the office. Some people were talking quietly and shadowy figures were seen passing between them and their campfires. Others were seen sitting in chairs around the fires, only visible due to the light of the flames dancing in their faces.

They entered the small, rustic office building. It was as small inside as it looked outside. Along the walls and on small shelves were camping tools and memorabilia for sale. Matches, lighters, pocket knives, coozies and the such. There was a single counter, lit by an old, dull desk lamp. A person sat behind it.

It was a woman in her mid-forties working on a cross-word puzzle. Her jowls moved into a frown as she noticed the group walk in. She sat her puzzle book down, pushed her reading glasses up and brought out a sign-in sheet from under the counter. On the wall behind her was an old Winchester Model 12 pump action shotgun, with a wood stock and fore-end.

"Welcome to Camp Dickson," she said monotonally for a thousandth time, "Names?"

Jon approached the counter and said, "My name is Jon Kilroy. This is Eve and Logan. We-"

"Ok, sign in," she grumbled as she spun the sign-in sheet towards them on the counter.

"Actually, there's something we need to tell you about," said Jon, "We found a dead body on the trail, 'bout fifteen to twenty miles south of here."

The woman showed no emotion as she said, "Oh?"

Jon said, "Yeah, looked like a bear attack."

"Ain't no bears 'round here. If this is sum kinda joke-"

"This is no joke, I assure you," said Logan, stepping forward, "Something out there killed a full grown man. We would have called the police but we didn't have service."

The woman took the three friends in, darting her gaze from over her reading glasses at each of them before saying, "Alright, I'll report it. You're at number seven. Check out's by noon t'morrow."

"Let us know if you need any more information," said Jon,

not convinced she believed them.

They exited the office and Logan said, "We reported it, that's all we can do."

"I don't feel right about it, though," said Jon, "I should have just asked to use the phone."

"Let's just try to forget it," said Eve, putting her hand on Jon's shoulder, "Like Logan said, we told someone and it's out of our hands."

"She said site seven?" said Jon, "Just wanna go to sleep."

"I think we all could use some rest and forget about what we seen," said Logan.

They hastily set up camp as the night afforded them little to no light. The music from another site had subsided, yet Logan lay awake. He could see their campfire casting dancing shadows on the side of his tent. They had hiked six hours that day and he was exhausted from it, but sleep evaded him.

Then he seen the fire cast another shadow on his tent. It was something on all fours, but it was hard to tell as the flames of the campfire kept the shadows moving in odd directions. Logan kept still, controlling his breath as he tried to listen, but no sound could be heard. Then he seen another figure pass, then another. A total of ten figures passed by the fire until there was nothing but normal shadows.

The silence was broken as a woman's scream shattered the

night. This was followed by an animalistic howl that sounded both high and low pitched at the same time. The air was filled with shouting, screams and the mysterious baying.

Logan threw on some jeans and a hoodie and slowly unzipped enough of his tent flap to poke his head out. In the tent next to him he seen Jon had done the same. Beyond their site, he could only see darkness and some campfires still smoldering. Every now and then he would see red lights blink instantly than go away.

"The fuck is going on?" Jon whispered, his voice barely carrying through the commotion.

"Don't know," whispered Logan back to him, "I think we're under attack."

"From who?"

"No idea, but we should get out of here."

"Roger that," said Jon, and his head disappeared back into the tent.

Logan turned back as well and got his pack ready, leaving his sleeping bag and pad. He had a pocket knife that he readied just in case. He slowly opened his tent up and stepped out, quickly followed by Jon and Eve from their tent. There were less screams but they were still echoing from further away as people tried to run.

"Get out of the light," said Logan, motioning for them to duck into the darkness behind their tents.

The three ducked down and Logan whispered, "Our best hope is to get to the office and bunker down there. Maybe the camp

13

curator is still there with the jeep."

"Jon, I'm scared," said Eve, her voice trembling.

"It'll be ok," said Jon, wrapping his arm around his fiancé, "Stay close to me."

"Keep low and quiet, stick to the shadows," said Logan, who had already plotted a path back to the check-in office in his head.

They snuck through the dark behind tents and around trees towards the building. The dull light from the desk lamp shown through the only window, showing them their goal. Every now and then one of them would stumble or trip in the darkness as they could not see.

After a few minutes of carefully navigating the maze of tents, they had made their way to the office, where the door was wide open. They could faintly see a blood trail leading into the building. At this point the screams were barely auditory as they were far into the woods.

Jon peeked around the corner of the doorway and seen the camp curator propped up against the counter. Scratches ran up from her legs to her torso, and she was coughing blood up from a punctured lung. The three dashed in and quickly closed the door, locking it behind them. Logan moved the desk lamp down onto the floor so they could still somewhat see but it would not shine through the window.

"What the hell is going on?" Jon asked the dying woman in a low voice.

"I... those things," she managed to painfully say.

"Shh, don't talk, save your strength," said Eve, who began checking her wounds.

"What things?" asked Logan.

"They're....monsters," said the woman, who passed out right after.

"We have to get her to a hospital," said Eve, "She'll die of blood loss."

"We can't leave," said Logan.

"What? But she'll die," said Eve quickly, "She's bleeding out."

"If we try to take her out there, there is a high probability that we'll face the same fate. We'd be defenseless in the dark."

Eve flashed her eyes at Jon and said, "Jon, tell him we have to get her help."

Jon lowered his eyes and said, "He's right, babe, I'm sorry. I won't risk our lives, no matter how much I want to help her."

Eve looked incredulous but decided to do what she could to help the woman. She pulled a first aid kit from behind the counter and started bandaging some of the more lethal wounds. She knew it was futile as the woman's lung was punctured and was filling with fluid, but she had to do something.

As she went to work binding the curator's wounds, Logan picked up the phone that was on the desk. He held the receiver at his ear and heard nothing. No ring tone, no busy signal, nothing.

Jon found the jeep's keys on the counter and pocketed them, saying, "We'll stay here tonight, but if we have to go at least we can use the jeep."

"Now you're going to steal her jeep?" said Eve, feeling lost.

"I'm not stealing it, I'm just borrowing it," said Jon.

"It's probably impossible, but we should try to get some sleep," said Logan, "One of us should keep watch for a few hours then switch off. I'll take the first shift."

Although they needed the sleep, they would barely find any this night. The screams finally subsided, but the three were anxious that whatever attacked the campground would come back. Jon finally got irritated of trying to sleep and told Logan he'll take up the watch, equipping himself with the pump shotgun that was on the wall. He found five shells in the counter and loaded them into it, before sitting behind the counter. Logan laid down on the hardwood floor, propping his head up with his pack. He would lay there sleepless until morning. Eve at least was able to get a few hours of restless sleep.

Jon got everyone up once the sun had risen and they opened the door to the office. What laid before them was a scene of mass carnage. Tents were ripped apart and bodies were everywhere. Men, women and children laid dead around the campground. Some bodies were intact, but most had limbs ripped off. Their blood was everywhere. Coolers holding food and beer were thrown around, their contents scattered along the ground.

The three stood there for what felt like ages before Logan finally spoke up, "This is not good."

"This is...I don't know what the hell this is," said Jon.

"Jon, I want to go home," said Eve.

"Yeah, we should head home," Logan agreed.

They got to the jeep and threw their packs in the back hatch. Jon sat behind the wheel and started the engine. Eve got into the passenger side and Logan jumped in the back seat. Jon turned on the FM radio and started switching through stations, most of which was just static or silence. Then one station he switched it to had a voice.

"-truly unprecedented. All across the United States, there are reports of attacks from large, humanoid creatures. The military is currently mobilizing across the country in response to this unknown threat. Everyone should remain in your homes and do not go out at night. I repeat, do not go out at night."

"We're under attack?" said Jon, thinking out loud.

"So this is going on everywhere..." said Logan, his voice trailing off as he got lost in thought.

"We can get back in five hours or a little less if I haul ass," said Jon.

And they left Camp Dickson. The trip that was supposed to be peaceful and meant to clear their heads was over. Rather than feeling hopeful and a part of nature, they felt hollow. They just wanted to get home and be with their families, but their journey back would prove more difficult than they could imagine.

Chapter 2 - Poplar Bluff

The three were able to drive to the Missouri border well within an hour. They kept checking their cell phones to call home, but service never came back. News updates on the radio kept them up to date as to what was going on, but each broadcast they heard took longer and longer, and each was more bleak.

According to what they had heard on the radio, the wave of these mysterious creatures started on the east coast of the U.S. with other countries all across the world starting to report their presence as well. Washington, D.C., Boston, Philadelphia and New York had already fallen, followed by Atlanta. The latest major city they heard that was attacked was Indianapolis, which was a little too close for comfort to Illinois. Some areas to the west had reported seeing the creatures but no large-scale attacks had happened yet.

Although the military was deployed quickly, they were defeated in every engagement. A few bases and forts held out but they were eventually attacked en masse. The last reported hold out was Fort Bragg in North Carolina, where the Army Airborne and Special Forces are based. Their fate was unknown as the news reports stopped not long after the three were deep into the Missouri Ozarks.

Eve gave up on the radio for the time being and said, "I still don't believe this is real."

Jon, driving as fast as he could up and down the winding, hilly roads, said, "I just hope we get a win in. I find it pretty damn hard to believe that our armed forces are defeated that easily."

"Blitzkrieg," said Logan while he watched trees zip by them through the window.

"Eh?" said Jon.

"Lightning fast attack. Doesn't matter how prepared you are if you're defeated before you can fight."

"Well that's bleak," said Eve.

"The truth usually is," said Logan.

"Gonna need to stop for fuel soon. We didn't have much to begin with," said Jon.

"Poplar Bluff isn't far," said Logan.

"We should decide which way to go back home from there. Could head towards St. Louis and cross the Mississippi river there, or head to Sikeston and go north," said Jon.

"Normally St. Louis would be quicker," said Logan, "But with what's going on, the city might be congested."

"So we head east, then," said Jon.

"Do I get a say in this?" Eve broke in.

Jon said, "You know a faster way?"

"My parents are in Chesterfield. I want to make sure they're ok."

Jon shook his head, "That's too out of the way. I'm sure they're fine."

"Well, I'm sorry my family doesn't live in Arborsville like you two. I have just as much right to make sure my family is ok as you," said Eve, furrowing her brow at Jon.

"It wouldn't take long," said Logan, "She deserves to see them."

"Thanks, Logan," said Eve, who then turned to her fiancé, "So?"

"G'dammit," said Jon, "Fine. Fine. We'll go to Chesterfield, but we ain't stayin'. Your mom and dad can come with us if they want."

The small, windy road intersected Highway 142, which ran north to south. There were few vehicles driving up and down the highway, but the ones that were there drove well over the speed limit. Others had heard the radio broadcasts and seen the news reports on T.V.

As they turned onto the highway, Jon said, "Feels odd

actually seeing other people."

"Hopefully they're going somewhere safe," said Eve, watching a car speed past them.

A road sign said POPLAR BLUFF 8 MILES, which prompted Jon to drive faster. More and more vehicles appeared on the highway, driving in either direction. Some were heading towards St. Louis for safety. Those from the city were driving away from it with all haste.

The area was less forested and hilly, instead consisting of large farmlands. Small businesses ran along the road every once in a while the closer they drove to their destination. They kept their eyes out for gas stations and there were a few. However, the lines of motor vehicles into each of them were so long, the three decided to take their chances in Poplar Bluff proper. One gas station had even posted a sign saying they were out of fuel.

Before long they seen the outskirts of the city. There were wide buildings that served as depots for semi-trucks and public storage areas on each side of the highway. Traffic was still steady in the morning hours, but otherwise it would appear nothing was out of the ordinary.

All three occupants of the jeep were tired. Eve was able to get some sleep back at the campground, but not much. She hoped they could get some rest at her parents' house before continuing on home. Jon drove like a man possessed, but even his unerring focus was hazy due to exhaustion.

Past the industrial park was an empty waterpark. All three looked at it as a place they would like to go to. Then all three realized it may be some time before they could, if ever again.

Further on the highway they had arrived at a commercial area. The first place they seen, as expected at almost anywhere, was a McDonald's. It reminded them of how hungry they were on top of being dead dog tired. Jon looked in the parking lot only to see it was empty and there did not appear to be any employees.

Around it were a couple more gas stations. On the same four-way intersection as the fast food restaurant was a large, chain grocery store called Field Foods and a bank. To the east of the store was more farmland. Jon pulled off the side of the road next to the general store to address the others.

"We should probably stop there to get some supplies," he said, "We're not far from St. Louis, but better safe than sorry."

"Agreed," said Logan, "But judging by the lack of cars in the parking lot, I doubt there is anyone working."

"I see someone in there," said Eve, squinting towards the windowed entrance of the building.

"Ok, let's get some fuel then we'll try it," said Jon.

He pulled back into the road and drove towards one of the gas stations that was not quite as busy as the others. He pulled into a line of other vehicles, in which he was the fourth. More vehicles pulled in behind them almost immediately. There appeared to be one person inside behind the counter, hastily ringing up everyone who

23

was buying fuel and other items.

Then they heard something in the distance. A helicopter.

"That a 'copter?" said Jon, starting to look around.

They looked in the direction they heard the rotor blades. Sure enough, a squadron of three military helicopters were flying towards them. The utility helicopters had two guns sticking out of each side panel.

"Venoms," said Logan.

"What?" said Jon, "They look like Black Hawks."

"No, they're Venoms. Black Hawks are used by the Army. You can see Marine Corps markings on the side of those," said Logan.

"I wonder where they're going?" asked Eve aloud.

"To some engagement somewhere, or perhaps reconnaissance. They may be seeing if those things have made it this far west," said Logan.

"Well I hope they kick ass, wherever they're goin'," said Jon as he pulled up to the third position in line.

The utility helicopters passed above them and continued on their way. They flew out of view after passing above the Field Foods store, but while they were still in ear shot, the three heard something else. It sounded much like the blades of the helicopters, but more quickly paced.

"More?" asked Jon, looking around.

"Jon, get us the hell out of here," said Logan, his face turning grim.

"Why, what is it, Logan?" asked Eve, who was starting to get scared.

"They're firing at something, and it's not far away."

"Well, what the fuck," said Jon, exasperated, "We can't drive very far. We're almost on E as it is."

"Go to the grocery store," said Logan, "Maybe we can hide there until-"

He was cut off from a car ramming them in the driver side. While they were talking, they failed to see the chaos that was beginning to stir around them. People were driving the wrong way down the road, and others were breaking into vehicles to find a way to run from what was coming.

Their jeep flipped onto its side, sending two passengers out of their seats. Everything inside the jeep scattered everywhere, hitting them and the windows. Jon was the only one not to lose his seat and he hung sideways from his seatbelt. Blood started forming on the side of his face where his head hit the window.

Logan groaned as he attempted to get to his feet. He was seeing double and blood fell into his vision from his eyebrow. He could hear Eve saying something, but it sounded like an echo.

Eve was miraculously unhurt. She managed to unhook Jon's seatbelt and the two of them crawled out of the busted windshield. Logan lost sight of them and for a moment thought he was being left there to die.

Until he seen Eve come back, saying something to him that he could not comprehend at the moment. She took him by the arm and pulled him over the front seat and through the broken windshield.

She put his arm around her shoulders to steady him and they leaned against the sideways front bumper of the jeep. Jon appeared from around the corner with the shotgun he took from the campground. He put his face inches from Logan's and spoke, but again, Logan could not understand what he was saying.

He seen Jon mouth "Fuck this," and his whole body was thrown over his friend's shoulder with a sudden, and powerful, jerk. With the blood running towards his head, and feeling lightheaded already, Logan soon passed out.

Jon was a strong man, but with adrenaline pumping into his veins, he barely noticed the dead weight of his friend on his shoulder. He and Eve were jogging alongside the opposite side of a ditch to the highway, as drivers were being wild in the road.

Ahead of them was their destination: Field Foods. Behind the building, the sound of gunfire grew louder. Then they caught the sounds they heard from the campground. The two-tone howl of whatever the things were that mauled their fellow campers.

With renewed vigor, they ran across the intersection they previously drove through. Cars, SUVs and pickup trucks sped past them, missing them by only a few feet on one occasion.

Once they made it to the large, paved parking area of the

grocery store, they seen one of the Venom helicopters fly low over it. One of its two engines was smoking. It seemed almost as if it would crash into the intersection, but the pilot pulled up and landed behind the three in the parking lot.

Out of the helicopter exited three marines and the pilot. They secured their arms and started running towards the same place Jon and Eve were focused on.

Once Jon arrived at the double glass doors of the building, he had to skid his feet to a halt, as the doors did not automatically open. He kicked it as Eve slammed her hand onto the window, shouting to let them in.

Others had the same idea and stopped their vehicles in the parking lot. Multiple people were now inbound to the store as Jon continued to kick the door.

A heavyset, squirrely-looking man with glasses walked up to the other side of the glass doors. He was wearing khakis and a long sleeved, button up shirt. A name tag pinned to his shirt named him as Oswald. Sweat had beaded on his balding head as he hit a latch and opened one of the doors.

Jon and Eve rushed in, still with Logan in tow. Behind them ran in the marines. They were followed by more people before the short man latched the door again.

He then went back to his task at hand, and rolled the security shutters down to block off the windowed entrance. Once he was finished, he turned around to a silent bunch of people. They all turned towards him, making his bald head sweat even more.

"Um," he said, "Welcome to Field Foods?"

Chapter 3: Cracks

Everyone but the marines moved to the back of the store, hiding behind shelves full of boxed and canned food products. The marines took up defensive positions amongst the checkout counters. The pilot kept his pistol at the ready while the other three marines trained their assault rifles on the gated entrance.

They could all hear thumping on the roof of the store as the invaders climbed around, seeking out their next targets. Everyone kept silent, mainly out of fear. It wasn't difficult for Logan as he was still unconscious.

After a few minutes, the assault the marines thought was coming never happened. The things outside had moved on and the occupants of Field Foods were safe for the moment.

The helicopter pilot, Lieutenant Joseph Ironson, approached

the civilians hiding amongst the long aisles of shelves. He unzipped his bomber jacket in relief and took his aviator sunglasses off. He said, "You can breathe easy for now, they're gone," he then looked at Logan's unconscious form, "Is he still with us?"

Eve, who had been cradling Logan's head in her lap, said, "Yeah, but he was wounded. I can treat him but I need bandages and stitches."

"Private Ritter has a first aid kit, I'll get it," said Ironson, who swiftly turned away to get the kit.

Oswald rubbed the sweat from his bald head with a handkerchief before standing and addressing the scared crowd, "It uh, seems we're safe for now. Help yourself to some uh, food in the store. I'll talk to the marines and see what they know."

"I'll join ya," said Jon, "I want to know what the hell is going on."

An elderly lady who was sitting next to her teenage granddaughter said, "I think we all deserve to know what is happening, boys."

The crowd began murmuring and Oswald said, "Uh, you're right. You're right. I'll ask them to uh, tell us all what we're dealing with. Right."

Private Ritter helped Eve patch Logan up, who had awoken. He had a hell of a headache and his eyebrow was swollen, but he'd be ok. Jon filled him in with what had happened since he passed out.

Oswald spoke to the marines and they agreed to tell everyone else what they were up against. The survivors were all gathered together in the break room of the store. Candles were lit as there were no windows. They cast a campfire-like glow upon the faces of the marines who were about to address everyone else.

Lieutenant Ironson, the highest ranking Marine of the squad, stood and began, "Yesterday, at oh-seven-hundred, there was a police report in Maine of attacks from unknown assailants. The first casualties found were the mangled remains of a well known hiker and his significant other.

"The attacks became more frequent over the course of the day, mainly from smaller towns. The national guard were deployed. No one knew what exactly the threat was until Manhattan fell."

He looked over at the other members of his squad, who all had grim expressions. He continued, "We are under attack from some kind of subterranean, humanoid species. They are faster than the fastest sprinter. Stronger than the strongest lifter. They can absorb a full magazine from an assault rifle. Some of the bigger ones can even take a shot from a .50 cal.

"They are ultra-intelligent and some reports say they can even speak to each other in their own tongue. So far the only way to kill one is a shot to the head, or complete decapitation."

"Bullshit," said a large, antsy man amongst the crowd.

"What part is bullshit, sir?" asked Ironson.

"You expect me to believe that we're under attack from,

31

what, mole people?"

Private Ritter stood up to his feet so quick it seemed like something might had bit him. He said, "Yeah, because that's exactly what we're fucking dealing with."

"Stand down, private," said Ironson. Ritter sneered at the civilian, but complied before the lieutenant spoke again, "I know it sounds farfetched, and I don't think I truly believed it myself until all armed forces in the states were called to fight. We fought them. We lost.

"We have been trying to radio HQ, but all military channels have gone silent."

Sergeant Dillian leaned towards Ironson and whispered, "You sure we should be telling them all this?"

Ironson whispered back, "No more secrets, Sergeant. The rules have changed."

The elderly lady said, "We're being judged. It's the apocalypse."

Her granddaughter elbowed her and said, "Shush, Grandma."

"Maybe it's aliens?" said someone else from the crowd.

Eve had taken Jon's hand. She believed in God, but never claimed to be overtly religious. After hearing what Ironson said, she might try to find a bible to read.

"Won't let anything happen to you," said Jon, looking deep into her eyes.

She remembered why she loved him after he said that.

She smiled at him as everyone began debating whether the invaders were mole people, demons or aliens. She looked around for Logan, who she seen leaning against the wall in a dark corner. He had his arms folded and a downcast gaze.

The couple got up and approached him. Eve said to him, "You ok, Logan?"

Unmoving, he said, "I am."

"A lot to take in, huh?" said Jon.

"Indeed," replied Logan, who appeared to be a million miles away.

"Are you sure you're alright?" said Eve, putting her hand on Logan's crossed arms.

He looked up at her and said, "You see the man there?" he pointed to a loudmouthed meathead-looking guy, "He's the one who said bullshit to Ironson. He may pose a problem. And the girl with the elderly lady. She is...promiscuous, so to speak. And at such a young age. I'd say she's sixteen or seventeen. I don't fully trust the marines, either, save for perhaps the pilot."

Jon raised an eyebrow and said, "How'd you figure all that out?"

"By watching, listening and reading body language."

Oswald's voice cut into their conversation, causing them to turn to the candle-lit area of the break room. He said, "Let's all take a moment to collected ourselves and uh, have something to eat, huh? P-plenty of food for everyone. We might b-be here a while."

"It's too dangerous to go outside," said Ironson, "Especially at night when they're out in force. Like the manager said, we might be here a while."

"Great," groaned Jon.

The days dragged on and soon turned into weeks. While cabin fever was setting in, Logan devoted himself to learning everything he could about the people they were stuck with. He couldn't bring himself to trust anyone else except for Jon and Eve.

Glenda, the elderly lady, became the cook, as she could do amazing things with few ingredients. Logan was right about her granddaughter, Tabby. She had propositioned him several times, only to be brushed off. She finally found a companion in Oswald, as they would disappear into his office during the late hours when Glenda was asleep.

Michael, the loudmouth, began spending time with the marines. He finally believed them about the invaders and kissed their asses to the point that they started making fun of him. Logan tried being cordial to the man, as he did with everyone else, but for whatever reason, Michael did not like him.

The marines stuck to themselves for the most part. They kept watch all day, every day and did not permit anyone to leave. They tried varying military, radio frequencies over the course of a couple weeks, but never heard anything from anyone. Cabin fever began taking them as well.

Logan asked Lieutenant Ironson how their helicopter was damaged. Apparently they had stumbled onto a roaming group of the invaders while flying at low altitude. There was a bigger one that managed to leap into the air and slash one of the engines. It seemed farfetched, even when Ironson called this particular creature a "Leaper," but Logan believed him.

There was a single mother and her child that Logan did not perceive as threats. Eve would play with the little boy to keep him distracted, but Logan knew it was to keep herself sane as well.

It was Christmas day, and Logan began to notice a decline in everyone's sanity. He tried to keep Jon calm, but their conversations usually ended in the larger man becoming agitated and wandering off to find something to break.

Logan noticed Eve was speaking less and less, while sleeping almost all day. He recognized it as a telltale sign of depression. Her normally jaunty demeanor had fallen to something else as she became less sociable.

He wanted to do something for them, anything, to bring their spirits up. It was partly to help himself too, as seeing his friends in such a state was bringing him down. So he began scrounging around the store and asking around.

He approached the single mother and her son first. The boy was playing with a toy plane, running around in circles as he had done every day they had been trapped in Field Foods. The mother was sitting on a fold-up chair with her legs crossed and her head in her hand.

"Hello Marissa," he said as he approached.

The mother nearly jumped out of her chair and blinked her eyes. She responded, "Oh! Sorry, was resting my eyes."

"Forgive me if I woke you."

"Nah, s'ok. What's up?"

"My friends, as with all of us, need a pick me up. Was wondering if you had any ideas?"

She brushed her unkempt hair out of her face and scrunched her face up. She said, "Uh, well, I've always found alcohol helps," before chuckling nervously.

Logan grinned so she didn't feel uncomfortable, then said, "You might be on to something. You happen to see any? Don't think I've seen any bottles."

She leaned in towards Logan and spoke quietly, "I think the manager, Oswald, is hording whatever booze there is."

"I see..."

Her son fell down onto the linoleum floor, making a smacking noise as he landed face first. His mother gave Logan a weary look as the boy began crying. She said, "If you happen to get your hands on any, let me know. I could use a drink. If you do, I'll give you my son's little game device. Maybe that'll make a good gift."

"You got it."

Logan thought about going to the produce aisle, which was full of rotten vegetables at this point, to ask Michael about gift ideas, but he passed it by. Partly because of the smell. Partly because he knew the conversation would end with Michael telling him to fuck off.

Past the produce aisle was a small section where liquor had once been sold. The shelves were empty. Logan looked closely at the shelves. He had to squint as the only light was whatever sunlight filtered in through the gated, front entrance. He seen a fine layer of dust around circular areas where there was hardly any dust. He deduced that the bottles had been removed not long after the survivors took up occupancy in the store.

He went to the back of the store and pulled out a flashlight. He flicked it on for light and knocked on the door that lead to Oswald's office. There was some muffled fumbling inside before the short, squirrelly man answered the door. His dress shirt was unbuttoned, giving way to his hairy gut.

Oswald pushed up his glasses and said, "Can I uh, help ya?"

"Merry Christmas, Oswald," said Logan, trying to be friendly.

"Oh, is it Christmas already?" said the manager while scratching his bald head, "I suppose it is. Merry Christmas to you, Logan."

"I'm looking for a gift for my friends and a birdy tells me you have some alcohol."

37

Oswald narrowed his eyes and looked Logan up and down before he responded, "Maybe I do, maybe I don't. What if I did?"

"If you did, then I'd like something for my friends."

"What do you have for trade?" said Oswald, folding his arms and propping the door open with his foot. Logan silently cursed how this normally twitchy man was suddenly a master negotiator.

"I... don't have anything, I'm afraid. Unless you're interested in my pocket knife?"

"Nope. Then I don't think I have any alcohol, sorry," said Oswald, "But if I did, I would take a pack of cigarettes for a bottle of rum."

Logan found himself befuddled, a feeling he wasn't used to. There was more to this man than a manager at an obscure grocery store. Logan had assumed he was a prude, but there he was, hiding alcohol, wanting cigarettes and spending time with an underage girl. Logan nodded and said, "I'll see what I can do."

Cigarettes...

Field Foods didn't sell them and the only people he had seen smoking were Marissa and one of the marines. It had been weeks since they had lit one up, though. He hung his head in defeat, his quest finished in failure.

As he began making his way to the break room, where he, Jon and Eve had taken occupancy, he heard footsteps behind him. The smallest of noises echoed loudly in the dank, smelly store, and Logan had been using this fact to his advantage to keep tabs on people.

He turned and raised the flashlight towards the noise. The beam cut like a laser through the dust and darkness. The footsteps stopped on the other side of a shelving unit.

"C'mon out. I've already heard you," Logan said.

A figure walked out from behind the shelves and into the circular light. It was Lieutenant Ironson. His years of military service were evident on his stony face as he looked at Logan, unflinching from the light.

"At ease, soldier," said Ironson. Logan couldn't tell if he was joking or serious as the man didn't show emotion.

Logan lowered the flashlight and said, "What brings you to the back of the store?"

"Just going for a walk, keep my mind focused. Needed time away from the squad, too."

"Trouble in paradise?"

Ironson looked in the direction of the entrance and said, "Suppose you could say that. Never thought this is how I'd be spending Christmas."

"Nor I. Everyone seems on edge," said Logan as he leaned against an endcap of toilet paper.

Ironson looked back over to Logan and seemed to stare right through him. He said, "They should be. We can't stay here forever and we can't leave, either. It's too dangerous."

Logan didn't respond. Ironson's words rang true with what he had been thinking already. Logan had been keeping tabs on their supplies and average usage. When they first arrived, there was plenty of food to go around for everyone. After almost two months, the produce and meats had expired that they weren't able to eat or preserve. The boxed and can goods that were left wouldn't last another month and their water supply was dwindling.

"How're you and your friends doing?" asked Ironson, "Haven't seen the girl very much."

"They're feeling the effects of being stuck, like everyone else," said Logan, "I wanted to do something for them for Christmas, but it seems I've failed."

"What were you thinking?"

"All I need is a pack of cigarettes," Logan said with a frustrated shrug.

"Never took you for a smoker."

"Not for me."

Ironson approached Logan and grinned, creasing his already creased face even more. He reached into his bomber jacket and pulled something out. He handed it to Logan, who shined the light on it.

It was an opened pack of cigarettes.

"Was keeping them for a special occasion, but sounds like you could use them more. Merry Christmas, Logan."

Logan took the pack and checked inside. There were only a few cigarettes left, but it might be enough. Logan said, "Thank you,

Lieutenant. And Merry Christmas to you."

The pilot walked off and Logan immediately revisited Oswald. He was able to negotiate a pint of rum in exchange for the cigarettes. Oswald was more surprised than charitable in the exchange and immediately lit up as soon as Logan gave him the pack.

Logan first went back to Marissa and gave her a glass of rum. She gave Logan the electronic game as promised, without her child knowing and wished him happy holidays.

Equipped with a couple glasses, most of a pint of rum and a little video game device, Logan went back to the break room in high spirits. As he approached the door he heard muffled yelling from within. He thought about waiting, but he had grown accustomed to the arguments between his engaged friends.

He opened the door to the room that was lit with a lantern. Jon and Eve were in each others' faces with heated looks. As Logan entered they turned to him in unison and went silent.

"Tell him I can't help how I feel," Eve blurted out.

"No, tell her we need to leave. This place is fucked," said Jon, gesturing wildly with his muscled arms.

"I want to see my parents more than anything, but we wouldn't last a second out there," said Eve.

"Like I said, I'd protect you. I still have that shotgun."

"Will you both just stop," said Logan in a commanding tone, which made both Jon and Eve shut up, "It's Christmas and we're going to make the best of it."

He approached Eve and handed her the game. She took it and powered it on. It chirped in it's simple electronic noises as she stared at it.

She was still heated but Logan seen her face lift a bit as she said, "I had one of these when I was a kid. Thanks, Logan."

Logan looked at Jon and held up the rum and glasses. He said, "How about a drink?"

Jon's chest stopped heaving and he said, "Sure."

As they shared the drink and forced themselves to gulp down the warm liquor, Logan said, "I know things aren't easy right now, but we need to stick together. We'll eventually have to leave this place, and it might be sooner than we think."

Eve had sat on a bench and kept her attention on the game, which was a crude racing game. She failed over and over, saying, "Shit," each time.

Logan poured himself and Jon another drink. He said, "Care to partake?" to Eve, shaking the bottle in the air.

There was an electronic crashing noise from the game and she said, "You made me wreck. Yeah, gimme that."

She took the whole bottle and chugged three shots-worth of rum. Logan and Jon looked at each other with grins. Logan knew how well Eve could hold her liquor. She couldn't.

"Well she's done for," said Jon, taking a sip from his glass.

"I give her about an hour before she passes out," said Logan.

Eve gave a disgusted look, burped and said, "Ugh, I'm not that bad."

"Yeah, ok," laughed Jon.

They talked and laughed about the good, old times as they finished the bottle and got hammered. Sure enough, within an hour, Eve curled up on a pile of blankets and passed out in a drunken stupor.

Logan began to feel tired himself and he said, "Well, Christmash washn't all bad."

Jon hiccupped and slapped Logan on the back. He slurred, "We're shtill fuckered, but you're you're right. We gotta shtick togeter."

"We-hic! We will," said Logan, "Think I'm gonna pash out, man."

"Yup," said Jon, then slid off his chair and passed out on the cold, hard floor immediately with no blankets.

Logan laid out on a table and let sleep take him. He knew the arguments would keep coming if things didn't change soon, but he would rest easy knowing he gave his friends at least one good night.

Chapter 4 - Memories Don't Die

The old Buick rumbled down the narrow, country road. A storm had been brewing since that morning, and it had finally sprung from the heavens. The windshield wipers were useless in the torrential downpour.

The driver pulled the car off the side of the road and put it in park. The headlights were swallowed up in the rainy night, barely illuminating twenty feet in front of the car.

"Why'd we stop?" asked the passenger. He was Abe Foster, the meek, older brother of Logan, the driver.

"I feel like I don't know you anymore," said Logan, staring out into the wet darkness.

"Oh c'mon. Can we keep going, I need to get home."

"You have to stop."

Abe sighed and scratched his skinny, tattooed arm. The skin art barely hid healing and fresh track marks. "Don't worry about me, bro, I'll be fine."

Logan shot his glare at Abe and said, "It's not you I'm worried about, Abe. It's the next woman who crosses your path. You almost killed the last one."

Abe narrowed his eyes and said, "Stay out of my business."

"It is my business. You're my brother. What happened to you?"

"Leave it alone, Logan."

"How many need to suffer before you realize what you're doing? Obviously prison isn't working."

"Fuck you, man. You don't know me," said Abe, opening the door and marching out into the rain.

Logan followed suit, not content on just letting his brother walk away. He shouted through the howling storm, "Yeah, just run away like always! I'm trying to help you, but you make caring so damn difficult."

The brothers converged in front of the car, casting long shadows in the dancing rain. Abe puffed his chest out and said, "Ya know what, I'll walk to the trailer."

"Fine, but I'm done. Don't ask me for rides anymore and don't ask Mom and Dad for money."

Abe, who had begun to turn to walk up the gravelly road, spun on his heels and marched up to Logan. "Don't tell me what to do. You ain't nobody."

"And you are?"

Abe pushed Logan, who was barely able to keep his footing. His brother no longer looked like the person he grew up with. He looked like a feral animal, backed into a corner.

"Is this what you want? Huh?" Abe said through gritted teeth.

Logan stepped forward and pushed Abe back. "I just want my brother back!"

Abe caught his balance and swung on Logan, nicking him in the cheek. Logan charged him and they tumbled down into a ditch. Like wet rats, they grappled in the mud. Fury had taken hold of both of them as they shed each other's blood.

Abe got the upper hand and straddled Logan's torso. He put his hands around his brother's neck and began to squeeze. "You don't know me. You don't know me!"

Logan couldn't breath, but managed to pull an arm out from under Abe. He punched him in the nose, forcing the abuser to lighten his grip. Logan let loose a flurry of punches until his brother fell backwards.

Logan stood and barely managed to see his brother on the ground before him. They were both covered in mud and drenched to the bone.

"I won't let you hurt anyone else," said Logan, letting a darkness into his mind that matched the night around them.

"I'll..do what I...want," said Abe, spitting out a tooth.

"Not anymore," said Logan. He brought his foot up and...

And Logan awoke in Field Foods, sweaty yet chilled. A nightmare?

No, it wasn't. As Logan rubbed the sleep out of his eyes, he tried to think of something else. There was no running from his past, however. He had lived with what he had done to his brother for the last year.

Part of him had wished he had gotten caught, went to prison like his brother did so many times before. But it never happened. No one questioned him, as no one cared about Abe. Outside of Logan's family, Abe was only known for being a drug addict. It was Logan who figured out what he had been doing to women. It wasn't difficult to deduce after seeing the face of the last woman Abe beat half to death.

Logan wanted to help Abe. He loved his brother, his only sibling. They grew up together, played video games and watched movies with one another. Once Abe became an adult, he got in with the wrong crowd and he became estranged from his family. He began doing things that were unforgivable to Logan, which pushed him to do what he did.

Abe's face before Logan ended him would be forever etched into his mind.

Logan didn't notice Jon sitting on the floor, staring at him until the former corrections officer said, "You always look so glum after waking up?"

Logan looked down at Jon, his face dimly lit by a lantern. Wisps of breath were coming out of his mouth. Logan had no idea how long he had been up or how long he had been watching.

"Bad dream," said Logan.

"It's the liquor," said Jon, rubbing his face, "I feel like crap."

"Same," said Logan, but he felt bad for other reasons.

Jon grabbed a bottle of water from one of the tables and chugged almost all of it. Logan wanted to tell him he should take it easy with the water, as their supplies would be running low soon, but he didn't care to. He was too distracted.

As his friend laid back down next to a still passed out Eve, Logan took a flashlight and exited the break room. The rest of the store was still dark and quiet in the morning hours.

He approached a small hallway that housed the restrooms. The plumbing had stopped working over a month ago and the smell was pervasive. With the marines not letting anyone outside, they had no choice but to keep using them.

As he approached the door to the male restroom, he heard muffled voices coming from inside. It was difficult to hear as whoever was speaking clearly intended for the conversation to not carry to unwanted listeners.

Logan switched off the flashlight and placed the palm of his hand on the door. He slowly, ever so slowly, opened it barely a centimeter. Light from a lantern shown through the tight opening and the voices, still low, were finally audible. Logan recognized each speaker.

"-only last a few more weeks at most," said Private Williams.

"What are you suggesting exactly?" said Ironson. He sounded exasperated, which put Logan on edge, as the military man never showed emotion.

"What he's sayin' is the food'll last longer if its just us four, brother," said Private Ritter.

"We could do it while they sleep, eh?" said Williams.

"This is insane!" said Ironson, "I will not take part in killing innocent people over a few cans of food."

"That's your damn choice, but do you want to eat for a few weeks or a few months?" said Williams.

"We've lost radio contact with er'yone. We're on'r own now. No one to answer to, s'why not make our lives as good as possible?" said Sergeant Dillian.

"You will answer to me. I am your commanding officer and I am telling you that you will not do this," growled the pilot.

The other marines scoffed and chuckled at the grizzled vet.

"Look, it's gonna happen either way, Ironson. We just gotta wait for the right moment, eh?" said Williams.

"It'll have to be sooner than later."

"I'm done talking about this," said Ironson.

Logan heard footsteps walking towards the door. He had nowhere to run off to and they would be opening the door in a matter of seconds. He decided to stand his ground and opened the door first.

For a moment, the air was tense. The three marines, pilot and Logan stared at each other. Their breath formed puffs of condensed water vapor as they sized each other up. Logan's heart was racing, but he steadied his breathing to match theirs.

"Mornin'," Logan said, breaking the silence.

"What're you doin' out there?" said Dillian.

"Just woke up and had to take a piss," said Logan, struggling to keep a nervous quiver from his voice.

"You hear anything, huh?" said Williams.

"Leave him be," said Ironson, putting himself between Logan and his squad. He turned to Logan and said, "We'll get out of your way."

Logan put his back against the door to let them pass. The pilot looked forward with a furrowed brow. Each of the other marines eyed Logan as they walked by. Sergeant Dillian was the last to exit, but he stopped right in Logan's face. The look on his face was dangerous, but that could have just been his natural expression.

"Stay out of our way," he said to Logan," And have a nice fucking day."

He turned and left. Logan breathed a sigh of relief and was more ready than he was before to relieve himself in the urinal. He had to tell someone what they were planning, maybe even tell everyone. Jon and Eve would be the first to know, as he wanted to keep them safe above all else.

After relieving himself, using the collar of his shirt to block his nose, Logan ran back to the break room. Jon had fallen back to sleep while cuddling with Eve, who had started to wake up.

"Eve?" said Logan as he bent down to his laying friends.

She brushed her long, matted hair to the side and looked at Logan with one eye open. She only appeared half awake and said, "Hey Logan," while elbowing Jon's arm off her.

"We need to wake up Jon. There's something I need to tell you."

After waking Jon up, Logan explained what he overheard. Jon agreed they should warn the others, but it would be difficult to gather everyone without clueing the marines in. As far as Logan knew, the marines did not suspect he knew about their plan. He told Jon he had a plan, but he would need his help.

After midday, Logan executed his plan with the help of his friends. Jon approached the soldiers and told them he sighted something moving out in the parking lot. No one had left Field Foods since they got there, but the marines had kept a dutiful watch out the front, gated doors and the high windows of the store.

As Jon and the marines went to the front of the store, Logan and Eve gathered everyone silently in the store room. Once everyone was gathered, Logan hastily explained what he had overheard and suggested they band together to overpower their would be attackers.

"That's a-a very serious accusation," said Oswald, sweat

beading on his balding head.

"They've protected us this long, why would they want to hurt us, sonny?" said Glenda.

"Sounds like you're making this up," said Michael with a disgusted look, "How dare you insult our military."

Logan blinked in surprise and said, "I'm not making this up, and I would never insult our armed forces. But what I'm saying is true, and if we don't act-"

Michael walked up from the crowd, his face distorted in anger. He said through gritted teeth, "My father was a marine, you hippy fuck!"

Eve stepped up to this man and said, "You have to listen. We are all in danger."

"Get the fuck out of the way, bitch!" said Michael, backhanding Eve in the face. The force of the blow sent her down to the ground.

As Logan watched Eve be struck down to the ground, his mind went back to his brother. How could a man do this? He knew things were desperate with the invaders from underground forcing them to hide, but to resort to violence when all he was trying to do was help them...

Logan could have tolerated himself getting hit like that, but not Eve. The girl he seen as a sister. She was trying to help Logan and she got punished for it. Logan narrowed his eyes as the darkness crept in.

52

Something in Logan broke.

Oswald stepped out of the crowd.

Logan drew his pocket knife out of his back pocket.

Oswald said, "N-now that was uncalled for."

Michael turned his back on Logan and said to Oswald, "Have you been listening to what these fucktards are saying? Who gives a fuck about that bitch."

In an instant, Logan had leapt behind the man. He reached up, grabbed his forehead and yanked him back as hard as he could. As they tumbled backwards, Logan buried the three-inch blade of his pocket knife into the man's neck. Three times he plunged the blade into flesh before they toppled to the ground. Blood spurted from the man's jugular and his voice was lost in watery gargle.

As the man bled out, Logan stood, covered in blood and shaking. Everyone's eyes were on him, wide and shocked. His adrenaline was pumping and he didn't know what to do from there. Maybe he should run?

Then he seen Eve in front of him. A red mark had appeared on her right cheek, a stark contrast from the beauty of the rest of her face. Yet, when his eyes passed into hers, his adrenaline calmed and he snapped out of it.

"Logan..." she said.

"I...I..." he said, his voice trembling even more.

Tears welled up in his eyes as emotions started to get the better of him. He dropped the knife and fell to his knees. He noticed the blood all over him and the only thing that kept him from freaking out was Eve.

She held eye contact with him and said in a calm, reassuring voice, "Just breath like me. In and out, slowly. That's good. Don't worry about the trembling, it's your body's natural reflexes kicking in."

Logan matched his breathing to Eve and the trembling started to subside. Part of him was glad he did what he did, the dark part of him that was powerless to help the women his brother beat. For the most part, however, he struggled with what he just did.

"Well, someone started the g'damn party without us," said someone.

Logan and Eve looked towards the entrance of the store room. There stood the three marines, the pilot and Jon Kilroy. It was Sergeant Dillian who spoke and he had his rifle trained on Logan.

"So you did overhear us, eh?" said Private Williams.

"Let's jes do it, right here right now," said Ritter, unsafetying his weapon.

"N-now there's no reason for a-anymore violence," said Oswald, sweat dripping down his face.

"Exactly," said Ironson, who had turned to face his comrades, "We can ration out what is left of the food and plan out what to do next."

The pilot unholstered his sidearm, backed up and pointed it at Dillian's head. Williams and Ritter pointed their rifles at Ironson.

Jon, seeing he was in the line of fire, slowly backed away. Logan had gained control of himself enough to know this was going to get ugly and he picked up his blood-soaked pocket knife. He motioned for Eve to hide, who crawled away behind a shelving unit.

"I said stand the fuck down," said Dillian. He looked at Ironson but kept his rifle pointed in Logan's direction.

"I don't know what happened here, but no more people have to die," said Ironson with a look of pure focus, "But if you won't listen, I'll do what I have to."

"Williams?" said Dillian.

"Yeah, Sarg?"

"Open fi-"

He was interrupted by a loud bang. Ironson had shot Dillian between the eyes. Another shot rang out as Williams fired into Ironson, striking him in the left shoulder. Before Ritter could react, Jon was on him. Like a wrestler, Jon picked up the marine and threw him on the ground. He straddled his torso and wailed on him with fist after fist.

Ironson fell to the ground and Williams opened fire into the crowd of people. They all attempted to get away. Some did, but some did not. Oswald, Tabby and her grandmother were riddled with bullets from the assault rifle. Marissa took her son and hid with Eve, narrowly avoiding being shot.

Logan charged at Williams with his pocket knife. The private seemed to almost enjoy slaughtering innocent people. What he did not enjoy was an already bloodied blade stabbed into his chest. He pushed Logan away from him and began to raise his rifle at him, but he was hit by several rounds from Ironson's pistol. The pilot was still alive and steadied his weapon on his knee so he could hit his target from his location on the ground.

Then, as if nothing had happened at all, there was silence again. Jon had made short work of Ritter with his bare hands, as he had almost eighty pounds on the marine. Williams and Dillian were dead, shot by their commander.

Chapter 5: The Three Become Four

Eve poked her head out from behind shelves and totes once everything had gone silent. Her mind struggled to comprehend what had just happened. She had seen dying people at the hospital but was never a part of how they got there.

Her gaze settled on the carnage, seeing the bodies of Williams and Dillian laying before Ironson. He was on his feet, holding his shoulder. Oswald, Tabby and Glenda were on the floor motionless near where she was hiding. Jon was pacing back and forth muttering under his breath while Logan leaned against the wall with his gaze downcast.

"Is it over?" asked Marissa from behind her; her voice trembled while she held her crying son.

Eve turned to her and said, "Get your son out of the stock room. Hide his eyes. He shouldn't see this."

Marissa nodded and stood with her son in her arms. She thrust his face in her bosom as she jogged by the dead and worried. When she had exited the stock room, Eve approached her fiancé.

"Knew something like this was gonna happen," Jon said once he seen her. He rubbed his bloodied knuckles as if it were a minor inconvenience.

Eve ran to the safety of his embrace and he held her tightly. For all the arguments they had been having while trapped in Field Foods, she still loved him. Loud and obnoxious, sure, but he always kept her safe.

Ironson said to the couple, "I'm sorry for what they were trying to do. For...what they did do."

Eve let go of Jon and noticed the blood dripping through a tear in Ironson's bomber jacket. She said, "Let me check that for you."

The pilot held up a hand and shook his head. "I'm ok. The bullet only grazed me."

"The mark on your face," said Jon, "Is that what made Logan go nuts?"

Eve nodded and looked over at Logan, who stood quietly on his own. "Michael hit me and Logan..." - she couldn't find the words to describe the brutality in Logan's eyes as he stabbed the man who struck her.

"Michael had it comin' then," said Jon, "I woulda done the same thing."

Eve was thankful for Logan's expedient readiness to help her, but she was torn. How could someone so easily be ready to take a human life? If the roles were reversed, she couldn't have done the same thing. She spent too much of her life trying to save lives.

"Thanks for the help," Ironson said to Jon.

"They were gonna kill us all, I had to do something. Logan overheard you and your squad talking and tried to tell the others. Guess they didn't listen," said Jon.

"I could tell you were trying to distract us," said Ironson, "But the others were on to you. They were smarter than they looked."

Eve had been focused on Logan as they spoke. She was worried about him. He was always the quiet type and there was a point in time she helped him through a depression. It was part of the reason she was more than happy to have him come on the vacation with her and Jon. To try to get him out of his funk.

"Go talk to him," said Jon, "You're better at these kinds of things than I am."

Eve agreed, Jon would make things worse by giving Logan and "atta boy" or something nonsensical. She walked up to Logan in his dark corner. He didn't move and had his eyes closed.

"Are you ok?" Eve asked quietly.

Logan didn't respond.

She stepped closer to him and his eyes opened. Even in the near darkness she could tell he was bothered, hurt. It was an odd feeling for her to have compassion for the killer and not the victim.

"What just happened?" he asked in a low tone. His voice quivered as he brought his arms tighter around himself.

"I think you know," she said, trying to sound as calming as she could, "But it's over now. Can't undo it."

"When I seen him hit you," Logan said, "I felt like someone else took the wheel. I couldn't just let him walk away and keep saying those things."

"I understand, and I'm thankful for you helping me," she said, but she didn't really understand. She was no stranger to blood and wounds, but in many ways was innocent to it.

"I'll be ok," said Logan, "I just need a minute to myself."

Eve nodded and left him alone. Jon had been waiting near the door that led out to the store. When she walked up to him, he said, "He ok?"

"I really don't know, Jon. He seems lost."

"Well, let him have a minute. Ironson said he wanted to talk to us. Let's go find where he went," said Jon, taking Eve's hand.

She was ready to leave the stock room, anyways. Too much death. As they entered into the store's sales floor, they were greeted by some sunlight. They searched up and down the aisles for Ironson, eventually finding him hunched over the short stack of what was left of the bottled water. He was filling a rucksack with other packs around him, bulging with other food supplies.

He heard the couple approaching him and looked over at them. He stood and said, "Been filling the rucks up. There's enough supplies to last at least a couple weeks, if we ration them."

"We?" said Jon, looking over at Eve then back at the pilot. "What'd you need to talk to us about?"

Ironson stood, but kept checking the rucksacks. It looked like he was counting the supplies over and over in his head. As his eyes passed between the packs and the couple, he said, "The last radio contact I had with anyone was with St. Louis MEPS. Marines, Army, everyone in the area from any branch found their way there. The place is like a fortress now. They were in contact with a group called the Marauders or some such. Former biker gang turned road warriors, but they'll be inconsequential. You help me get there, you'll have as safe a place as any to stay."

Eve's face lit up. It wasn't far from where her parents lived. She said, "Jon, we might be able to see my family if we go with him."

Jon's expression did not change. He folded his arms and quipped, "What's the catch?"

Ironson said, "No catch, except that we have to actually get there. The city is overrun for the most part and MEPS is downtown."

Eve said, "Jon, we should go. We could see my parents along the way if it's not too dangerous."

Again, Jon did not react to Eve's sentiment. She was used to him not listening to her when he was talking business, but it was starting to piss her off. As much as she loved him and liked how safe she felt around him, he wasn't without his faults.

Jon said, "What's your plan on getting there? If the city's overrun, won't it be impossible?"

"We'd need to recon the city to find the safest route," said Ironson, going back to packing foodstuffs.

Logan appeared next to the couple. He still didn't look like himself, but at least he left the room of death. He said, "The Metro system. The dark could be our ally if those things aren't there."

"That could work," said Ironson.

"At least it gives us an option," said Jon, nodding towards Logan.

The creases on Ironson's face creased even more before he said, "We should take the arms and armament off my squad. It may seem morbid, but we should arm ourselves before we set out."

"You go ahead," said Eve, wincing as she looked back to where the stock room was, "I'm going to try to find Marissa."

The men walked off to pick the gear off the corpses of the two marines, like carrion on roadkill. Eve went the opposite direction. She heard items clanking around in the front of the store, so headed that way.

The front gate was already up, flooding the entrance of Field Foods with the morning sunlight. It was a welcome sight as everyone had been operating with little to no light for the past couple months. Eve found Marissa there.

The mother looked manic as she gathered items and stuffed her pockets with any kind of canned or boxed food she could find. Even a few, remaining candy bars. Her son sat on a checkout counter, watching her. He looked confused.

"Marissa?" Eve said in a soft manner as she approached.

Marissa ceased whipping her body and items around to see who was speaking to her. When she seen Eve she said, "I'm taking my boy out of here."

"Come with us," Eve said, taking another step towards the woman, "We have a plan to-"

"I am not going anywhere with that...that freak," Marissa said, twisting her face in disgust.

"Logan?" said Eve, "I know it's hard to take in what he did, but you'll be safe with us. He was only trying to defend me, even though it was maybe an extreme reaction."

"Forget it," said Marissa, finishing her packing and throwing on a down coat, "I thought he was an ok guy, but the way he just killed Michael. I'll take my chances by myself."

"What about your son?" asked Eve who was genuinely worried about the boy.

"He's my responsibility, not yours," Marissa said, who may as well have thrown daggers with the look she gave Eve.

"You're right," said Eve, putting up her hands and backing off, "Just please be careful."

Marissa grabbed her son's hand and marched out of the store. Eve got her first whiff of the outside air in a long time. It was colder than she expected it'd be and chilled her to the bone.

Eve still didn't want to go back into the stock room, so she started searching around the store for warm clothes. She found various sweat pants and shirts, coats, socks and jeans. Some of Tabby's old clothes would fit Eve and some of Michael's would fit Jon.

As she finished gathering the items up, the men had come back. They threw the military gear and weapons on the pile with the clothes and began divvying it all up between them.

They threw on extra layers of clothes at Eve's suggestion. Logan and Jon equipped the tactical vests. Ironson didn't take anything, he was content wearing his Marine Corps BDU and bomber jacket.

Jon chose to keep the pump shotgun he had stored away in a secret spot. Ironson broke down how to use the M16A4 rifles to Logan and Eve. The weapon felt heavy in Eve's arms, almost foreign. She had fired a .22 revolver at a firing range on one of her and Jon's dates, but it was low caliber and lightweight. This eight pound killing machine almost dwarfed her and she hoped she would not have to use it.

When they started a last minute search of the store for anything else useful, Eve couldn't help but pull Jon to the side to have a one on one discussion. She said, "You were ignoring me earlier."

Jon blinked and scratched his beard, "No I didn't. When?"

"When Joseph was telling us his plan. I was saying that place he wants to go to was close to my family and you didn't say anything," she said, crossing her arms and maintaining a stern posture.

"Babe, c'mon," said Jon, throwing his arms to the side in disbelief, "I wasn't trying to ignore you. I was thinking about keeping us safe is all."

"I just want you to know that I have a say in all of this, too," she said in a determined tone.

Jon brushed her blond hair behind her ear and said, "Of course you do, babe, of course you do. Just don't go crazy at me over every little thing. We have bigger things to worry about, wouldn't you say?"

Eve slapped his hand away from her ear and said, "I'll give you something to worry about, dick," before storming away to join Logan and Ironson.

"This is your last chance to change your mind," said Ironson when they had gathered back together.

Logan checked the safety on his rifle, slung a rucksack over his shoulder and said, "I don't want to stay here any longer."

"Yeah, I'm ready to go," said Eve, who struggled to pick up a heavy rucksack. Jon reached out to help her but she turned away and growled, "I got it."

"Hoo-rah," said Ironson, "We have five to six hours of light left. Let's hoof it."

They exited out into the chilled air. The dank smell of Field Foods ceased to assault Eve's senses as she breathed in the fresh air. She hoped she could forget what happened there. Forget what Logan did. Forget the dead marines.

She seen Ironson take one last look at the abandoned helicopter, sitting amongst the effigies of long parked cars. He didn't say or express anything, but Eve knew he was saying goodbye to it in his own way.

Chapter 6: The Black River

Jon wasn't a trusting person. He kept people at arm's length outside of his personal circle of Eve, Logan and his family. So when Lieutenant Joseph Ironson decided to lead them away from Field Foods, he had his doubts. Granted, the pilot had helped them against the marines when they went mad, but the alpha in Jon was uneasy with letting another man lead.

Ironson had explained that they should hike along the Black River to U.S. Route 67, which would take them all the way to St. Louis. There, they could find a working vehicle and drive the rest of the way. Since they didn't know much about how the invaders hunt, Ironson speculated that the river would help hide their scent. It'd also provide drinking water.

Jon didn't argue with the plan. Eve wasn't happy with him for some reason and Logan wasn't talking much. He went with it for the time being to keep the peace.

Not far out of Poplar Bluff, farmlands gave way to more forest and more hills. The river was just a hop and skip away. Jon knew it was the eastern reaches of the Missouri Ozarks, but it didn't look how he usually seen it. He had visited this general area during summer, when the trees were lush and green. As the group trekked through it, in the cold of December, their view was leafless trees and little to no wildlife.

As they stepped onto the shore of the Black River, memories came back to Jon. No one was speaking so he let his mind wander. Not two years prior, Eve, Logan, himself and other friends had floated down this same river. The sun was beating down, burning everyone's skin, but they were too drunk to notice.

He and Logan had wrestled in the water, laughing and trying to get the upper hand. Logan was quick and technical, swimming underwater and popping out behind Jon. The former corrections officer was stronger though, and when Logan would get his arms around him, he'd just toss him over his shoulder, splashing water on everyone.

Between that last float trip and their doomed hike, Jon had noticed Logan would visit less. His bright and enthusiastic smile diminished. He always seemed distracted. Eve had told Jon he was depressed, but Jon wasn't emotionally equipped to help. Eve was, however, and Jon trusted Logan, so he would let the two of them spend time together. Anything to get his friend back to normal.

He had been so lost in thought, he barely noticed the loud crunch he made with every footstep. The shores of the Black River comprised of yellow-orange stones and pebbles.

"Kilroy," said Ironson.

Jon looked over and seen that everyone else had gotten off the stones and were walking on the frozen soil and underbrush. He immediately took the hint and got in line with everyone else before they continued onwards. Their footsteps were quieter, but the fallen trees and brambles made movement more difficult.

The full cold of winter was starting to set in, but it didn't bother Jon much. He had been used to standing out in the cold for hours on end when he worked at the prison. The experience steeled him against the elements.

Jon looked up at his fiancé's back; she walked in front of him. Even with multiple layers of clothes on, he couldn't help but look at her backside for a second. He loved her and her beauty was what attracted him to her in the first place. Once he got to know her, he seen she was much more than just a pretty face.

Her gait was uneven and she was hunched forward, breathing heavily. Jon knew the pack was too heavy for her.

"Want me to take it for a while, babe?" he asked.

"I got it," she said without looking back.

Still upset. Jon shook his head and didn't say another word.

He didn't understand why she was acting this way. She said something about ignoring her, but he didn't remember any instance of that. If they're in the god damned apocalypse, someone has to think about how to keep everyone alive. Would that not trump feelings?

They marched for hours with few breaks and even fewer words. Everyone was on edge, expecting to get attacked by the things at any moment. When the sun started to disappear beyond the trees, Ironson stopped the group.

He explained, "As far as I can tell, those creatures track their prey during the day and come back to hunt in packs during the night. We should find somewhere we can hide before it gets too dark."

"Didn't they attack during the day before?" Jon asked, thinking back on the day they got to Field Foods.

"They'll fight back if they have to," said Ironson, "Let's get a fire going to eat some grub, then settle down for the night."

They found an overhanging cliff that would provide cover next to the river. Roots of trees atop the cliff dangled down through the dirt and stone, allowing them some semblance of comfort.

They built a small fire on the stony shore of the river. Canned vegetable soup would be their supper that evening. They huddled close to the flames as they as they ate. The warmth was enticing and gave them respite out of the cold.

"I could sit next to the fire forever," Eve said while she was sitting on her knees, holding her hands out over the campfire.

"Warmest I've been all day," Jon said as he huddled closer to his fiancé. She had a displeased look on her face, but didn't move as Jon put his arm around her.

Ironson stood after he finished eating and said, "Foster, come help me cover up where we're going to sleep."

Logan nodded and followed Ironson into the forest.

"What's wrong?" Jon said once they had left.

Eve sighed and closed her eyes before she said, "You always feel like you have to make decisions for me."

"No I don't," Jon said.

"I just want to know I'm going to be heard. I'm in a sausage fest with you three, and you all think you know what's best for everyone."

Jon hugged her tightly and replied, "Of course, babe. I'll make sure you get a say."

"See? You're doing it again," she said, shrugging Jon off of her, "You don't get to say when I make a decision."

"I just don't know what I'm doing wrong," said Jon, starting to get flustered, "But whatever, make any decisions you want."

"Thanks, I will," said Eve.

Jon sat down and leaned back on his hands. He grumbled, "We could die any minute and you're worried about this."

Eve shot her gaze at Jon and looked as if she was about to explode on him. Instead she stood and said, "I'm going to help

Logan and Joseph."

"Sure, go ahead," said Jon, shaking his head.

He tried to wrap his head around what she was trying to say.
She wants to make her own decisions? Fine, but when he said he'd
let her, she got even more angry. Just when he thought he had the
woman figured out...

Tired of contemplating the argument, he got up and snuffed
the fire before helping the others block up the small cliff. They put
sticks and logs around the sides of the exposed roots. They wouldn't
stop any attackers, but it would help camouflage them in the night.

When the sun went down, the cold intensified. The river was
already freezing over before light faded, but the makeshift blinds
broke up the breeze. Out of necessity, Eve latched onto Jon while
they bedded down. It kept them both warm. The couple were flanked
by Logan and Ironson. Jon wrapped his arms around his fiancé and
tried to get some sleep.

Jon awoke early in the morning, before the sun had come up,
to a bone shattering howl. It was the same he had heard back at
Camp Dickson. The sound stunned him for a moment as the others
roused quickly from their slumbers. The howl was close, but it was
difficult to tell from which direction.

"The hell?" whispered Jon, bringing up the pump shotgun
from amongst the gear set at their feet.

"Stay frosty," said Ironson, who already had his M16A4

propped up on a root. Jon could barely see him scanning the area in the darkness and could just see the profiles of trees on the other bank of the frozen river.

Then they heard what sounded like hooves on ice. The rushed steps of something running in their direction. Ironson held his fist up, which Jon knew meant to hold fire. For Logan and Eve, it was probably fear that stayed their hands more than his silent command.

A shape appeared as it ran along the far side of the river. It was followed by eight more, larger shapes with glowing blue eyes. They darted alongside and in the river, cracking the ice. They howled and growled as they ran with incredible speed at their quarry.

Within a few seconds they dove onto the unfortunate source of their ire, their eyes turning red before they attacked. They chomped and tore at flesh and bone. Eve grasped Jon's hand as they listened and watched the ravenous feasting.

When the shapes ended their meal, they ran off the way they came from and silence fell once again. The four party members breathed a collective sigh of relief. Jon waited until they were long gone before he sat his shotgun back down.

"We're going to have to be extra careful today," said Ironson, who was getting his pack ready for travel. "Was hoping we wouldn't run into them on the river."

"They looked so big," said Eve.

"Aye, their damn huge. Those were the smaller ones. We're better off avoiding them," said Ironson, "Let's get some grub before we head off."

The sky began to break into orange hues when the group made ready to depart their temporary home under the cliff. They all watched in different directions, taking as long as was needed to make sure the coast was clear. They seen and heard nothing out of the ordinary, except the silent void of the forest.

The icy layer atop the Black River was fine and easily breakable. They refilled bottles with water. On the other side of the river they seen a massacred deer that they seen fall earlier that morning. They took in the gory scene before setting off.

They trekked in relative silence, afraid of alerting something to their location even when the creatures' activity was less during the day. After a few hours of walking along the river, it was Jon who finally broke the silence in an attempt to lift their moods. He nudged his fiancé in the arm and said with a grin, "So, when we find somewhere safe, we're going to have to repopulate, if you know what I mean."

Eve rolled her eyes then responded, "A world full of Jons...no thank you."

"Hey, c'mon," he said, curling his lips in an obviously fake frown. He could tell she was still not over their argument, but a smile forced its way onto her face. "See, I knew you'd see it my way.

We got a civilization to rebuild."

Logan was just ahead of them, between the couple and Ironson as they walked between the forest and the pebbly shore of the river. He had said little to nothing since leaving the grocery store, so it was almost a surprise when he spoke up, "Would it be better to rebuild civilization or save what is left of humanity."

"Aren't they the same thing?" said Eve.

"Depends on how you view them," Logan continued as he picked up any flat stones he came across and skipped them across the halfway frozen river. "One might say that in order to build a civilization, you have to sacrifice humanity. We are nurturing beings, who are meant to love one another and show compassion. But in order for civilization to work, we require class systems to divide manual labor from-"

"Let's keep the chatter to a minimum," Ironson cut in without turning around as he walked.

Logan threw a skipping stone particularly hard, sending it skipping all the way across the river to the other bank before replying, "Fine, never mind."

The protective side of Jon wanted to yell at the pilot. His friend had finally said something and was shut down immediately. He knew, in their dangerous situation, that it was probably for the best, but it didn't stop him from glaring at the back of Ironson's head.

At midday they decided to stop for a quick lunch. The forest was less dense here and the rocky bank of the river went fairly far inland. There was a blue canoe flipped upside down a few feet away from the water. Near it was several columns of rock art, with larger stones at the bases and consecutively smaller rocks the higher they climbed into the air. The tallest one was a foot and a half tall.

Jon popped the fingers in his hand and said under his breath, "Challenge accepted."

As the others ate canned peaches and pears, Jon set about making his own column of rock art. During their float trips in the past, anytime he would see rock art he would make his own next to it that was just a little bit taller. So he would do this time as well, as when he was finished, his column stood at two feet.

He puffed his chest out proudly with his hands on his hips and looked at the others for validation. Eve and Logan were sitting next to each other on the canoe, watching a man who, although not much taller than Logan, was more accustomed to a gym than an art studio. In unison, they golf clapped sarcastically.

"Tell me that isn't impressive," he said, gesturing at his creation with both hands, "It's probably the tallest I've ever made."

As he looked at his friend and fiancé, their expressions turned from amused to horrified. Ironson, who was trying to contact MEPS with what little power was left of his walkie talkie, looked past Jon and his rock art, sharing their pale look.

Jon turned around and at the edge of the forest was one of the creatures. It was standing on all fours, like a canine, save for its forepaws were humanlike with talons at the ends of the fingers. It was larger than the three had expected it to be and its skin was dark and leprous. A trail of black hair grew from the top of its head, down its back and wrapped between its legs, where one might find it's genitalia. Its face looked almost human, save for a lack of a distinguishable nose, lips or ears. Its mouth was large with larger teeth, and could be larger still if it dislocated its jaw like a snake. The worst part of it were its eyes, bright blue orbs that seemed to almost suck the soul out of the travelers.

"Oh fuck," said Jon, who reached down to grab his shotgun. As he did the thing's eyes switched from blue to red, illuminating the group in a red hue.

"It's marked us," said Ironson, who sounded like his tongue had fallen into his throat, "It needs to die or we're dead come nightfall!"

"Already on it," said Jon, pumping his Winchester to ready it.

As he shouldered his weapon, the creature stood on its back legs to its full height of eight feet. It howled that terrible two-toned cry, making the humans cringe as the hair stood up on their necks. Jon fired at the thing, but the sound of its call lowered his accuracy and the shot grazed its arm. It seemed unaffected by the attack, spun on its heels and ran on all fours away from them into the forest.

Chapter 7 - Out of the Frying Pan...

Lieutenant Joseph Ironson had a reputation for ruthless efficiency during his time in Iraq. Countless times he transported Marines in heated areas of operations or provided close air support. He was never physically wounded even when he would return with his helicopter riddled with bullets.

The only wound he suffered was when his wife and child were killed in a car wreck with a drunk driver. It was the only thing that pulled him from his duty and made him contemplate what he was fighting for. He was overseas to protect his family, but didn't even have a chance to say goodbye.

Not long after he returned stateside to bury his family, the invaders came. The man who had known nothing but victory in all his military operations began losing along with the rest of the United

States military branches.

When he seen the creature mark them and run off, it was the most vulnerable he had ever been in this conflict.

He led the three friends into the woods to chase the thing. Its travel was slowed through the brambles and trees, but so were they. The group was already at a speed disadvantage and he knew there was no way they could keep up. Ironson used broken limbs and imprints in the frozen ground to track it.

Ironson was tireless as he focused on the mission at hand: killing the creature. He was impressed with Jon Kilroy's ability to keep up with him. Logan was just behind but started to slow down, and Eve was gasping for oxygen.

Eve stopped, half leaning, half falling onto a tree with sweat streaming down her face, "I...I can't go on."

Ironson cursed under his breath but knew he wasn't with fellow soldiers. He stopped as well and said, "We have to keep going. If we don't find it and kill it, we'll be dealing with a larger threat."

"That thing is running twice as fast as we are," said Logan, wiping his scarred brow.

Jon piped up, clearly full of adrenaline, "Why don't we keep going. They can catch up."

"We need everyone on the front line with this thing," said Ironson, who was growing increasingly agitated, "Tuck your balls in and keep going!"

Eve and Logan shared a distraught look but they listened to the pilot. They kept going as quick as they could, but distance separated the group in half. Logan and Eve were soon out of view behind Ironson and Jon.

The two, more fit members of the group continued onwards. Ironson began to think Logan was right, but he had to try, even if he went on by himself. He had seen what happens when a person is marked firsthand. It never ended well.

As they ran, ducking and juking around trees, Ironson said, "Good to see you keeping up, Kilroy."

Without looking, Jon said, "Gotta redeem myself. I'm a better shot than I showed back there."

The creature's howl echoed against the trees, making both men jump in unison. They heard gunfire after the unnatural call, not far up ahead. Small arms fire? Maybe a shotgun. Shot after shot rang out, like an audible beacon telling the followers which way to go.

The forested land was getting steeper the further they ran. Eventually they could not run at all and had to start pulling themselves up by the bases of smaller, younger trees. They climbed up towards where they heard the gunfire, which had subsided.

They reached a clear, flat plateau. In the middle of the clearing was a forest ranger watchtower that stretched above the tops of most of the wintering trees. At the base of the watchtower stood someone in a black cloak and hood. At their feet laid the creature, its head split open in a black, gooey mess.

Jon and Ironson began approaching the figure, but a shot rang out from the top of the watchtower. The dirt at their feet blasted upwards and a high pitched voice called down at them as they froze, "Not 'nother step!"

The figure at the base of the watchtower raised a peculiar looking weapon and said, "Guns on th'ground, naw!" in a low voice.

Ironson placed his handgun on the ground, as did Jon who looked like he might do something stupid for a moment. They raised their arms in the air and Ironson said, "My name is Lieutenant Joseph Ironson, helicopter pilot of the United States Marine Corps. We were tracking that thing after it marked us. We are no threat to you."

The figure in front of them raised their hooded head towards the top of the watchtower and shouted to whoever was up there, "Wotcha think?"

After a short moment the high pitched voice called back down, "Bah, fine! C'mon up, but Rachel's gonna keep yo guns fer th'moment!"

Jon leaned towards Ironson and whispered, "I'll be damned if they take my gun."

Ironson responded in a low tone as the hooded figure approached them, "Stand down, Kilroy."

As Rachel walked nearer, Jon lowered his hands and said, "Name's Jon. I-"

The figure stood three inches taller than Jon, which was

noticeable when they got up close. When Rachel looked at Ironson, he seen the face of a woman staring at him through her hood. She was a large woman, whose muscles were evident through the black cloak.

She picked up their firearms and turned towards the watchtower. "Well, c'mon," she said without turning to them.

They followed her, walking past the corpse of the creature that had marked them earlier. Ironson was relieved it was dead before it could get back to a nest and relay the humans' whereabouts with its pack.

He was unsure about what to think about Rachel and the person up top. Jon and Ironson were still alive, so he gave them points for that. He couldn't help but feel like something was...odd. Rachel had a certain look to her that was off-putting, and her eye twitched eerily.

They followed the large woman up the spiraling staircase towards the top. The view was like none other as, once they reached the top, they could see the hills of the Ozarks and could even just make out where the Black River cut its way through the forest.

When Logan heard gunfire, he set forward with renewed vigor. Eve was just behind him but looked like she might collapse at any moment. He felt sorry for her and said, "I know it's tough, but we need to keep going. Jon and Joseph might be in trouble."

"I... I know, I'm coming," Eve said. It was clear she was

running on fumes.

They continued until they found the hilly side of the plateau that the others had climbed just minutes before. Logan pressed upwards while Eve leaned against a tree at the bottom.

"Wish I had thought about it and grabbed some water before we took off," she said.

Logan forgot all about leaving their supplies on the river bank in the rush to follow the creature. He said, "We'll have to go back for that at some point. I'm going to go take a look up the hill. You need help up or?"

Eve shook her head and said, "Go on, I'll follow in a sec."

Logan climbed upwards until he found the top. He seen the watchtower and the dead creature on the ground, but there were no other indications that the other members of his group were there. He leaned out over the top of the hill and motioned for Eve to come up. He stayed a moment to see if she needed help, but she was making her way up just as awkwardly as he did.

He shouldered his M16A4 rifle and looked around until Eve had reached his location. As she stumbled into the clearing she said, "Thanks for the help," while brushing dead leaves and dirt off her jeans and sweater.

"Sorry, thought it looked like you were ok," he said, looking up at the watchtower.

"Just kidding," she said, finally catching her breath again but then the seen the dead creature at the base of the watchtower, "Oh god, was that it?"

"Think so," said Logan, "Took a blow to its head. At least we don't have to worry about it hunting us tonight."

"Do you see Jon or Joseph?" she asked, slinging the rifle off her back and into her hands.

"I don't, but maybe we can get a better look up top," he said, pointing the barrel of his weapon towards the top of the former ranger tower.

"Uh, I'm not going up there," she said, already pale at the aspect of climbing all the way to the top.

"Still afraid of heights?" Logan asked, even though he knew she was.

"Just go on up, I'll stay here," she said.

"Ok, I'll be right back."

He carefully climbed the wooden steps that wrapped around the metal struts of the tower. Halfway up, the steps started creaking and the cold wind seemed to make the tower sway back and forth subtly. He could swear he heard voices at the top, but thought the breeze was playing tricks on him.

Closer to the top he definitely heard voices. Was that Jon's voice? He quickly made his way up that last few flights, lowering his weapon as he thought he was safe. When he was only a few stairs away from the top, he was forced to stop.

A short person wearing a black cloak and hood stood in front of him, pointing a revolver directly at his head. He froze and did not move his rifle up. They had the jump on him.

"Forgive my trespass," he said, trying to not look threatening, "I'm only looking for my friends."

"Drop yer gun," she said in a high pitched voice, cocking the hammer back of the revolver.

"Ok, I'm putting it down," he said, sitting the military issued weapon down on the top step in front of her.

Behind her, he seen Jon barge out of the door of the tower. Jon grinned and said, "Hey, it's ok. That's the guy I was telling you about. Eve with you, I hope?"

Logan was confused, but responded, "Yeah, she stayed below."

The short person lowered the revolver and said, "Well, tell'r to git on up," before turning back to go inside.

Out in the woods, a pair of eyes watched as Eve slowly made her way up the watchtower. Unbeknownst to the group, they were followed from Poplar Bluff by a spirit of vengeance. The eyes were waiting for the right moment to pounce, and that moment may be close.

The room atop the tower was surrounded in windows. It was messy, with two makeshift beds along the walls made of piles of blankets and sheets. There were a couple of coolers locked with padlocks in the corner and in another corner leaned a couple of firearm-looking weapons. Black cloaks hung on the wall, the same kind the two occupants wore. The messiness of various eating utensils, cups, plates and fish bones could be forgiven if it was not for the smell of something rotten. It might be the rotting remains of fish guts, but Logan thought it might be something else.

Rachel kept their weapons slung over her strong shoulder, but at least no longer kept her odd looking weapon pointed at them. The other female had her hood taken down, revealing an older woman whose face could be likened to a troll. Her grey hair looked like it was falling out in strands. She introduced herself as Maud.

Logan had been keenly observing everything around him, but mainly kept his interest in the two women. The day's events had taken up occupancy in his mind and let him forget about Field Foods. Like an owl in a tree, Logan's head rotated around, taking everything in.

"How did you kill that thing?" Logan asked as he leaned against a windowed wall. Jon and Ironson were leaning against the opposite side of the room while Maud sat with Eve on the floor. Rachel kept suspiciously near the only entrance into the room. She rocked left to right, shifting weight between her feet.

"Shock'm then shoot'm," said Maud, "Trick we learned."

Rachel held the weapon up as if she was selling it and explained, "Benelli M4 tactical semi'matic shotgun with laser sight. Modified'r with an amped up stun gun. Shock'm with a million r'so volts, ram the barrel down their damned throats, then boom, they deader than a doorknob."

"Surprisingly intuitive," said Logan, "You come up with that?"

"Nah, we-" Maud started to say.

"Yes, sure did," Rachel cut in.

The others did not notice the interruption, or did not care, but Logan took note. He said, "How long have you two lived up here?"

Rachel put her weapon back to the ready, but did not point the weapon at anyone. She said, "Since the beginnin' of the shit."

Maud reached over and began playing with Eve's blond hair, twirling it between her skeletal fingers. Eve looked uncomfortable, but did not stop her. "We like it up here," Maud said.

"Now that we've proven we're friendly, think we could get our weapons back?" asked Jon.

"You get'm when you leave. Gotta protect r'selves too, ya know," said Rachel.

"What's with the cloaks?" asked Ironson.

"Nasty monsters can't mem'ize us if they can't see us," said Maud, "Can walk safe at day."

Logan crossed his arms as he started thinking these two may not be the magnanimous saviors they appeared to be. He eyed the coolers in the corner and said, "It's a strategic location, and the river would provide you with water and food. Have you run into anyone else out here?"

"Few here n' there," said Maud who was absolutely

transfixed on Eve, "Never stayed long."

"Speaking of staying, we should get going," said Logan to his friends.

Rachel stood up straight and ceased her rocking. She said, "Why not stay longer. Won't find 'nother place safer than here."

"Thanks for the offer," said Ironson, narrowing his eyes behind his aviator sunglasses, "But I think it's time we continued on our way."

Rachel brought her weapon up in one hand and pulled Maud towards her in her other hand. "Hey!" exclaimed the older woman as she scrambled to her feet, then immediately grabbed the other modified shotguns in the corner.

"No," said Rachel, her Benelli pointed directly at Logan's chest.

"That smell isn't fish is it," said Logan, fearing his growing suspicions were correct, "And I think the other people you met ended up staying longer than they intended."

Even though her face was more or less hidden under her hood, he could tell from her heavy breathing that he was right. She said, "A'ight, fine. We get hungry and gotta make due."

Trapped like rats. Logan figured the two women would wait for them to starve, or try something stupid and shoot them. He never thought it would end this way. Never wanted to be part of a meal for another human.

Chapter 8 - ...Into the Fire

Maud, as old as she looked, skipped around the outside of the square room like she was a kid again. She tapped on the glass with her tiny hand with a devilish smile on her face. Logan had been telling himself he wouldn't hurt another human being, but the constant rapping of old knuckles on glass was starting to change his mind.

Jon and Ironson discussed ways to break through the glass or attack the door, but all plans ended with them dead. Jon paced around, huffing and puffing while Eve sat on one of the makeshift beds, her arms wrapped around her legs. Logan had not moved from his leaning spot on the wall as his mind raced for other options.

"Good going, Joseph. 'Stand down' you said. We let them do

this," Jon hounded as he stomped around.

"They had us from the beginning," Ironson said without revealing his emotions, "Even if we took out the big one, Maud still had the high ground."

"Starting to rethink our deal, if I'm honest," said Jon while he glared at the pilot, "We got this far and already shit's gone bad."

Rather than responding, Ironson sat on one of the beds and folded his arms. Logan had been watching them argue, but was more interested in Rachel pressing her large face against the glass. She was licking her lips and seemed to take pleasure in their distress.

Logan had an idea. Maud had tired herself out and stopped skipping, but she still walked around the room. As she passed by where Logan was he turned to the window and said through the glass, "How do you know Rachel?"

Maud cocked her head and said, "Why ya wanna know?"

"I figured we're gonna die here, may as well make conversation until the inevitable," he said, trying to sound as friendly as he could.

Maud shrugged and said, "She's m'daughter."

"So you gave birth to her?"

"I did. She was a biggun baby," said Maud, a crooked, remembering smile shining from under her hood. She stretched her arms out as if she was holding a baby Rachel.

"Our friend here, Eve, is pregnant," said Logan, hoping his plan would work, "Surely you want to give her the same chance to have a daughter as you had."

Maud's smile faded. Rachel had heard them talking through the glass but did not hear what was said. She marched over to Maud, but kept her gun pointed at the room's occupants. She struck her mother in the shoulder with a strong fist, almost knocking her over, and said, "Dun talk to'm. They'll try to poison yer mind like others have."

Rachel walked back to her position at the top of the watchtower staircase. Maud's mood changed but she said nothing more as she leaned against the railing, looking out over the trees. Eve scrunched her nose up at what Logan said. He knew she never wanted to have kids and she would hate the idea, but their situation was desperate.

Logan let enough time pass so that Rachel would no longer be on edge. He went to the door and looked out at the towering, cloaked woman. He said, "Ever hear the phrase: give a man a fish you feed him for a day, teach him how to fish you feed him for a lifetime?"

"Yeah, so what," said Rachel disinterestedly.

"I could teach you how to fish the river. Then you won't have to resort to...this," he said, gesturing towards his friends.

"I know how to fish. Ain't no more," said Rachel, spitting over the edge of the tower.

"All the fish are gone?" asked Logan, who was shocked.

"A'most. Not enough to keep us goin'."

"Maybe we can make a trade?"

"What kinda trade? We have yo guns, a'ready."

"We stashed some food. We could give you half if you let us go," he said, wondering if their packs would even still be on the rocky beach.

"Bullshit. Stop talkin'," said Rachel, kicking the door to back Logan up, which he did.

He took back his position on the wall and folded his arms. Maud tapped on the glass behind him, not threateningly like before, but to get his attention. She asked, "How far long is she?" as Logan turned towards her.

"About a month in," responded Logan, who said a random time that he knew would be far enough for her not to show a bump.

Rachel shouted to her mother, "I said stop talkin' to'm!"

Maud cringed and shrunk back to the railing. Rachel turned her gaze towards Logan and reprimanded him, "You say anything else to mammy, I'ma shoot ya!"

"Was a good try," said Ironson from where he sat on the bed.

"Quiet," said Logan in a low enough tone that he could not be heard through the glass, "She still believes me."

"I ain't dying in here," said Jon, balling up his fists, "And if I do die, I'm going down swinging."

"Take it easy, Jon," said Logan, "We aren't dying here. Just try to stay calm."

"Stay calm? How in the hell can I stay calm?" Jon said with a burning leer.

"Because you aren't helping anything and only making things worse for Eve," stabbed Logan.

Jon looked down at his fiancé, who had not said anything this whole time. His face lost its menace and he calmed down as he sat next to Eve and put his arm around her shoulders. She rested her head on his chest and they started having their own, unheard conversation.

Not much was said as the day ticked on. A few times Maud went over to her daughter and spoke to her in hushed tones. Rachel would become agitated and Maud would walk away again. The sun began yawning and was looking to settle in the western horizon.

As the sky turned from shades of blue to purple, Maud spoke to her daughter once again. They were less hushed this time and the group could hear her as she said, "Should least let the girl go."

"I dun believe fer a second she's preggers," said Rachel, tired of her mother talking about this again.

"Well, I'ma let'r go anyways. She's got purty hair and her kid'll have purty hair too!" said Maud, who turned towards the door.

"Nah, you ain't," said Rachel, pulling her feeble mother away from the door.

"Ow! Rachel, ya hurt me," said Maud, who's knees shook as she struggled to regain her balance.

"Sorry, mammy, but we need all we can git," said Rachel,

who offered a hand to help Maud.

Maud brushed away her hand and eyed one of the modified shotguns that was set down at Rachel's feet. She grabbed one and shouldered it, pointing it at her daughter. The group watched intently, waiting for a moment to act.

"What you doin', mammy?" said Rachel, who did not raise her weapon.

"We're lettin'r go, Rachel. I ain't killin' no babies," said Maud with shaky knees.

"Ain't doin' it," said Rachel as she started to raise her own weapon. She would not get it to her shoulder before Maud shot the shotgun into the air. The unexpected loudness made her drop her weapon and the force of the gunfire made Maud drop her own gun.

Far away, they heard the creatures begin to howl.

Logan knew this was their moment, but before he could say anything, Jon ran at the door, busting it off its hinges. He tackled Rachel like a linebacker, making her lose her balance. They toppled down the stairs and out of view.

Eve rushed to the wall where the hooded cloaks were hanging as Logan and Ironson collected three taser-modified shotguns from the ground outside. As Eve removed the cloaks she seen a couple of boxes of shotgun shells and stun gun cartridges in the window sill that were hidden before. She took those too. They peered down the staircase and seen Maud looking over the railing, howling in emotional pain. Jon was not there.

They ran as quick as they could down the stairs and past Maud, who did not notice Logan and Ironson, but seen Eve. She grabbed her by the hair in a shriek, forcing Eve to fall back onto the stairs. Logan stopped to help, but there would be no need. Eve jumped back to her feet and slapped Maud, sending the frail woman flailing backwards.

They ran down the staircase that spiraled down to the ground. The air was cold like before, but Logan was glad he did not smell whatever it was that pervaded his senses in the watchtower. He did start smelling something else though. A fire?

About halfway down, they seen Jon sitting on a landing. He had the wind knocked out of him but he was still conscious. They ran down to him and Eve started checking him for injuries. Besides a few splinters here and there, he looked ok.

"Where's Rachel?" Logan asked.

Jon pointed down to the ground and said, "She fell."

Ironson sniffed the air and said, "Does anyone else smell that? Smells like a fire."

As if it was on cue, they started to see smoke rise from the bottom of the watchtower. Logan looked over the edge and the base of the tower was ablaze. He seen someone at the base aiming a rifle at him. He ducked back from the edge just in time as a shot rang out, hitting the railing just behind Jon.

"Remember me, boys?" called the voice from down below.

"Oh, shit, it's Ritter," said Ironson, "Where are our rifles?"

"Down with her," said Jon, pointing down again as he got to his feet.

Another shot rang out. Ironson shouldered one of the shotguns and fired it down at his former squad mate. From above, Maud screamed and slowly began making her way down the stairs. All the while, the creatures howled. Their calls echoed up to the plateau.

From above, Maud fired her revolver down at the group. One shot hit the wooden stairs ahead of the group. Another pinged off a strut, sparking as the bullet hit the metal. The shots were wide, but still made Logan flinch each time she pulled the trigger.

They began moving downstairs, trying not to get shot from either of their foes. Jon fired a shotgun upwards and Ironson shot his downwards as they moved. It was more covering fire than anything, an attempt to suppress both their foes.

They were on the second to last case of stairs before they felt the heat of the fire. The stairs leading up to them were completely engulfed in flames. It was climbing upwards towards the survivors. Beyond the inferno they seen Ritter, his face lit up in a maniacal smirk.

"You're dead, Ironson!" he shouted at them.

"You're crazy, Ritter!" the pilot shouted back at him.

Although both Maud and Ritter were firing weapons at the group, the true threat was about to raise its ugly head. All around Ritter, at the edges of the forest and from within foliage, red eyes lit up. The Marine turned and fired futilely into the trees.

"We need to put on the cloaks and climb down," Logan said, hastily. They all donned a black, hooded cloak and left the remaining ones behind. Save for Eve, they slung the modified shotguns on their shoulders from the gun straps. They began to climb down towards the fire.

It was almost completely dark out when the creatures made their attack. All at once, half a dozen of the fiends ran out of the forest and congregated on Ritter. He tried using his rifle to keep them at bay but there were too many of them and they made short work of the soft, human body. His limbs were thrown about as they fought each other for the good, torso meat.

The group were about ten feet off of the ground as the watchtower began to moan from the stress of the fire. Their hands began to burn as the metal heated up. "We have to jump," said Ironson, who was already leaping off of the struts. He landed beside the fire, searing the edges of his cloak, but he managed to roll away from it. The others followed him, landing less gracefully than he did.

The fire raced onwards up the watchtower and they could hear Maud's scream go from anger to horror. Nearby, they seen Rachel's body engulfed in flames, but Jon's Winchester shotgun was just out of the fiery grasp. He gave his modified shotgun to Eve, who had twisted her ankle on landing, and snatched up his lucky charm.

Their presence had not gone unnoticed, as Ritter was consumed in seconds. The creatures dropped to their haunches, like canines rearing for an attack. Their round, pupilless eyes flashed red at the cloaked four. It seemed the cloaks were working. The creatures craned their necks and flashed their eyes red again.

One brave creature approached the group, snarling with its large toothed maw. The mowhawk-like hair on its head prickled back and forth as it desperately tried to mark its prey. The group raised their weapons as it drew nearer, fear powering their desire to survive. They had nowhere to run. To their front prowled the large, yet maybe confused invaders. To their back the watchtower blazed.

Logan brought a hand to the stun gun that was attached to the bottom of the semi-automatic shotgun by electrical tape. He aimed center mass of the creature and pulled the trigger of the stun gun. It hit its mark and the creature stood straight and fell like a plank of wood to the ground. Jon rushed at it with his handy Winchester, stuck the barrel into the creatures stuttering mouth and pulled the trigger. The creature's head exploded into black, gooey bits, causing the rest of the creatures to howl at the group in unison.

Jon backed up, looking back and forth at his enemies, waiting for another to spring up. Eve gave Logan a replacement cartridge for his stun gun. As he was putting the new cartridge back in, another creature began running at their location. Ironson stunned this one and repeated Jon's charging maneuver.

Another creature fell, then another. Two creatures remained, hissing and snarling at the humans who figured out how to kill them. Logan and Eve put these creatures down before they could make their own attack.

Covered in dirt and the gooey blood of their enemies, the group stood triumphant. Logan was a little less afraid of the things than he was before, but feared facing a larger group. The cloaks did their job in helping to befuddle the creature's mark. They could be beaten. They could be killed.

Chapter 9 - Omega

They stayed the night beside the heat of the blazing watchtower, taking turns keeping watch. Out in the forest they heard the creature's calls far away. The sound sent chills down Logan's spine, but they now had a way to defend themselves at night, and could move pseudo-safely during the day.

The morning sun rose, peeking through the trees at the survivors. The scene it lit up looked like a battle had been fought there. The watchtower was no longer on fire, but it was a charred remain of what it used to be, only held up by its metal struts. The creatures they fought the night before laid dead in a half circle around where the group had jumped off the tower. Rachel's body was charcoal, burned with their M16A4 rifles and Ironson's pistol.

Ironson had last watch and he was standing before what was left of Ritter's corpse when Logan stretched himself awake. Jon and Eve were still snoozing as the smoldering tower still offered more warmth than they had felt for a while.

Logan approached Ironson, who heard him coming and said, "There was a time where he, the rest of our squad and I were family."

Logan did not really know what to say, so just said, "I suppose it'd be like if Jon and I turned on each other. I wouldn't want that to happen. He's more of a brother to me than my actual, blood brother."

"Your brother still out there?" asked Ironson, who picked up Ritter's M4 Carbine and began wiping blood off of it.

Logan hesitated. Of course his brother wasn't out there, but he had never told anyone what had happened. For a moment he thought about confessing, but couldn't bring himself to tell the pilot. Instead, he responded, "He was in prison last I knew."

Ironson was looking right into Logan's eyes, as if he were reading the younger man's mind. He continued to clean the rifle and responded, "If you don't mind me asking, what'd he do?"

"He used to beat women, but there was one that really sent him over the deep end. He had problems with drugs, too."

Logan was usually good at reading people, but Ironson hardly ever showed emotion. No eye twitches, no frowns or smiles. He always spoke the same and in a monotone. Logan just could not get a bead on what was going through his head.

"If it were my brother, I would have done something about it," Ironson said in a flat tone. He plunged the barrel of the rifle into the ground next to where his former comrade laid in pieces.

Logan looked down with a, "Yeah..." that trailed off. Then, to change the subject, he said, "Why not keep the rifle?"

"Stock is broken," said Ironson, turning away from Ritter's gore, "It's useless."

Logan looked over at where the modified shotguns laid and said, "I guess we could take those. They've already proven useful."

Ironson nodded and said, "Benelli M2, Kal-Tec KSG and a SPAS-12. With Kilroy's Winchester 120, that's a helluva arsenal. Not cheap, either. Wonder how they got them."

"Guess we'll never know," said Logan.

"Oh well," said Ironson, patting Logan on the shoulder as he walked past him, "Let's get these knuckleheads up and get back to our supplies."

Logan nodded at him and seen a glint of metal in the grass. He walked over to it and seen it was Maud's revolver. Upon closer inspection, he noticed it was a snub nose .357 Magnum. It had one bullet left in the cylinder. He picked it up and put it in the previously empty holster in his tactical vest.

When they reached the beach, their bags had been ransacked. Canned goods and bottles of water were spread all over the beach. They could not tell if anything had been taken at first, but when they gathered everything up, they only had two rucksacks worth of items left.

"I bet some damn raccoons did this," said Jon, swinging the straps of one of the packs over his shoulders.

"Normally I'd agree," said Logan, noticing that the canoe was gone, "But we haven't seen a single wild animal out here and the canoe is gone. Maybe someone came back for it and took our supplies as a fortuitous gift."

Ironson took note of what he had put into his pack, shouldered it and said, "Either way, we have far less supplies than we did before. Gonna have to take it easy on food until we get to St. Louis."

"I remember what happened last time a marine tried to ration food," said Jon with a glare.

Ironson swiftly turned to the bearded man and marched up to him, saying, "If your memory is that good, you'll remember that I was on your side during that."

He stopped a couple feet away from Jon, who said, "Yeah, you're on our side until you aren't."

"You got a problem?" said Ironson, taking another step forward.

"Jon, stop," said Eve, hobbling over to her fiancé, "He hasn't given us a reason to not trust him."

"Just like we trusted those women. Then what happened? Oh yeah, they tried to eat us," said Jon, balling his fists.

Logan stepped between the two men, holding a hand up at each one, "What happened was unfortunate, but it doesn't mean we should fight each other. We worked as a group to overcome that debacle and we survived. All four of us played a part and we're all standing because of it."

Jon shifted his gaze to his friend and blinked away his anger. He said, "Yeah, I guess so. Let's get going," before marching off along the river.

Ironson shrugged at Logan before setting off as well. Jon stopped to help Eve walk before continuing onwards, while Logan brought up the rear, carrying the two empty packs.

Travel was slower than normal, with Eve barely being able to walk. They had to stop more often when the pain in her ankle flared up. She never asked to stop, but they would out of respect. Jon and Ironson shared few words as they walked.

They had divvied up the shotgun shells and stun gun cartridges between them. Logan took the Benelli, that had once been used by Rachel. Eve took the KSG due to it being lighter and smaller. Ironson took the SPAS and Jon kept his Winchester, even though it wasn't modified like the rest.

Along the way they seen the remains of a fight. Several creatures were dead, floating in the river past them and a few more laid motionless on the rocky beach. The group gave them a wide berth, even though they were most certainly dead.

They found remains of their supplies in and along the river, but most of the cans and boxes were smashed and spilled. They scavenged what they could and left anything open or destroyed.

During one of their breaks, Logan searched the nearby woods for a walking stick for Eve. He found one that was strong and straighter than others he seen. Using his pocket knife, he stripped the bark off and smoothed the knots on it. Whittling wood used to be one of his favorite past times while camping in the past and he had not had an opportunity to do it for a long time. It also helped him push back the memories of recent events.

He presented it to the engaged couple and said, "Thought this might help you walk."

Eve's face brightened and she said, "Oh, thank you so much, Logan," before giving him a friendly hug.

"Nice one," said Jon, admiring the carving.

"I was starting to feel like a burden," Eve said as she tried the walking stick out by putting her weight on it.

"You're no burden at all," Logan said as he picked up some crackers and munched on them before they headed off.

The river was still wide and deep this far south in Missouri. The forest on each side began opening up to farmlands and small subdivisions. The houses were up on hills above the river, but some had paths leading down to little docks. One dock had the blue canoe they had seen earlier tied to it.

"Should we check out the houses for the rest of our supplies?" asked Logan from the back of the group.

"We shouldn't take any unnecessary risks," said Ironson, dismissing the idea without stopping his gait.

"But they took our stuff," said Jon, furrowing his brow, "We already don't know how long it'll take to get to St. Louis and we're all armed."

Ironson stopped and turned to the rest of his companions. He said, "It's not going to take that long if we keep moving."

"It's too dangerous," said Eve, "I agree that we should keep going."

Logan noticed blood on the canoe and dock. It trailed up to a white, single story house that had a wooden deck at its back door. He said, "I'm going to check it out."

"We should keep going," said Ironson, his voice a touch louder than normal.

"Logan and I'll go take a look," said Jon, already starting up the grassy hill, "Stay here with Eve. Should only take a minute or two."

Ironson said, "You got five minutes. If you don't find anything then double time it back here."

"Thanks for the permission," said Jon, shaking his head.

He and Logan held their shotguns at the ready as they approached the back deck of the house. The trail of blood went up the steps and to the back, sliding doors. A bloody handprint was on the glass door and along the edge of the doorway.

Jon kept his back to the siding wall and peered into the home. He could not see much other than a kitchen area connected to a living room with some furniture, an entertainment center with a television that had not been turned on in months and a hallway leading to bedrooms.

Logan stepped on the opposite side of the sliding doors as his friend and slowly opened it. Silence greeted them and Logan said, "Hello? Anyone there?"

There was no response so Logan peeked his head in and said, "Hello?" again. Still nothing.

The two crept in and scanned the inside. The blood trailed onto the carpet of the living room and into the hallway. Another hand print was on the wood paneled wall next to the entrance of the hall. The two friends nodded to each other and Jon took point, holding out his Winchester at the ready.

The blood went under the first door they encountered and they mimicked their positions as they did outside, standing with their backs against the wall on each side of the door. Logan knocked on the door and was met with silence once again.

Jon took the door handle and turned it slowly until it unlatched. He pushed the door open while staying behind the wall, in case something tried to attack them. Nothing happened, which prompted both men to peer into the room.

It was a small bedroom with a boarded up window. A dresser sat with half of its four drawers opened and clothes hanging out of it. The bed was unmade, with sheets and blankets thrown on it haphazardly. Sitting on the floor was a person wearing the same black and hooded cloak as they were, leaning their back against the bed. The blood trail ended at the cloaked figure, who appeared to be holding a photograph in a picture frame.

They appeared unarmed as Jon and Logan stepped in with their weapons raised. The hood turned slowly towards them, putting them both on edge. "Won't be any need for that," said the figure, painfully in a gruff voice.

"Never can be too sure," said Jon, keeping his firearm trained on the man.

Logan slung his modified shotgun over his shoulder and took a knee next to the wounded man, who, with great difficulty, pushed his hood back to reveal his face. He was an older man with white hair and a face that had seen much hardship in his life.

"You're wearing a cloak like us," said Logan.

"Yup. Used to be a group of us, but don't recognize you," he said before coughing up blood, which drained down his stubbly chin.

"Is that canoe yours?" asked Logan.

"Yup, again. I take it those supplies were yours?"

"Yeah, you stole 'em from us," said Jon, unrelenting in his

aim at the man.

The man tried to chuckle but it only made him grimace before saying, "Finders keepers, I thought, but I didn't get far with it. Got ambushed by the burrowers on my way back home. Took care of some, but they left me a little present." He opened his cloak to show multiple gashes and stabs in his torso.

"Maybe Eve can help," said Logan, starting to stand up.

The man grabbed Logan's cloak and pulled him with a pathetic pull. He said, "Don't even. I'm not long for this world. My vision is already fading," before looking back down at the photograph.

Logan followed his eyes towards the photo and almost gasped at what he saw. He seen the man, not as rough and clean shaven. He was smiling and standing between Rachel and Maud. Both women looked happy and Maud looked far less crazy than when the group met her.

"Since you have those weapons and cloaks," said the man, "I can only guess my wife and daughter are dead."

"Damn..." said Jon, lowering his weapon and bowing his head.

"I'm afraid so," said Logan, wincing at having to tell the man they killed his family.

"It's ok. They weren't who they used to be. I hadn't seen them for about a month now. My daughter, she was...always a confused girl. When the burrowers came, she couldn't take it, neither could my wife. We had a good sized group but they..." the man coughed again, spit mixing with blood.

"Save your strength," said Logan, putting his hand on the man's shoulder.

"Got none left," the man said, "That revolver was mine. It got any bullets left?"

"One."

"Well, you better make it count then," said the man, who pointed at the dresser, "There's some slugs for the shotguns in there, a box of stun gun cartridges and my journal. Take it all. I just ask you let me have my revolver back."

Logan felt sorry for the old man. He took out the revolver from his vest holster and unloaded the bullet, handing them to the man separately. Maud's husband smiled and said, "You're a smart one, but don't worry, got no intentions of using the last bullet on you."

"You want us to stay a little longer?" asked Logan, who felt odd about leaving the man to his fate.

"Nah. Go ahead and take what you need then be on your way."

"What's your name, old man?" Jon asked.

The man grimaced in pain but smirked and said, "You can call me Omega."

Jon raised an eyebrow and said, "Uh, ok then."

"I guess we'll leave you to it, then," said Logan, who stood and walked to the dresser. Like Omega said, all the items were there. His journal was leather-bound and looked like it had been kicked around in the dirt a few times. Logan put the items in his empty rucksack, but kept the journal with him.

As Logan and Jon turned to leave the bedroom, Omega said, "Few miles up the river is Hendrickson. If you're heading that way, I'd avoid it if I were you."

"Why?" asked Jon.

"The burrowers have a nest there. There's more about it in my journal."

"Thanks for the supplies, and I'm sorry for-" Logan began.

The old man waved at him and interrupted, "Don't. Just try to be good men from here on out."

"Farewell," said Logan, as they turned and closed the door behind them.

Before leaving, they checked a few kitchen drawers and found some batteries and few medical supplies. Logan packed what he found away, feeling guilty for destroying the man's family.

As they exited the home and walked back down the hill to Ironson and Eve, a loud shot from the revolver rang out. Ironson began to ready his weapon, but Logan told them what had transpired inside. Before moving on up the river, Logan took one last look at the house, wondering what he would learn from Omega's journal.

Chapter 10 - The Journal

They spent the night in an old fishing shack near the river. It was rickety and probably hadn't been used for years, but the wooden walls gave the group respite from the wind. Winter was growing harsher with each day and Logan felt like he would never know warmth again.

Through the night they heard the invaders howling from afar, hunting their unknown quarries. While Logan was on his turn to stand guard, he felt a numbness in his toes, but ignored it to keep his attention on potential threats.

His eyes had adjusted to the dark and he could just see the still forms of his friends laying huddled together in the middle of the shack. Eve had been upset at Jon before the events at the watchtower, but Logan wasn't quite sure what about. Jon and

Ironson had an uneasy truce, but who knew how long that'd last. Logan did his best to keep the peace between them, but he feared they would eventually come to blows.

Standing there, looking out the broken window to a still, moonlit river, Logan felt alone. More alone than he had ever felt. Jon used to try to set him up with girls, but none of them proved much more than a one-night stand. He just couldn't really connect with anyone, no matter how much he tried. He had known Jon since high school and had known Eve for ten years. Other than them, who else did he have?

"No one," Logan mumbled aloud while looking up at the moon.

"No one what," Jon said quietly from behind him.

Logan hadn't heard him get up while he was lost in thought. He turned and said, "Nothing. Your turn to stand guard?"

Jon stretched and joined Logan at the broken window. He said, "What's on your mind, man? We haven't really talked since we left Field Foods."

What should he say? That he was jealous of Jon and Eve's relationship? That he had been lying about what really happened to his brother? That he felt like he was losing his way?

"That Omega guy said try to be good men," Logan said, finding his voice, "But what does that mean?"

Jon looked at Logan, who was ready for a smartass comment. The bearded man said, "We have to protect each other. Bleed, sweat and struggle for one another. Eve may be my fiancé, but we're brothers, Logan. I know you'll do whatever it takes to protect her. You've already proven that. I just want you to know that I'm here for you too. Ain't no one gonna break the three of us up.

"That's kinda what I think he meant by be good men. Watch each other's' backs and fight for one another. We've seen how people crack when there's no Internet anymore and I don't think it's gonna get any easier."

"I do miss the Internet..." Logan said.

"Oh God, me too," Jon said with a chuckle, "But I'll settle with being alive for now."

Logan wasn't expecting something like that to come out of Jon's mouth, but then again, Jon was never dumb. They had myriads of deep discussions over the years about the meaning of life or what it all means. Logan genuinely felt better and was thankful for his friend, even if he was a bit of an asshole sometimes.

"Gonna try to get some sleep," Logan said.

Jon nodded, picked up his Winchester and leaned at the window. Logan laid down, his back to Eve, who was sandwiched between him and Ironson. Eve turned and buried her face into Logan's back and put her arm around Logan's torso. He immediately looked at Jon with a look of protest.

Jon just smiled and whispered, "Careful, I'll kick your ass," before waving his hand, "Don't worry about it. It's too damn cold."

Logan awoke early in the morning and gingerly moved Eve's arm off of him. Ironson wasn't in the shack and in his resting place was Jon, tucked into the fetal position. Logan didn't want to wake them, so he got up, threw his cloak around him and exited the shack.

He found Ironson squatting next to the river, looking at something in his hands. His own, black cloak swayed gently with the breeze. When Logan's feet crunched into the rocky shore behind him, he stood up and tucked away whatever it was.

"Morning, Foster," Ironson said.

"Morning," said Logan then poked his thumb at the fishing shack, "They aren't up yet."

"Let them sleep a little while longer. Eve needs to rest her foot anyways," said Ironson before he blew into his hands and rubbed them together.

"Think it'll be ok to build a fire?" Logan asked.

Ironson nodded and said, "Affirmative. The cloaks seem to work well enough. I'm going to scout the perimeter."

Ironson walked up river past a copse of trees. Logan was curious what he was looking at but paid it no heed. He had secrets of his own he didn't want found out.

After Logan built a small fire and let his body warm up, he pulled out Omega's journal. There were some scribblings about hunting and Omega's interactions with neighbors. Logan skipped past most of the early writings to find when Omega first seen the creatures.

115

October 30

Ran across weird thing in the woods. Same woods I hunted for thirty years. Never seen anything like it. Looked human but wasn't. Stayed downwind like always. It didn't see me. Told Rachel and Maud to stay inside.

Told Gregory about it. He and his wife seen it too. He hunted with me before. We went back out.

October 31

Those things are evil. It didn't see me again. It seen Greg. Blinked its eyes red at him. Found Greg and his wife dead. Some kind of mark?

Need to gather everyone together. Don't know how many of those things there are. James' place might work to hold out in. He's paranoid and safe.

November 12

Had twenty people. The things came in force last night. Now we have ten. Got past our defenses.

Found some cloaks. They protect us during the day. It confuses the things. Can scavenge for supplies safely at day. Food and fuel getting low. Slim pickings.

Worried about Rachel. No more pills. Hope she can keep it together. It'd take five men to take her down.

November 17

Lost someone else last night. Too damn hard to kill those things. Lost eleven people and only killed one of them. Got an idea. It's risky. Maybe my last entry if it goes awry.

November 20

It worked! Used one of James' stun guns. Dropped it like a rock. Shotgun to the head finished it.

Bucky went missing. Don't think it was the things. Eight of us now. Have to be extra careful.

Rachel and Maud spending time in the old watchtower. Strategic location with a good vantage point. Don't like being away from them. Rachel is struggling. They're my family.

Logan was completely immersed in Omega's findings and took to heart every bit of information he learned. He was so swept away in the mind of this man, he didn't hear Jon and Ironson arguing until they were already shouting. They were on the opposite side of the fire to Logan.

"It's not her damned fault she can't move very fast!" Jon shouted, pacing around like a caged lion.

"Didn't say it was, Kilroy," said Ironson, whose normally stoic composure was starting to crack as he raised his own voice, "All I said was we would've made it to the highway by now."

"You're the dumbass that said to jump," said Jon.

"Jon, stop, I'll try to move faster today," said Eve, who limped up with her walking stick.

"No babe, you haven't done anything wrong. This jackass is goin' to get his lights knocked out," said Jon, his face turning red.

"It was either jump or burn. Which would you have rather done?" said Ironson.

"Gentlemen," said Logan, stowing away the journal and standing up, "Er, and gentlelady. We should be on our way."

The arguing men hushed up and began gathering their supplies. Both throwing things in their bags like they were throwing a baseball. Logan didn't get it. Jon was always hotheaded, but he really had it out for the pilot. He'd maybe try to talk to him about it later.

Eve hobbled over to Logan and said, "I feel like we're the only sane ones."

Logan folded his arms to warm his hands and said, "I know what you mean."

"I just wish Jon would calm down," she said, watching her

fiancé angrily pack.

"You can tell me to shut up if you don't want to talk about it," said Logan, "But what was it you were upset about? Before we got to the watchtower."

Her eyes still on her fiancé, she said, "He ignored me and started to speak for me. I want him to know I'm a part of the group."

"Oh," said Logan, "I had no idea."

"Im sorta over it with what's going on, as long as he doesn't do it again," said Eve, who then looked at Logan and smiled, "I'm glad you're here though."

Logan grinned and felt less alone than the night before.

"Guess we better get going, then," Eve said.

As they were walking, or limping in Eve's case, Logan shared his findings with the group. Ironson pondered, "Wonder if others figured out ways to kill those things."

Jon responded, his voice seething in sarcasm, "How can one guy survive for so long, but you guys didn't stand a chance? No offence."

Ironson ignored the snap in Jon's voice, and said, "We tried using brute force. For every creature we took out, there'd be a hundred more behind them. They knew where to put their numbers. We didn't have much time to react so we threw everything we could at them all at once. I'm guessing out here, they don't see many threats, so we only see small contingents."

119

"So there's an advantage to keeping to a small group," said Logan, thinking out loud, "How many of those things do you think there are?"

"No idea. Millions, probably," said Ironson.

Everyone fell silent, only hearing the flowing water of the river next to them. Logan tried to imagine what millions of those things could do. How could humanity have any chance, even with all the technology. He concluded that war machines were designed to kill fellow humans, not aliens, demons or whatever the invaders were.

"It's sad that we've focused on killing each other over the millennia," said Logan, breaking the silence, "And never thought about being defied from other beings."

"Maybe we can do things differently, now," said Eve, "If there's any coming back from this, we can change."

"I hope you're right," Logan responded.

"Where's your family, Joseph?" Eve asked.

After a prolonged moment, the pilot responded, "They died before this all happened."

"Oh..." said Eve, "I'm sorry, I didn't mean-"

"It's fine," cut in Ironson, "Let's just get to that damned highway."

At midday, they stopped to share a couple of fruit cocktail cans. Logan was waiting for them to stop so he could continue reading the journal, which he was becoming obsessed with.

December 1

Branching out further for supplies. Food getting real low. Went to Hendrickson to search for survivors. No one there but the creatures. Thousands of them. Burrowing into the stoneworks there. Think they live underground.

Seen a burrower larger than the others. They're usually eight foot or so. This one was bigger than that. Skin looked smooth. Had an almost human face. Barked orders at the smaller ones. Some kind of leader? I call him the Enforcer.

Another missing person when I got back. Seven of us now. Some are talking of leaving. Can't blame them. I won't be leaving. This is my home.

December 10

Almost gave up writing this. Found why people went missing. Knew Maud was slipping but...Not sure how to say it. So I won't.

They're staying at the watchtower now. I'm staying home. Everyone else has left.

December 18

Killed three burrowers. Used to hunt before. Going to hunt them now. Damn them.

December 25

Merry Christmas to me. Killed five more of them.

December 28

Not much to say. Using the canoe to go upriver. Killed four more burrowers. Haven't seen other animals. Need food.

January 1

That's it. Can't stand being alone. Miss my wife even if she's...Going to the watchtower. If they kill me then...

Well, then great.

That was the last entry. Logan figured he came to see his family and when he left, he found their supplies. He wondered how they passed each other without seeing one another, or maybe they just did not see Omega.

"We shouldn't follow the river all the way to Hendrickson," said Logan as he closed the journal and ate a peach out of one of the cans.

"Didn't that guy say there was a nest there?" said Jon, helping Eve to her feet.

"Yeah, his journal said he seen thousands of them there," said Logan, getting ready to travel again, "So we should head north, and bypass it completely."

"The less I see those things, the better," said Eve, "It's a good thing you read that journal, we could have walked right into their home."

"So we head north from here, then," said Ironson, "Good work, Foster."

They had to cross the river to continue north. They found a spot that was not too deep, only came to their knees. The water was freezing though and they had to step through frost to make it across. Once they were across they made a small fire and dried out their shoes or boots and socks. Hypothermia was not something they wanted to worry about out here.

While they were waiting, Logan noticed a tall, metal structure to the northwest. He remembered reading about a stoneworks in Omega's journal and figured it had to do something with it.

Eve sat on her knees next to Logan, who had his feet bare and next to the fire. She leaned down, looking at his feet and said, "Logan, your toes."

Logan looked down and noticed a couple of his toes on his right foot were bluish-white. He said, "Yeah, they're a little numb. A few of them are tingly."

"You might have frostbite," she said with a grim expression on her face, "Are you able to walk ok? Sometimes it makes you clumsy if it gets really bad."

"As far as I can tell, I'm ok," Logan said, starting to get worried, "Does it really look that bad?"

Eve picked up a small twig and pushed the skin of his toes with it. She said, "Do you feel that?"

"No."

Eve tossed the twig aside and said, "You can have one of my socks."

Logan shook his head and said, "No no no. There's no point in you getting it too. Will it get better?"

Eve shrugged and scrunched her face as if she were trying to hold back bad news. She said, "It can, but it needs rewarmed. Even after we that, you'll get blisters and need to stay off your feet for twenty-four hours."

Jon and Ironson had been watching and listening. They both checked their feet, but they seemed fine. The two then looked at Logan, as if they were waiting for him to decide what he wants to do.

Logan finally said, "We can't stop. We're already getting to a point where we'll need to ration our foodstuffs. Maybe if we find a vehicle on the highway we can stop for a moment, but not right now."

Ironson breathed out a visible sigh and said, "We'll see how it is when we get to the highway. For now, we need to move out."

They gathered everything together and got ready to travel. Logan cursed his body. Why him? He had never broken a bone, never gotten seriously injured before the invaders came. It was cold, for sure, but he didn't imagine he would lose parts of his body from it. He tried to push it out of his mind and decided he'll deal with it when the time comes.

They had a short walk through some woods before coming across a farmhouse and a barn, with fields all around it. One of the creatures prowled a few acres away in one of the tundra-like fields. The group moved low and silently at Ironson's command. Even with their cloaks, none of them wanted to call attention to themselves.

Beyond the farmhouse was a road that split in two directions. A sign pointing northwest said HENDRICKSON 3 MILES while another sign pointing north said MO-172 8 MILES. They followed the road northwards, as Jon said 172 crossed over Route 67. It was a narrow country road that went up and down forested hills.

As they walked, a single snowflake fell. Logan paid it little heed and was surprised it hadn't started snowing already with how cold it was. Clouds rolled in and a devastating wind howled through the survivors.

Chapter **11 - Friend or Foe**

Eve was able to walk easier, but she kept the walking stick anyways. She appreciated the gesture from Logan and thought throwing it off to the side of the road would look disrespectful. So she kept it for the time being.

She pulled her cloak around her body, as the others had started doing, to protect herself from the harsh winds. Snow was hitting her in the face like tiny bullets as the ground began to disappear underneath the ever growing layer of powder. She swore the temperature dropped twenty degrees. Her hand went into one of her pockets to check her phone for weather updates before she realized that wasn't a thing anymore.

"We should stop at the next house before we start along the highway," said Ironson, wiping snow off his aviator sunglasses.

"Yeah, it'll be dark soon and my balls are already freezin' off," said Jon, wrapping his cloak tighter around him.

"We agreeing, now?" asked Ironson, bemusedly.

"That it's cold? Hell, yeah. That you're a good judge of character? Not so much," Jon responded.

Ironson shook his head and continued westward on 172. The others followed, and Eve overheard Logan say to Jon, "Give him a break, no one could have known what would happen."

"I'm just making sure it doesn't happen again," said Jon.

"Beating a dead horse never helped anyone," said Eve, her jaw quivering under her hood.

"Maybe you're right, but he doesn't speak for me, all I'm saying," said Jon with an air of finality. He was a stubborn man and his time as a corrections officer made trusting others a chore. Eve wished she was more like him in that regard; she knew she was too trusting at times.

"Sounds familiar," Eve said under her breath. She hoped he understood why she was upset with him after he said that, but he probably wouldn't. As much as she loved him, he was so thick headed. Whatever, she was over it anyways. Or so she told herself.

Where the two highways met was somewhere to stay, and thankfully enough, as it was nearly night. There was an old, single story hotel, that looked questionable enough, with rooms in a line, forming a long building. In front of it was a truck stop and places to fuel up. All around the two buildings was an orange, gravel parking lot that was almost all the way covered in snow. There were a few semis parked in the gravel lot and an abandoned truck at the fuel pump.

"Hotel or truck stop?" asked Ironson as they looked at the location from across the highway.

"That hotel looks creepy," said Eve.

"Truck stop it is, then," said Jon, starting to walk towards it.

"Wait!" snapped the pilot, stepping up to Jon, "We may not be the only ones who have found this place. We should make sure we're not alone."

"What if there is?" asked Jon, turning his lips into a frown, "You just gonna give 'em your gun and bend over for them?"

There he goes again. Eve seen the look on Jon's face. He was ready to rumble. She's only seen him look like that a few times before, and it always ended with a fight. Even with the thick beard, she could tell he was about to snap.

What she didn't expect was Ironson's reaction. His face turned red and he balled his fists up. He said, "That's e-fucking-nough! I don't make the same mistakes twice, but if you wanna have a go, let's do it."

Jon dropped his pack and thrusted his Winchester into Logan's arms before stepping towards Ironson. He said, "I'm always ready," and the next word he said particularly scathingly, "Lieutenant."

Ironson swung one of his balled up fists at Jon, who ducked and retaliated with an uppercut to his opponent's jaw with surprising speed considering his height and bulk. He followed up with a jab with his left hand that the marine pilot caught and twisted. Ironson used the momentum to throw Jon to the ground with a great amount of force.

"Both of you, stop this!" shouted Logan, "We're all on the same side here."

Jon got up and said with an angry glare, "Tell that to the pussy," before charging at Ironson. They clashed but Jon was able to get his arms around Ironson's waist, and picked him up before dropping him to the ground. He straddled the pilot, who grabbed Jon around the neck and pulled him into his chest. Jon tried to swing, but he was pulled too close to connect.

Eve was shaking her head as they fought, but something else caught her attention. Across the highway stood a young man, watching the action. He wore a thick, tan coat over overalls, which all hung loose on his thin frame. His head was covered in unkempt, red hair.

"Uh, guys?" said Eve, pointing at the voyeur.

Logan looked where she pointed and shouted, "Jon! Joseph!"

Ironson, who was still on his back but somehow had control of the scuffle, looked over after them. He seen the young man and pushed Jon off him. Jon grunted as he rolled into the road, but when he stopped he also seen the stranger.

"Ya'll alright?" he said with a Southern twang.

"We're fine," said Jon, throwing up puffs of snow as he got to his feet.

Logan raised Jon's shotgun towards the newcomer and said, "Friend or Foe?"

This prompted the stranger to raise his hands. He said, "Easy, friend, I ain't no foe. Why don't you come on inside and get warm."

"We're keeping our weapons," said Jon, shooting a glance back at the pilot.

The wind picked up, making the young man bow his head and try to protect himself from the snow by raising up the collar of his coat. He started back towards the truck stop and said over his shoulder, "Your choice, but I'm goin' in."

Logan and Jon shared a quizzical look. Logan said, "Let's go in with him, it's freezing out here. We should remain cautious, though."

"Don't get too close to them and keep your firearms ready," said Ironson, wiping blood from his lips, "I'll take a look around the perimeter before joining you inside."

130

"Alright, alright," said Jon, "Let's see what this guy is all about and hope he doesn't try to eat us."

As they followed after the red head, Eve could only think about getting warm. Her mind didn't work like Jon's, always ready for a fight. Or like Logan, who observed everything. It was difficult to think about anything else but getting out of winter's grasp.

From whence they came, the creatures' call could be heard. The sharp notes of their communication sang over the thunderous howl of the wind. The group collectively sped up to the doors of the truck stop.

Ironson said, "Gonna make sure they don't have any surprises for us."

"Just don't get caught outside with those things," said Logan, "Can already hear them hunting."

"I'll keep an eye out. Now go on in," said Ironson, marching away from the entrance and around a dark corner.

Logan, Jon and Eve stepped into the confines of the truck stop, which was surprisingly warm compared to outside. The building was divided into a small convenience store at the entrance, and a restaurant further in. Every window was boarded up with haphazardly nailed in planks of wood.

Most of the shelves of the store were devoid of useful items, left with memorabilia and cleaning materials mostly. The cash register at the counter next to the front door was on its side, already looted of its money. Eve scoffed at how anyone could think money was useful anymore, but still checked to see if there was any change leftover.

The restaurant was lit up by a few oil lanterns, placed on empty tables where diners used to sit at to eat. All around the sides of the dining area were boots with built-in tables. One door led to the kitchen and another led to the restrooms. To Eve's left, there was a fireplace with a fire already made within, the source of the warmth she felt when they walked in. Sitting on the mantel were various bottles of high dollar liquor. Half of them were empty or only contained a few shots worth.

The red head was speaking with two other people huddled close to the fireplace. One was a girl, who looked to be no older than twenty. She had long, dark hair and a clean, cute face. She wore a Metallica t-shirt underneath a black, leather jacket and lycra pants.

The other person was a man in his forties. He had dark hair as well and was slightly overweight. He wore a red, goosedown coat. When the three approached, he stood up, only coming up to Logan's chin in height, with a warm look. When he seen they were armed, however, his expression changed and he stepped between the cloaked group and the girl.

He looked as if he was trying to act tough, but his eyes betrayed his act. He said, "N-now, we don't want no trouble."

Logan responded, keeping his modified shotgun at ease, "Nor do we, but we're prepared to deal with trouble if need be."

The red head said, "Look, ya'll don't seem so bad, but take it easy, ya? We're just passing through."

"So are we," said Jon, who held his Winchester in the crook of his arm, as if it were his baby, "How do we know we can trust you?"

"How about this," said the red head, who reached behind a table. He brought out a bolt action hunting rifle with a scope. It was covered in a woodland camouflage paint. This made Jon raise his weapon at the red head.

Jon growled, "How about that? How about I just shoot you now and be done with it."

"Please," said the target in Jon's iron sites. He slowly carried the rifle, nonthreateningly, towards them. He laid it on a table before them and stepped backwards. He said, "I don't know fully well if we can trust ya'll, either, but that's the only gun we have. My name is Danny Childs, by the way. That's Astrid Skalder and her daddy, Eric Skalder."

Eve, who thought the whole show of force was unnecessary, shook Danny's hand and said, "I'm Eve Parker. Sorry if we're a little skittish. We've had some...bad experiences with people we've met."

"Then we have more in common than we may think," said Danny, looking Eve up and down.

She was used to guys looking at her in such a way. Jon always said he never seen anyone look so good in scrubs when she'd come home from the hospital. Even Logan had told her before that she was beautiful, which would embarrass her coming from him.

She knew she looked better than most and her assets were perfectly proportioned, so she didn't mind the odd look or catcall here and there.

But for some reason, when Danny looked at her, it made her uneasy.

Jon eased up and said, "Don't get any ideas. Name's Jon Kilroy," while thrusting his hand towards the meek Danny.

The snow began to build up outside, forcing Ironson to pull his cloak tighter around him as he investigated the grounds. He found nothing suspicious at the end of the hotel, which he was not surprised, as it was pitch black out and most of the hotel room doors were locked.

He had been hearing the creatures call out all around him, but they sounded far away. He took note of it nonetheless and began making his way back to the truck stop building.

He really did want to make sure everything checked out, but he almost left the three. He had one of the packs of supplies and could have easily just walked away. His fight with Jon earlier made him think they were not worth taking with him, but it was Logan that made him stay. He seemed a little weird and eccentric, but he made Ironson feel like part of the group. Friends were in short supply in this new world, so he would try to make amends with Jon at some point.

When Ironson entered the restaurant, Danny, Eric and Astrid re-introduced themselves to him. Everyone had gotten comfortable and sat in chairs around the fireplace, save for Danny and Astrid, who sat in a corner booth and spoke to each other in hushed tones. Danny's hands were all over the girl, but she seemed to tolerate it.

The marine made sure to be aware of any new building he entered. Of any possible exits and threats. This building had only two exits, the front door and a door out the back of the kitchen. Eric looked out of shape, but it was hard to tell if he could handle himself. Danny looked like he could get blown over by a stiff wind, Ironson wasn't worried about him. Astrid didn't seem to be a threat, but she had a wry smile when Danny would touch her. Their relationship was superficial, Ironson concluded, possibly just physical.

Logan had his boots off and set his socked feet near the fire. He was leaning back in the chair, letting his toes warm up. Hopefully that would help, as Eve's sprained ankle already slowed them down enough. They didn't need anything else to keep them from getting to St. Louis. Ironson made sure not to mention it, though, thinking it would spark another confrontation with Jon.

He wasn't afraid of the bearded man; he had fought more skilled fighters before. The pilot just didn't want to shake the boat any more than it was. And since they had met a new group, it would be tactical to keep the peace between his own squad.

Eric looked nervous about the newcomers, but he said, "We

lived just outside Williamsville to the west a ways when those things came. At first people started just disappearing, but one night they came hard. My daughter and her boyfriend, Danny, were at my ex-wife's house. She...didn't make it. We've been wandering ever since, finding food n' such as we go, but finding less and less as time went on. We only got here last night before we try to figure out what to do next."

"Why don't you come with us?" asked Eve, rubbing her hands in the warmness of the fire. She meant well, but Ironson didn't approve.

Mirroring Ironson's thoughts, Jon said, "Don't think that's a good idea. More people means more mouths to feed, and you don't have a way to protect yourselves, save for the Remington."

"We don't want to be a burden on anyone," said Eric, "Is there any way we could borrow some food, though? If you have any to spare."

Ironson said, leaning back in his chair, "Got anything to trade?" knowing full well they didn't. He had already scoured the room with his eyes and seen nothing else of value.

Eric looked over at the marine pilot with an empty look then said, "I'm afraid we don't. We have a few bottles of water, but from the looks of it, you don't really need it."

Eve said, "Surely we have something we could give them?"

"You gonna volunteer our stuff?" asked Jon with a frown.

Eve squinted her eyes at Jon and said, "No, I just dunno how much we have left."

Ironson already had an idea of what was left. He knew there was a dozen bottles of water, that could be replenished, and twenty-five to thirty separate cans or boxes of food. Between four of them it might last them a week, and if they didn't find a vehicle, they'd need every bit of it.

"There isn't enough, Eve," said Ironson.

"Right, ok," Eve said, "Sorry, he knows better than I do how much we have."

Eric slouched over and looked at the floor. He said, "That's ok, was a long shot. I'm probably done for anyways."

Eve said, "You don't know that. We may not be able to give anything, but there have to be places that haven't been fully looted yet."

"I don't mean that," Eric said, "I mean, well, earlier today I was out checking the hotel rooms and I seen one of those things."

Logan, Ironson, Eve and Jon looked over at him in unison as he continued, "It seen me and, I can't be sure, but its eyes seemed to turn red for a second before it ran off. I'm not sure exactly what it means, but it can't be good."

"We need to start fortifying this position right now," said Ironson, standing up in a hurry.

"Why's that?" asked Eric.

Logan pulled on his boots and said, gravely, "Because you've been marked, and they'll come back tonight."

Chapter 12 - The Marked

Astrid Skalder loved her father, almost as much as she loved her mother. When they divorced she was a little kid. She struggled with being shared between the two. As she got older, she learned to deal with it. Alcohol and the occasional joint helped her cope. Danny Childs would usually supply her with both, which is why she kept him around.

She didn't really love him, but refused to believe that she was using him, as some had suggested. He was nice enough, but he was never really her type. Give her a smoldering look, muscles and a bad boy attitude any day.

Upon seeing Logan enter the truck stop, her heart skipped a beat. He wasn't particularly muscled, but he was tall and fit. She liked his dangerous look and sharp eyes. The scar on his eyebrow gave him an air of badassness. The cloaks seemed odd, but it was almost zero degrees outside, so maybe they were for warmth. As far as she could tell, he didn't notice her looking at him. Danny didn't notice either.

The friendly atmosphere disappeared in an instant when her father told the newcomers about seeing the creatures. She was confused as to what the problem was. They had seen the creatures before, and there was never any issue. Then again, the creatures never seen them, either.

The four cloaked newcomers were checking their weapons hurriedly. Shotguns with tazers attached by electrical tape? She wondered what the use of those would be, but they looked cool.

Eric was standing too at this point. Astrid wasn't used to her father looking scared, as he had kept her and Danny safe through this whole ordeal. Eric said, "What do you mean, I've been marked?"

Ironson picked up some chairs and said, "If those things see you, they leave a mark on you then come back in packs. I don't know exactly how it works, but they will sure as shit be back tonight."

Danny was also on his feet, looking frail compared to the others. He said, "What ya'll need?"

The cloaked people were moving tables and chairs around. Ironson said, "We need to barricade the front door with every table we can, and put the chairs in the back door. The windows are boarded up and might slow them down, so their main entry will be the front door. The shop will be a kill zone for anything that gets through."

Jon placed the Remington rifle in Eric's hands and said, "You know how to use that thing?"

"Of course I do," said Eric. Astrid wasn't so sure. As far as she knew, he had never fired a gun in his life.

"Aim for the head, anything else is wasting ammo. We need someone to watch the kitchen in case they come through the back," said Ironson.

"I'll watch the back," Danny said.

"What do you want me to do?" asked Astrid, looking back and forth between the others.

Logan stepped forward and said in a soft tone, "Stay next to your father, or you can go to the kitchen. It might be safer back there."

Their eyes met as Logan spoke and she would have done anything he wanted her to do in that moment. She said, "I'd rather be with my dad. Thank you for what you're doing."

"Thank us afterwards," said Logan, who rushed away to help the others blockade the entrance.

The room looked a lot bigger without all the tables and chairs. Darker too, since the oil lanterns were moved to strategic locations in the gift shop. The front door was barely visible from behind the stacks of restaurant furniture.

140

Jon snatched up the fullest bottles of liquor and took whatever rags he could find from the kitchen. He stuffed the rags into the bottles and said, "Last resort, we set the bastards on fire."

"Good thinking, Kilroy," said Ironson, "We need any advantage we can get."

Danny had already disappeared into the kitchen, so Astrid decided to go check on him. He was sitting with his arms wrapped around his knees and rocking back and forth. How weak.

"You ok, Danny?" Astrid asked while pulling her hair up into a pony tail.

"Y-yeah, I'm good, darlin'," he said before quickly getting up and putting on a tough persona.

From outside, the invader's two-tone howl broke through the blizzard's wind. Danny flinched and said, "Go on back in, I gotta keep watch."

Astrid was ok with leaving him there, she felt safer with the others anyways. She went back into the dining area. Jon, Eve, Ironson and Logan stood in a line in the open area. They held their weapons ready and looked prepared for battle.

Eric was sitting at a corner booth next to a boarded up window. He had the rifle on the built-in table, but was looking out the window through gaps in the wood. Astrid went over and sat next to him.

"I see something out there," he said, "Hard to tell through the storm, but there's something moving."

141

"Everyone keep your heads and stay frosty," Ironson said while keeping his eyes on the front door, "The slugs we got should help with our accuracy. Jon, you're the only one without a tazer, so be careful."

"Roger that," Jon said.

As the howls came closer, Ironson said, "Everyone get ready."

Time seemed to stop for a while. Eve listened to the crackle of the fireplace. The creaks of the building as it was pounded by wind and snow. Her own, labored breathing as she tried to gain control of her nerves.

The creature's howls had stopped and made her leerier of what was coming. The Kal-Tec shotgun she held was smaller and lighter than the others, but it felt heavy. To keep her wits, she practiced moving her steadying hand to the tazer trigger.

She was flanked by Jon and Logan, so she felt safer. They both stood, motionless, watching the front door with their weapons at the ready. She wondered if they were just as scared as she was.

"You ok, babe?" whispered Jon, keeping his eyes forward.

"Yeah, I think so," she whispered back, "You?"

"I'm ready."

From behind the standing sentinels, Eric said as quiet as he could, "I don't see them anymore."

"Enough chatter," ordered Ironson, "Don't say anything
142

unless you're calling out shots."

Jon sighed heavily and shook his head, but said nothing else. Eve was proud of him for keeping his mouth zipped, but she knew it was because they had bigger fish to fry.

Save for the ambient sounds of the fireplace and the blizzard outside, the silence was unnerving. Eve could've sworn her heart was outside her chest. How much time had gone by? Few minutes? Half hour?

Then there was a knock on the door. A simple knock as if someone was there to check if the truck stop was open. Eve and Logan exchanged anxious, yet confused glances.

A second knock. This time it was more forceful, like if it were the police. Eve looked back at where Eric and Astrid sat. The father was struggling with the bolt action of the rifle. Astrid leaned over and helped him before he put his eye on the scope.

A third knock. Much harder. The hinges loosened and the door hit up against the stack of tables. Eve gulped down her nerves and counted silently to herself to steady her hands.

The door knocked a fourth time. Louder and angrier. The small flames of the oil lanterns flickered as the winter winds were let in for the smallest of moments.

The next knock would surely bring the door down. Eve took a deep breath and waited.

But nothing happened. For a full minute, it was like nothing had even happened. What were those things doing? Eve had been seeing them as mindless killers up until this point, but would rabid animals knock on the door? She felt like they were being toyed with.

Then the window next to the booth Eric was sitting, as reinforced as it was, shattered inward. Wood and glass sprang out like it was fired from a cannon. The muffled sound of the wind roared as snow shot in through the opening. The father covered his head, far too late, as his face was cut from the debris.

In the window, leaned in a creature from the darkness. And it howled that terrible howl, almost breaking Eve's eardrums. It looked down on Eric, who had not even noticed it was there yet, and flashed its orb-like eyes red at the man. It was he who they had come for.

On the opposite side of the building another window was blown open as a creature jumped through, snarling and looking for victims. It was like they did not even notice the wooden barricades nailed to the window sills.

Tears formed at the edges of Eric's eyes as he looked up into the gaping maw of his doom. The creature drooled and loosened its jaw like a snake. It clamped down on Eric's head. He dropped the rifle on the table and tried to push it away, but his hands slipped off the slimy, leprous skin.

In one flick of its neck, the creature bit the head off of Astrid's father, who was frozen while watching it happen. Blood spout up like a geyser, covering her in it. Tendons and nerves stretched until they snapped as the creature raised its head to chew.

The cloaked guards were taken by surprise and had no time

to react. There were only seconds between the two creature's entering and Eric's beheading. Eve wanted to freeze in fear, but that would mean the rest of their deaths. She raised her pump shotgun at the creature that was halfway inside the window. She breathed out and pulled the trigger.

Black goo sprayed out of its head as it fell backwards into the snowy darkness. Eric's headless body slumped over onto Astrid's lap, covering her in even more blood. She screamed so loud her voice went hoarse.

As this fight happened, Logan stunned the second creature and Ironson finished it off with his own shotgun. Danny emerged from the kitchen, his eyes wide at the scene. He immediately backed up into the kitchen. Eve seen his pants were wet before he disappeared from view.

The front door knocked again. This time with so much power that it shattered in two. One of those menaces rushed in on all fours, scraping the floor with its talon-like hands and bristling its black mane as it looked upon the humans.

Ironson stunned it and as Logan turned to back him up, another window was forcefully opened next to him. He ducked, but was not quick enough as a talon sliced his face. Blood splattered on the ceiling as Logan fell down, his eye covered in blood.

"No!" shouted Jon as the thing raised its too human-like arm to finish off Logan. Jon shot a slug into its neck before it could. It turned to Jon, wounded, and flashed its eyes red at him. Jon pumped his handy Winchester and finished it.

Jon pulled Logan away from the window and said, "You ok, man?" as Eve and Ironson took care of the creature at the door.

Logan looked up at him with a bloody gash across his face, running from his forehead to his nose. He responded, "I think so, hard to see, though."

Another wave of the invaders came in. Simultaneously, three more jumped into the building's openings. Two of them were brought down immediately, Eve claiming one kill and Ironson the other, but the third was too quick and rushed the marine pilot. He tried to dive away, but no human on earth was as quick as the deadly invaders. It stabbed a claw into Ironson's side and threw him against the wall, all but knocking him out.

Logan stunned and killed it, but there were more howls outside. He said, "Get ready for more," as Eve bandaged his face to at least stop the bleeding.

She went to Ironson and said, "Let me look at it," but he was not moving anyhow. The stab wound was deep and blood was pouring out of it. Stab victims happened every now and then in the hospital, but she never had to treat them during a fight. She held Ironson's side tight, her medical background keeping her from panicking.

The howls carried into the building as more of the things entered. Jon and Logan were the only two able to act as Eve did everything she could to help the pilot. Jon said, "It's time to light this fucker up!" and he rushed to the fireplace.

Logan followed him and they used the flames of the fireplace to light the Molotov cocktails that were sitting on the mantel. Jon threw one at the front door and hit a creature in its chest. The alcohol ignited and flames burst everywhere, covering the general store area in an inferno. Logan threw his across the room and the ground was lit aflame at the feet of one of the creatures. It shouted at him as the blaze kept it away.

"We have to go!" said Logan, picking up the packs and throwing one to Jon. They shouldered them and got Ironson to his feet.

Eve took the third pack and went to Astrid, who was hiding under the booth table. She bent down and said to her, "C'mon, it's time."

Astrid stuttered and had a thousand-yard stare. Eve felt for the girl, losing her father in such a way, but she had no time to sit and talk with her. She yanked the girl out into the open. Astrid fell forward with a "Hey!" before Eve dragged her to her feet. Eve slung the hunting rifle onto her back and followed Jon and Logan. They were carrying Ironson between them.

Jon kicked the kitchen door open to see Danny sitting in a puddle of his own making next to an old stove, looking just as scared as Astrid, if not more so. "Get up, you pussy!" Jon shouted at him while kicking the red head's feet.

He stood with wobbly knees and they ran out the back door.

147

They were met with high powered winds and snow pelting them in the face. The cloaked ones pulled their hoods tighter and they all rushed towards the motel, listening to the howls of the creatures on their way.

As they approached the longer building, they seen a ghastly-faced head appear on the roof. The creature snarled, baring its long, sharp teeth. Like a lion about to pounce on prey, it reared back for its attack.

Eve fired her weapon at it, hitting it in the face, crippling its vision. It was pure reaction and firing her KSG at those things was becoming more familiar. The creature fell backwards onto the roof and thrashed about as they started checking doors. The first few were locked, but the third was open.

They rushed into the dark hotel room. Jon and Logan threw Ironson onto the bed, unsettling the layer of dust that had been sitting there for who knew how long. The girls and Danny entered behind them and shut the door.

The room was dark, but the window curtains began to glow orange as the flames outside grew. Eve peeked out the bottom of the window, lifting the curtain just high enough to see out. She watched as the things rushed into the truck stop just to run back out as the flames grew.

From what Eve could tell, the only creature that seen them was the one dying on the roof, but she knew they were far from safe. She watched and waited as one by one the creatures ran south, in the direction of Hendrickson. They had killed their previously marked prey.

Chapter 13 - While Inside Room 106

No one slept that night. Logan's right eye was covered in a bandage but his eye itself did not suffer any injury. He did have one hell of a headache and Eve said he would need stitches under normal circumstances.

Ironson was in and out all night. They had no painkillers and the puncture in his side torso caused him to lose a lot of blood before Eve was able to use a quikclot on it. It was not fatal as far as they could tell, but could have hit a kidney. Eve kept a close eye on him, telling the others that she feared exsanguination.

Astrid looked as if her soul had left her body. Even when Eve and Danny were wiping the blood of her father off of her face, she stared forward into nothingness. She did not speak or acknowledge anyone else. Nor did she move from her spot on the floor all night.

The blizzard, if it were possible, only became fiercer when morning came. The truck stop had stopped burning and still had parts of the building that were intact. A foot layer of snow had covered everything and continued to grow.

Jon was proud of Eve in the fight and in taking care of everyone else. Eve though Logan and Ironson were wounded, it could have been much worse. Jon didn't know the new people well enough to feel sad for Astrid, but the brutality of how her father died. Damn...

"Well we're in a spot," said Jon as he and Logan leaned against the wall on opposite sides of the curtained window. They had opened it enough to let some light in, as dull as it was from the cloud cover.

"Joseph won't be able to travel like this," said Logan, looking over at the Marine lay in pain.

"He's in bad shape," said Jon, scratching is bearded chin, "How's your head?"

"Hurts like hell, but I'll be ok."

"Another scar to up the badass meter," said Jon, trying to keep things light.

Logan looked over at his friend, clearly not in a joking mood. He said, "Hardly a badass, my friend. I think we killed or wounded seven of them, but there were more. And there will be more tonight."

"Ya think so?" asked Jon. He wasn't a dumb guy, but Logan thought differently than he did. Jon thought they had won.

"These things aren't dumb," said Logan, "They may not have been able to mark us, but they know there are people here. I can only assume they'll send more to finish us off.

"In Omega's journal he wrote about a larger creature. It gave orders to the smaller ones, if you can call these things small. They will surely somehow communicate to their leader about the attack."

"It'd be nice to kill the bigger one then," said Jon, more as a side thought.

"What if we did?" asked Logan, "Cut off the head?"

"And how exactly would we do that?" asked Jon, who thought the idea was ridiculous.

"We go to Hendrickson, wait for it to come out and kill it the same way we did the other burrowers," said Logan, his uncovered eye lighting up.

Jon thought for a moment before replying, "Even if we did, who is to say we don't get swarmed by the smaller ones. Didn't the journal say it looked like there were thousands there? We couldn't even get close if we wanted to."

"We could in the blizzard. And the hunting rifle would give us enough distance. You make one or two shots count and it could bring it down," said Logan, standing up, "But we'd have to leave right now. Hendrickson is a little less than ten miles away."

"Whoa, whoa, wait a minute," said Jon, waving his hands to calm his friend's anxiousness to go back out, "First off, I ain't putting Eve in that much danger. Secondly, the best man for the job is laying passed out in the bed. And thirdly," he brought his voice low and leaned towards Logan, thrusting a thumb in Danny's direction, "I don't wanna take that pussy with us on something like that."

"Just you and I go. You've fired a rifle before, and from what you used to say, you were a good shot," responded Logan, "That fixes all three points."

Jon blinked at him as he started to think it might work too. He looked over at Eve, who had been listening from her position on the bed next to Ironson, and said, "What do you think, babe?"

She said, "We can't go anywhere with Joseph like this, but we can't stay or else we'd get attacked again. As much as I can't believe I'm going to say this, I think it's worth a shot as long as you stay safe."

"It's hardly safe," said Logan, "But we're stuck between a rock and a hard place. Unless...Danny, you know anything about the pickup truck out there?"

Danny, who had been trying to talk to his girlfriend, looked up and said, "Huh? The truck? I reckon it'd run but it has no fuel."

"What about the semis?" Jon asked, "You try them or see what cargo they had?"

"They're locked up, but I doubt they got any gas," said Danny.

153

"If we can get one of them running, we could get to St. Louis in a matter of a couple hours," said Logan, "We might be able to siphon fuel from other vehicles on the highway, if there are any."

"So, wait, what do you think we should do then?" asked Jon, not really following Logan's train of thought, "Go take out the big bad, or try to get a vehicle going and run?"

Logan thought on it for a long moment. He replied, "If we try to get a vehicle going and can't, then we risk another attack. If we can manage to kill the lead burrower, then we potentially have more time to find transportation. Or...yeah. Or we can do both.

"While you and I are out, Danny can see about getting something going. He could use Joseph's cloak to move around relatively safely while he checks things out. Even if he can't find a way to get a vehicle to work, we'd buy ourselves some time and be safe at least another night."

"I ain't going out there, no sir," said Danny, looking frightened.

"You're a real piece of work," said Jon, furrowing his brow with a disgusted look on his face, "We did what we could to help you guys out. In this together now, whether you like it or not. Stop pissing yourself and help out."

Danny stood up in a huff, twisting his gaunt face in a mix of embarrassment and rage. He said through crooked, clenched teeth, "I'll make you eat your words, mister."

"Bring it," said Jon, raising his fists.

154

Logan put his arm in front of Jon. He looked over at Danny frustratedly and said, "He's right, Danny. We may barely know each other, but we all need to do our part."

"Well I ain't goin' back out there. Sure as hell not," said Danny.

"Don't expect any of our food then," said Jon, "You help us get the fuck out of here, you get to eat."

Danny's eyes went wide and his mood changed real quick. He said, "Please, don't let me starve. I'll help you, sure enough. I'll find us some gas. Just please don't leave me with nothin', sir."

"That's more like it," said Jon.

Danny reminded Jon of inmates he used to have to deal with when he worked at the prison. Quick to anger, but even quicker to back down in the face of losing something. He hated thinking about his time at the prison and who it made him. It hardened him. Put up armor against others. That was something he was trying to correct, especially when it came to Eve.

"Do what you can to get fuel into that truck or get the semis working," said Logan before turning to his friend, "You ready to do this, Jon?"

"Nope," said Jon with a shrug, "But let's get to it."

Logan and Jon repacked one of the rucksacks with enough canned food and bottles of water to last them two days. Eve, who had taken it upon herself to be in charge of provisions, gave them

155

enough shotgun slugs and stun gun cartridges for the journey. Logan packed it all up and put the pack on over his cloak.

Jon checked the Remington hunting rifle. It appeared in working order and had five rounds left in its magazine. He slung it over his shoulder and made sure his Winchester pump shotgun was ready as well.

Before they headed out, Eve gave Jon a long kiss and said, "Please be safe."

Jon put a rough hand on her cheek, gazing into her eyes and said, "I'll be ok. It might be sometime tomorrow before we make it back."

Eve squeezed her fiancé in as tight a hug as she could, resting her head on his wide chest. She said, "I love you, you big, dumb asshole."

Jon replied, "Love you too, babe," with a kiss on the top of her head before they let go of each other. He couldn't lie to himself, he didn't want to let her go.

Logan had given them time to say goodbye, but he had to tell Eve, just loud enough so only she could hear, "Make sure Danny does his part, but if things start to get ugly tonight, think of yourself first."

Eve nodded, but said, "I won't leave Ironson like he is, but I can take care of myself if I have to." She gave Logan a hug before the two friends opened the door with some difficulty as the snow had built up against it. They walked out into the blizzard.

Eve watched out the door as her fiancé and best friend walked out beyond her sight. In truth, they were only twenty or so feet away, but the wind was so harsh and the snow fell in such multitudes, that it was like it formed a wall between them.

She shut the door, but hated doing so. She felt like it was the last time she was going to see them, but immediately put the thought from her mind. To distract herself, she gave Ironson a manual check on his vitals. He was still passed out, but hi breathing and heart rate were normal.

Behind her, in the corner of the hotel room, Danny had been sitting with Astrid. He was no longer trying to talk to her. As Eve sat on the bed next to Ironson, she couldn't help but feel Danny's eyes on her back. She had caught him looking at her with enraptured longing a few times over the course of the night.

She wasn't a violent person, but she was ready to deal with him if it came to it. This new world had begun to change her outlook on life. No longer could she have fun, work hard and live how she wanted. Everything was changing around her and she had to change with it. Her naivety began to give way to clarity.

Chapter 14 – Uncertainty

Logan pulled his hood over his face as far as it would go.
The biting wind seeped through the bandage on his face and into the
slash wound on his face. He groaned in pain, but carried on.

He looked over at Jon, who kept in step next to him as they
trudged through the snow. The larger man's hood covered his face,
only revealing a portion of his ever growing beard. It was speckled
with snow that got caught in the hair and revealed a wispy breath of
air with every other step.

They kept to the road as visibility was so low that a creature
could pass by them and neither of them would notice. The snow was
lower there as well, and they had to make good time to get to
Hendrickson before nightfall.

Logan was scared, no way around it. A few of the invaders at a time weren't too difficult now that they had some practice. Approaching a nest, though. There could be thousands, if not more, of the things there.

"This plan better work," said Jon over the storm.

"It will," said Logan, who was unsure himself, "It has to."

"This is better than waiting for them to come kill us, at any rate," replied Jon.

"We don't really have a choice but to try to hit them where it counts," said Logan, "We've been running away ever since this all started. Now it's all or nothing."

The two friends fell silent and the expression on Jon's face turned grim. If they failed, or were incorrect, Eve and the others would surely die that night. Logan noticed his friend lost in thought and was almost taken aback by Jon's sudden silence.

He shared the sentiment, however. Part of him felt like they were marching to their deaths. He tried to think positively, but all he could think about was what would happen if they failed. He had come to terms with dying; part of him felt like he deserved it after what he did to his brother. The thought of losing Jon and Eve was more unbearable. Instead of letting his fear take him, he tried to use it as armor.

"We can't fail," he said aloud, but his words were taken by the wind and away from Jon's ears.

In room 106, Ironson had awakened. He looked drained and weak, a stark contrast to his normally powerful presence. He looked around, not exactly sure how he got there, but did not complain. The bed was comfortable and he was ok with not moving for a while, but his military mind didn't sleep.

"What's our status?" he asked in a strained voice upon seeing Eve.

She had been looking out the window, holding her chin in her hand. Her breath formed a fog on the window as the water vapor from her breath froze against the cold glass. She heard Ironson and her expression turned from worry to elation. She picked up a water bottle and sat next to Ironson on the bed.

"Alive, for now," Eve responded.

The pilot rubbed his eyes and looked back and forth before looking up at Eve. He seen a beauty in her he had not noticed before, but he would never dishonor himself by hitting on a taken woman. Even if he and Jon did not see eye to eye all the time.

"How do you feel?" Eve asked, uncapping the plastic bottle.

"I'll live. Where's Foster and Kilroy?" he asked as Eve helped prop his head up with some pillows so he could comfortably drink.

She glanced out the window before saying, "We couldn't run away with you as injured as you are. So they're going to go kill the leader creature thing."

"Leader creature thing..." Ironson repeated, raising an eyebrow before realization came to him, "They're going after the

160

nest?"

"Yeah," said Eve, her voice trailing off.

Ironson looked out the window as a memory flooded his mind. He said, thinking out loud, "It's suicide. My squadron of helis were providing support for a platoon, forty-three marines. We knew those things had a nest in the AO so we were moving cautiously. The platoon was ambushed by, had to have been almost a hundred of them. They were all killed and eaten. We didn't even take out a third of them."

Eve looked down at her hands and said, "They didn't think they had a choice. We weren't sure if we could get a vehicle going and we'd be sitting ducks here."

Ironson tried to sit up in bed, but the pain in his side shot through his torso. He growled and laid back down, punching the soft covers of the bed in frustration. "We have to help, somehow," he said.

"Danny is outside trying to find a running vehicle," said Eve, "He's been out almost as long as they've been gone."

"Go help him," said Ironson, taking another sip of water, "I'll be ok here. Those two don't know what they're getting themselves into."

Eve nodded and said, "Ok, I'll come back to check on you in a little bit," before throwing her cloak on and grabbing her modified shotgun, just in case.

Although the fights at the watch tower and the truck stop

could be considered victories, Ironson knew full well the position they were in. They had yet to run into a large contingent of the invaders, which there no doubt would be at the nest. He felt useless and frustrated that he wasn't with Jon and Logan. He wanted to fight.

As she entered into the brutal storm, Eve looked around for Danny's whereabouts. She couldn't see past the half-standing truck stop so trudged to where she knew the pickup truck was.

Once she was close enough to see it through the snow, she seen the driver side door was left open. She approached it and peered inside it. Keys were hanging from the ignition but there was no sign of Danny.

Over the rushing wind she heard a clanging sound, like metal on metal, coming from the direction of one of the semi-trucks. She walked towards the sound until she could see what was going on.

Danny was hitting the back door of the semi-trailer with a crowbar. A chain winded through the latches of the door and a key lock kept the doors shut. As Eve approached, she took note of how weak each of Danny's strikes were. She could probably hit it harder than he could.

"Any luck?" she said when she got close to him.

He jumped, obviously not knowing she was outside and held the crowbar defensively until he seen it was her. He said, "Jesus H. Christ, you scared me right good. This thing is locked up pretty tight."

162

"Have you tried using the crowbar on the semi windows to see if there's a key in there?" she asked, thinking that would have been the first thing she would do.

Danny looked like she just said the best idea ever and said, "Well, nah, I didn't. That'd be the smart thing to do though, I reckon."

He stood there just looking at her. He seemed dim-witted, but the look in his eyes made Eve cringe. She said, "Let's go try it, then."

"Sure," he said as he followed her to the front of the semi.

She climbed up to the door and looked down to Danny to ask for the crowbar. He was looking under her cloak at her buttocks, but quickly stood straight and looked at her sheepishly in the eyes. Wondering if he was going to be a problem, she asked, "Can I have the crowbar?"

He replied, "Yeah, here ya go," innocently enough, handing her the crowbar. She didn't want to turn back around because she could feel him watching her, but she had a task at hand.

She leaned away from the truck and swung the crowbar into the window. It cracked the glass, so she hit it again. It broke the second try, shattering glass into the cab. She cleared any excess glass with the crowbar so as not to cut herself, then reached in and unlocked the door.

"Unlock the other side so I can help look, if you'd be so kind," Danny said up to Eve.

She brushed loose glass shards down onto the floor. Then

reached over and unlocked the passenger door and motioned for him to walk around to it. He ran through the snow, opened the door on the other side, climbed up and slammed it shut.

"There has to be something in here," she said to him, looking in every nook and cranny, "Try to find some keys or anything else that'd be helpful."

"Yes, ma'am," Danny said, flashing his eyes down at her chest. Not much to look at, though, since she was wearing layers and a tactical vest.

As they were searching the cab, Eve wanted to break the awkward silence. She said, "So, Astrid seems like a nice girl."

Danny shrugged as he opened the glove compartment and said, "She's a'right. In truth we had only been goin' out a few months before the things came. Now, I dunno, can't talk to her."

"Well, she just watched her father get killed," said Eve, "She's in shock. I'll talk to her when we go back inside."

"Can if ya want, but I'd rather stay in here with you," Danny said with a wicked look. He placed his hand on her thigh and began moving it up towards her waist.

Through pure reaction, Eve took the crowbar and slammed it into his shoulder. He squealed and recoiled back as far as he could go into his seat. Eve held the crowbar at him and shouted, "You touch me again, I'll shove this up your ass, you sick fuck!"

Danny's face contorted in terror and he said, "W-why'd you do that?"

"Get the fuck out," Eve said.

Danny fumbled the door latch on the door before finally being able to open it. He rushed out and disappeared into the blizzard. Eve used the bent end of the crowbar to shut the door behind him.

Eve shut her eyes and let her nerves settle, taking deep breaths. She had hit Danny before she even knew what was going on. Where did that reaction come from?

She searched a few minutes more before she dropped the sun visor on the ceiling. A pair of keys fell into her lap. Without a word, she jumped out of the semi cab and headed back to the trailer doors.

She tried the key in the lock and heard a click as the lock fell off the chain. She unwound the chain around the handles and unlatched one of the doors. The doors swung open with a metallic creak and made Eve's jaw drop as she viewed what was inside.

Although the cloud cover made it difficult to see what time of day it was, Logan guessed it was about noon. He and Jon had made decent time, walking five miles towards Hendrickson. The blizzard winds had relented and their visibility widened.

They decided to stop briefly for a break to eat and drink something, taking cover amongst some trees alongside the road. Logan pulled a can of vegetable soup from his pack and two bottles of water that looked more like slushies as they were half frozen.

They did not want to stop so long to make a fire, so they

attempted to gulp down the soup as is, taking turns sipping it. Both Jon and Logan scrunched their noses at the coldness of the soup, but it was sustenance.

"I miss home," said Jon, who had not really spoken much about his feelings since everything went to hell. Jon had opened up to Logan before, but those moments were far and few in between.

Logan looked over at his friend, surprised at his candor. He replied, "Haven't thought much about it since we left Poplar Bluff, but now that you mention it, I do too."

"St. Louis sounds safe if MEPS is as good as Ironson says, but it'd be nice to know if my family is ok," said Jon before choking down the cold vegetable bits and handing Logan the half full can.

"Wish I knew, too," said Logan, "We're out in the thick of it with no way to communicate. We can't even tell the time as it is."

"I left my g'damn watch back at the campground," said Jon, "Feels like that was so long ago."

"If we make it back from this, I'll find you another watch," said Logan, finishing the soup and slurping what water he could from the almost frozen, plastic bottle.

Jon looked over at Logan with a grin under his snow-covered beard and said, "You damn well better to make up for dragging me out here."

Logan slung the rucksack onto his back and they climbed up the road to continue their mission. Logan's mind went back to his mother and father in Arborsville. He hoped they were safe.

166

They trekked southwards, their cloaks fluttering in the wind. The closer they got to their destination, the more anxious Logan became. There was no way to know for sure what would happen, but he remained stalwart. He kept his head on a swivel, looking for any threats as they walked. The only things that moved save for them were the leafless trees on the side of the road and the snow dusting over dunes.

After a few more hours, the snow relented, but the wind was just as fierce as it was the night before. The cloud cover started to dissipate, letting some sunlight through like bright beams of hope.

They approached a sign alongside the road that said HENDRICKSON 1 MILE. They turned to each other and Logan said, "This is the last stretch."

Jon drew in a long breath and released it before saying, "Ok. Let's kick some ass."

Chapter 15 - The Nest

Hendrickson was a small hamlet. It was divided into two halves by the Black River and consisted of mainly residential areas scattered amongst woods. On its southern border was the rock quarry. The village had no commercial district.

When Logan and Jon looked upon it after the collapse, it looked like a ghost town. Just outside of town, along highway 67, was a forested hill that gave them enough cover to scout out the area.

Jon had climbed a tree to get a better view. The lack of leaves made it easier to see the surrounding region, but the dampness from the snow made it difficult to climb. He slipped a few times, cursing as he regained his footing. When he reached the highest he could climb, he scanned around using the scope of the rifle to give him a better view.

The wind had died down for the moment, allowing sporadic spurts of snow to fall slowly. Logan stood at the ready below the tree in case a creature made its way to their vantage point.

What put Jon off more than why they were there, was the eerie stillness. Here and there he would hear howls in the distance, but between the cries was absolute silence. He could hear his heart thumping underneath his layers of clothing.

Jon viewed the hamlet to the northeast, seeing snow-covered roofs of a few houses between wooded areas. Several of the creatures roamed there and almost looked as if they were playing. He brought the rifle to his right and noticed the Black River almost frozen over. Further to his right he seen the quarry.

Just outside the stoneworks was a leaning sign that said RIVERSIDE STONE WORKS. Beyond the sign were huge piles of gravel and rock, looking like scaled down mountains with their snowcapped peaks. Machinery and conveyers lead to and from the heaps. There were a few vehicles there, mainly large haul trucks and excavators. Beyond the heaps, the ground dipped down, beyond Jon's view, into the quarry proper. Between the quarry and the highway was a processing structure that stood higher than where the two friends were. Conveyers led into this building and large storage cylinders stood around and on top of it. A gravel road led from 67 to where this building was, being the main entrance to the quarry.

But the stoneworks isn't what caught Jon's attention as he gazed down at it from across the river. It was the myriads of creatures there. They were climbing in and out of the quarry, some were carrying carcasses, but Jon was too far away to make out what they were. Some would run from the woods surrounding the stoneworks or along the river. He noted that the creatures were different colors; many had darker skin as he was accustomed to seeing, but a few had hues of red or purple and their manes were longer than the others.

"There's a shit-ton of them," Jon said down to Logan as quietly as he could.

"You see the leader?" Logan asked in the same tone.

"Don't think so," said Jon, keeping an eye glued to the scope, "There's some different colored ones, but I don't see one that's obviously bigger. I can't see down into the damn quarry from here, though."

Logan asked, "Is there a place where we can get a better look?"

Jon looked south along the highway to the gravel elevator building. He said, "Yeah, but it gets us close to the quarry. Uncomfortably close."

"If the bigger one is down in there, we don't have a choice," said Logan.

Jon swung the strap of the rifle around his shoulder and began to climb down. He slipped again with a "G'dammit," but

170

managed to get to the ground safely.

They heard howls coming from the direction of the quarry as they snuck across the bridge where the highway crossed over the Black River. Halfway across the bridge was a red car that had crashed into the railing. Its front bumper and headlights were smashed in, causing the front, two tires to flatten. Logan looked inside as they passed it, but it was empty and they keys were gone.

Once across the bridge, they could see the processing and storage facility to their left. It towered over a large parking lot where one of the large, hauling trucks was parked. A long ladder on the side facing the highway led up to the top of the building

They ducked down low in a snow-filled ditch and Jon whispered, "We get to the top of that place and we can see everything. Might even be able to see the truck stop from there if it was clearer."

"Is there a way up other than that ladder?" Logan asked.

"Don't tell me you're scared of heights too," said Jon, rolling his eyes.

"No, it's just...it's a long way up a slippery, metal ladder. You almost fell off the top of the tree."

Jon looked as if Logan had just slapped him and said, "I was in full control, thank you very much. I meant to slip to test my footing."

"Yeah, sure," said Logan, "Anyways, we should get to it while there's none of them around."

They kept low as they approached the tall, metal building. Next to the ladder was a closed, roll-up door that was big enough for one of the hauling trucks to enter into.

When they reached the ladder, Jon said, "You wanna go first?"

"Not really," said Logan, looking up at the ladder that seemed to ascend into the sky.

"Well fuck. Rock, paper, scissors then," said Jon, holding his right fist in his left palm.

"Ok," said Logan as he brought up his hands in the same fashion.

"One, two, three," said Jon as they hit their palms in unison.

Jon had rock.

Logan had paper.

"Lucky ass," said Jon. He turned to the ladder. Each rung was covered in a line of snow. He began to climb up and Logan followed. The ladder was cold, biting into their skin, but they climbed on.

Further up, Jon looked down, but was unphased by the height. Logan was concentrating purely on climbing and keeping his head upwards. Jon joked, "Stop looking at my ass."

"Can we just keep going, please?" said Logan, his hands shivering, "Feels like my hands are going to fall off."

"Alright, alright, just trying to lighten the mood," Jon laughed.

They continued upwards and Logan said, "How can you joke around at a time like this?"

"Dunno," his friend responded, "Looking death in the eye has a certain freedom to it. I almost died while working at the prison, I ever tell you that?"

"Yeah. An inmate beat a fellow officer and formed a mob. You beat them all single handedly."

"What?" said Jon, incredulous, "That's not what happened."

"That's how you told it, but I think we were drunk at the time," said Logan, keeping a steady pace up the ladder under his friend.

"The inmate got ahold of a gun somehow. We didn't keep weapons in the blocks, so no idea how that fucking happened. Anyways, he did end up beating a CO half to death and I was first to respond. I ran in, ready to kick some ass and found myself staring down the barrel of a gun. My whole life flashed before my eyes.

"There was an inmate who tackled and unarmed him. He got a whole helluva lot of good time for that. But still, when I looked at the inmate ready to shoot my lights out, I almost laughed. I felt...free, I guess. I dunno. It was like nothing really mattered if I'm going to die there in a place I didn't wanna be. It was the main reason I ended up quitting the prison."

"I didn't know you could think so deeply," said Logan, his voice lighter. It sounded like the Logan that Jon used to know and grow up with.

"Hey, fuck you, man. How about I kick you off this ladder," said Jon with a laugh.

The moment was not lost to either of them. For the first time in a long time Jon felt like they were friends in a normal world again. Why the moment was shared on a two hundred foot ladder was beyond him, though.

They finally reached the top of the building, taking a moment to catch their breath and warm up their hands. In one corner was one of the cylindrical storage silos. The sheet metal roof was solid and surrounded a large, glass window directly in the center. Jon looked down through the window and seen a conveyor that had been dropping sand into the center of the building when it stopped production. The conveyor ran through a gap in the building that led, like a slide, down into the quarry pit. The gap where the conveyer emerged was about ten feet below the roof of the building.

They ducked down next to the ledge that faced the quarry, just above the long conveyor. From here, Jon had a good look down into the pit. There was an excavator down there that was knocked over onto its side. The creatures were coming and going out of several cave-like holes in the side of the rock. Some stood along the sides of the quarry, almost as if they were guarding the place The amount of the invaders was staggering and Jon didn't bother trying to count them.

Jon looked through his scope down at the nest and said, "Holy shit, I thought there was a lot before."

"I can see some of the different colored ones, but do you see any that are bigger?" Logan asked.

"I don't."

"I guess we wait, but it'll start to get dark in an hour or so," said Logan.

As the creatures went about their unknown business down below, the two men watched and waited. Jon was ready to do whatever was needed. He was fearless in the face of a very possible death, but if it meant Eve was safe, then so be it.

Chapter 16 - The Enforcer

Jon and Logan suffered the cold breeze atop the structure until dusk. The snow had stopped falling and the clouds were dissipating. The waning moon rose as the sky turned from orange to purple. It was then that they heard the call.

It was lower and seemed to come from the earth itself. Several two tone calls were heard in answer to it. It caused Logan's hairs to stand on end, even more so than the cold, as he exchanged a knowing look with his friend.

Jon balanced the rifle on his knee as he looked down in the pit. All of the creatures seemed to congregate like they were waiting for something, even the ones who appeared to be standing guard turned their attention to the quarry.

The growl came again, making all the awaiting creatures cower in between their snarling. They appeared to be anxious, almost scared. From Logan's perch more than two hundred feet above, he could see the bioluminescent glow of the creature's blue, orb-like eyes lighting up the area. Like a thousand fireflies in a pit, they all stared towards one of the carved out tunnels in the side of the rock.

Jon used the scope of the rifle to guide his own view. He followed their gazes towards the opening in the rock as the growl came once more, but even louder than before. The creatures in the immediate entrance of the cave backed away, causing them to back into some of their own kin. They snapped their ugly mouths at one another in response.

A light began to shine from within the tunnel as the source of the low growls made its way to the open. "That has to be it," whispered Logan.

Jon made sure the rifle was ready to fire and whispered back, "I'd bet on it."

Again the growl came as the light in the tunnel shone brighter and finally revealed its source. The enforcer emerged, causing Jon to pause at the sight. It looked much like the other creatures with a few exceptions. Like Omega wrote in his journal, it was indeed taller than the other, already large creatures. Its skin was smooth, almost armor-like, which contrasted with the other creatures' slimy, grotesque skin. Another difference was how it had a nose and its eyes were smaller, human-like. Its mane of hair that started at the top of its head and ran down its back was a powdery white, speckled with dirt from being underground.

The enforcer looked around at its subjects, blinking its bright, blue eyes. It barked at different creatures and pointed in various directions. In packs of eight to ten, they left after being given their orders. The initial howls Logan and Jon heard seemed to just get the attention of the other creatures.

It was time.

"You got a shot?" Logan asked. He had already felt apprehensive about being so close to this congregation. With the presence of the larger creature, he steadied his breath to get ahold of his nerves.

"Damn thing is moving around," replied Jon, "I'm a good shot, but I already have to adjust for the wind. I'm just waiting for it to stop moving."

"Whenever you're ready," said Logan, "Just make it count."

"I fully intend to," said Jon, who stared at the enforcer through his scope with a menacing intensity.

The other creatures had always been jittery and wild, save for when they were marking their prey. The enforcer moved in slow, confident movements as if it were commanding its army.

After a few, long minutes, it was done with its unknown orders and stood in the center of the quarry amongst the others. Logan knew this was their opportunity. He watched Jon with wide eyes.

Jon breathed in as he adjusted his rifle, moving the center of the scope just to the left of the enforcer's head, into the wind.

He breathed out and squeezed the trigger.

With a shot that echoed around Hendrickson, the .308 bullet soared down at the Enforcer, hitting it directly in its head.

Black goo spout from the wound, but the thing didn't fall. It howled in either anger or pain as it looked up at the two friends. In unison, every creature in and around the stoneworks looked up as well and the sea of fireflies that Logan had been looking at turned red in his direction.

Jon brought the rifle's bolt back and reset it with hasted precision, took another breath and fired again.

He struck the enforcer in the chest, where a human's heart would be, but still it did not fall.

The creatures knew where they were and like flies to a corpse, they began running on all fours towards the structure.

Jon fired again, grazing the shoulder of the enforcer, who had begun lumbering towards them.

The creatures jumped at the metal building, snarling and biting at the two men's direction. Many slipped off, but the red and purple creatures were able to stick their talons into the walls and begin climbing up.

"We're going to have company," shouted Jon.

"Just stay on the big one," said Logan, "We have to bring it down!"

The enforcer seemed unphased by its wounds as it looked up at the friends from the base of the structure. Jon leaned over the edge of the roof on his belly and said, "Hold my feet!"

Logan slid over to him and grasped his friend's legs so Jon could concentrate on the shot. He took aim, breathed out and fired.

The bullet hit its mark, taking out the enforcer's right eye. It flailed around and howled before looking back up at its attacker. With no difficulty at all, it began climbing up the building, shaking the metal structure with every slam of its taloned hands.

"This g'damn thing won't die!" shouted Jon, bolting another bullet into the chamber of the rifle, "And its climbing up here."

Jon fired the last round in the rifle's five bullet magazine, hitting the enforcer in its arm. It began climbing faster, but it favored its uninjured arm.

"That's the last shot, pull me up," said Jon.

As he got his friend back to safety, Logan said, "What if we can't kill it?"

Jon dropped the rifle to the ground and readied his trusty Winchester. He said, "Then we're gonna take out as many of those damn things as we can."

Logan slung his Benelli shotgun from off his shoulder and the two men waited at the ledge until the things were close enough to do some real damage with their shotguns.

The first, purple creature made it within fifty feet of the

armed men. Jon pumped his shotgun and fired a slug down at it, making a hole in its face. It did not immediately kill the creature, but caused it to lose its grip and it fell to its death.

Logan targeted the next one and fired two shots at it. It shared the same fate as the one before it and fell. Again and again, Logan and Jon fired down into the climbing creatures. Some fell while others died from direct, shotgun hits. Others simply shrugged off the attacks.

Even with some dying, they were getting closer to the top of the building. Each one that the friends killed was replaced by five more as some of the regular creatures managed to get a grip in the metal and begin their climbs.

The enforcer had caught up to its quicker underlings and snarled at Logan and Jon. It's human-like face gave them pause, but only for a moment, for the creatures were about to reach the top.

The friends backed up away from the ledge. Jon turned to Logan and looked at him. Logan would never forget the look in his friend's eyes. For the first time ever, he looked scared.

"You should go," Jon said hastily.

"What? I'm not going anywhere, we're in this together," said Logan.

"Someone has to take care of Eve," said Jon, wincing at his fiancé's name as if it hurt him to say it out loud.

"I'm not leaving," said Logan, determined. He could see the mane of one of the creatures poke up over the edge.

"Dammit, Logan!" said Jon, who swung his Winchester around and pointed it at his friend, who froze, not knowing how to react.

"Jon, what're you doing?"

"You get the hell back to the truck stop and you do everything you can to protect her," said Jon, his eyes stern.

The first creature began to claw its way up over the edge.

Logan backed up towards the ladder, afraid his friend might actually shoot him. He looked over his shoulder at the ladder that descended into the dark, only the first few rungs were lit up by the pale moonlight.

Jon lowered his shotgun and with an apologetic look and said, "Go..."

It went against everything Logan wanted to do, but he began his climb down the ladder. Jon turned to meet his foes before he was no longer in view. It felt wrong, leaving his friend to die, but that look in Jon's eye stuck with Logan.

He climbed down as quick as he could, hearing gunshots and the roar of his friend, like a barbaric yelp it cut through the cold air. Then it was silent. Logan stopped clambering down to listen. He looked up at the top, hoping to see his friend start climbing down with him.

What he seen instead, was one of the creatures poke its head out over the ledge. It snarled and growled, as if to taunt Logan. Then it started climbing down, upside down, towards Logan.

"Oh, shit!" he exclaimed as he started to climb down as quick as he could, but the creature was gaining on him and others were starting to make their way around the side of the building as well.

He wasn't even halfway down, but he had to get down quick. He wrapped his hands in the edges of his cloak and grasped the sides of the ladder, then he kicked his feet off to the side as well and began sliding down in a controlled fall.

Seeing that its prey was moving quicker than it was, the creature leapt at Logan, missing him by a few inches. It plummeted down to its death, past the sliding man.

Logan hit the ground harder than he meant to and fell onto his back. If it wasn't for the snow build-up, he might have broken a leg from the impact. He was by no means safe, though, and he got up and started running towards the road.

He looked behind him and seen a creature on his tail. He skidded to a halt, brought his modified shotgun up and tased the thing. It fell face forward into the snow, allowing Logan time to shoot it in the back of its head with a shotgun slug.

He reloaded his weapon and a stun gun cartridge and continued to run. Until he seen lights ahead of him. For a moment he thought they were from the creatures, but as it got closer it looked more like headlights.

Jon watched as his friend descended down the ladder, out of view. Never did he think he would pull a weapon on a trusted friend, but it was senseless for both of them to die. He wanted to get his point across and it was the quickest way he knew how.

He turned back around just in time to see a red creature lunge at him. He shot it with his Winchester, hitting it in the mouth as it was snarling and ready to chomp down on some human flesh.

Another one attacked him, but its speed was too much for the man. Its claws slashed deep into Jon's shoulder. As he fell, he discharged his weapon into the torso of the thing, wounding it and making it fall back.

A third creature ran up on him, stabbing him in the leg, causing Jon to yell mightily. It was painful, but it fed his anger and he ended the thing's life.

The only creature left in view was the enforcer, who had reached the top of the building. It scrunched its nose as it looked down on Jon. It growled from its throat as it began lumbering forward.

Jon tried to get up, but the wound in his leg forced him back to the ground. He aimed his shotgun at the enforcer and shot every round he had left in it, hitting it in the chest every time. The creature began to slow down, but Jon had no time to reload.

He crawled to the window on the roof, leaving a streak of blood on the glass as he went. He glanced down at the dark drop below him, the only thing visible was the conveyer that led from outside about twenty feet below him.

With each inch, a pain shot through his body, like he was

being stabbed constantly. His vision began to narrow and his breathing was labored.

Just a little further...

The enforcer followed him onto the glass, opening its mouth wider than it looked like it should be able to. Jon looked down and moved a little more to his right before looking back at the creature and saying with a pained chuckle, "You afraid of heights too?"

The creature cocked its head as if it were trying to understand what Jon said. The man spoke again, "I ain't afraid of heights and I ain't afraid of you. Fuck. You!"

With the last bit of strength he had left, Jon got on his knees and slammed the butt of his gun into the window. It cracked like a spider web all across the large pane of glass before giving out under the weight of Jon and the enforcer.

They both fell into the darkness.

Down below, the enforcer had landed hard into the sand pile. It was dazed and severely wounded, but still it was able to walk away. It pounded on the large, roll up door to escape the structure. After a few failed attempts, it put all of its weight into it and bashed through the door.

It was met by a pair of blinding headlights pointed directly at it. Next to the headlights stood a cloaked man with a Benelli shotgun. He looked fearlessly at the creature, even though it began approaching him. The rest of the minions were running around the structure to aid their leader.

The headlights belonged to a Chevrolet Silverado technical truck, painted in green camo. Behind the wheel was Ironson, still wounded and blinking to keep himself conscious. In the bed of the truck was a mounted M240 machine gun. Eve stood behind it, making sure the enforcer's body was in her iron sights.

Logan shouted, "Light it up!" and he began firing his shotgun into the approaching enforcer. Eve squeezed the machine gun's trigger and together they unloaded into the thing.

With every bullet that pierced its body, black blood and gore flung out of its body and into the snow. Each step it took was more laborious until it couldn't walk anymore. It fell to its beastly knees as the machine gun and shotgun fire concentrated on its head. Its eye popped out and its jaw was shattered.

Finally, it fell and the gunfire ceased.

Knowing how tough this thing was, Logan ran up on it while reloading his shotgun. At point blank range, he unloaded every slug into its head, splashing his cloak with black blood.

When the gunfire ceased, the thing was barely recognizable. It looked like a lump of gore and organs.

"Logan!" Eve shouted, noticing all the creatures that had gathered around.

Logan turned to see they had all gathered around to see the death of their leader, but they did not approach. They snarled and snapped their mouths at the humans, but then something odd

186

happened.

They turned to their nearest, fellow creature and began attacking each other. Some ran off towards the quarry, but others fought each other to the death. They completely ignored the humans, instead tearing themselves apart.

Logan looked upon the scene with surprise and shock. He deduced that the enforcer was the only thing that kept them organized and willing to hunt. He watched as they killed each other until they had all fallen or fled.

Hendrickson had been liberated.

Eve jumped out of the back of the technical and checked on Ironson. He was slumped back in the seat, passed out, but breathing. As she checked his bandages, she said over to her friend, "Where's Jon?"

Logan looked grim and he looked up the ladder. Maintaining his gaze upwards, he said, "He made me leave him up there."

"You left him?" she said, her voice stern.

Hearing the tone in her voice, he turned to her and said, "Eve, he pointed his gun at me and told me to go."

She raised an eyebrow and softened her voice as she looked up the building, "Do you think he's ok?"

"I don't know, but I'm going to find out right now."

Chapter 17 - The Problem with Danny

Once again, Logan made the cold climb up to the top of the structure. He hoped it would be the last time, but he had to find Jon. They had been in danger the whole time since the invaders came, but they were always together. He feared the worst when he made it to the top of the structure and didn't see his friend there.

The moonlight gave off enough luminescence to see the scene of Jon's stand. Logan walked amongst the tattered remains of the red and purple creatures. He seen the streak of blood on the steel roof that ended at broken glass. He got down on his knees and peered down through the shattered window.

He seen only darkness at first. It took a moment for his eyes to adjust. Far below he could barely see the opening that the enforcer made to escape.

On the conveyer, twenty feet below, laid Jon on his back, motionless. His arm and leg dangled dangerously.

"Jon!" Logan shouted downwards, ecstatic that he actually seen his friend again.

There was no response or movement.

Logan looked around for any way to get down to him, but the only way he could see was dropping down on the conveyer where it exited the building. It was a long drop, too long.

He followed the conveyer with his eyes as it led down into the quarry. Down there, he seen a spot where he could climb up it. With more urgency than he had ever felt, he ran to the ladder to make his way down to tell Eve.

Jon opened his eyes. Above him was the window he shattered in a last ditch attempt to kill the enforcer. He felt cold and couldn't feel his leg. His shoulder felt like someone was constantly stabbing it with a knife. It was difficult to breath, and even through all the pain, he felt peaceful.

It could have been minutes or hours that he laid there, he couldn't tell. A euphoric feeling overcame him and his vision began to blur. He tried to blink it away.

He watched the stars twinkle in the sky as the remnant clouds of the storm had finally relented entirely. It reminded him of evenings where he and Eve would sit outside back home with each other in their arms and watch the sky.

Eve...would he ever see her again. He didn't care about how beautiful she was, or how successful in life. In that moment, he just wanted to be with her. How dumb he had been the last ten years to worry about things that didn't matter.

She's what mattered.

This man, who had spent his adult life trying to be as tough as he could, began to shed a tear. Everyone felt a million miles away and he felt so, so alone. Even though it sounded like he could hear someone's voice.

Then he heard it again, but a little clearer. Someone calling out his name.

He looked down the conveyer, towards the gap where it exited the building, and seen a figure enter into the moonlight. The reaper had come for him. It was his time to go.

"Am I dead?" Jon asked. He wasn't sure why that's the first thing he would say.

"Not yet," said the figure as it carefully made its way up the narrow conveyor.

When the figure was upon him, he was ready to go. If that's how it ends, fuck it, get it over with.

The figure took down its hood and revealed itself to be Logan. Jon's blurred vision could just make out the bloodied bandage on his face.

"Logan?" said Jon, confused. He still instinctively rubbed the tear off his face with his shirt sleeve. Logan would never let him live down crying, or so Jon thought. The look on Logan's face showed worry rather than jest.

"I'm here, buddy, let's get you out of here," Logan said as he cautiously moved Jon all the way onto the conveyor.

"I'm sorry I pointed a gun at you," Jon said.

Logan gave him a sympathetic look and said, "I get it. I wouldn't have left if you didn't do something like that, but why did you want to stay by yourself?"

"I was thinking of Eve," Jon said, his voice cracking, "She's a tough girl, but what the world has become, I just wanted someone to keep her safe."

"Well, if you seen what I seen, you'd know she doesn't need anyone to look after her. Right now, though, let's get you back down," said Logan.

He took the edges of Jon's cloak and wrapped him up as best he could. Then, with some difficulty, he began dragging him down the conveyer. He would move down a foot or two, then pull Jon the same distance and repeated this all the way down from the building and into the quarry. It took nearly an hour to drag him all the way down.

Once he got him down and into the bed of the technical, Eve grabbed her fiancé around the torso and hugged him, tightly. She said, "Don't leave me again, you ass."

Jon groaned in pain from Eve squeezing him, but he let her. He was glad to see her again, and looked at her with renewed love. Staring death in the face has a tendency to remind someone what is important. It happened once when he worked at the prison, and then again with the enforcer. He vowed that day to not take Eve for granted.

"I'm sorry to interrupt, but we should get him back to the hotel," said Logan in haste, "He's in pretty bad shape. I'll drive back."

Eve jumped in the back of the technical and cradled her fiancé's head as Logan got in the driver's seat, pushing Ironson over only as far as was needed. Jon looked up at Eve and caressed her cheek with his hand.

He said, "I love you," as Logan fired up the ignition. He heard Eve start to say something back to him before the pain came back he lost consciousness.

Logan and Eve carried Jon, who kept passing out, to room 108 after they arrived back at the hotel. They then carried Ironson to his own room, in 102. They figured they'd let Danny and Astrid keep room 106 for themselves and Logan would take up occupancy in the office to search for maps or anything useful. It was open and gave him a view of the area, so his choice was more tactical than comfortable.

As far as Logan could tell, their mission had been a success.

The drive back to the truck stop was devoid of the creatures, and it was night, their prime hunting time. He breathed easy knowing they were safe for the moment, but still worried about Jon.

Eve stayed in the hotel room with Jon while Logan wanted to check on the younger couple. More importantly in his mind, he wanted take the rucksacks of food and water with him into the office area.

He knocked on the door of room 106 and Astrid opened it.

She looked rough, her eyes sagged and it looked as if she had aged ten years. It contrasted vastly with how Logan first seen the confident girl. She brushed her dark, unkempt hair out of her face and looked up at the hooded man, her cheeks stained from where tears had cleaned off the dirt on her face.

"Forgive me for bothering you," said Logan, who was sympathetic for the girl for having lost her father the night before, "I just wanted to tell you and Danny that we were successful. We'll be safe for tonight."

Astrid looked over her shoulder and quickly back to Logan. She shuffled her feet as she said, "Okay. Thank you."

"How are you holding up?" Logan said softly.

She avoided his eyes and played with the frayed ends of her dark hair. She said, "It's tough, ya know, but I'll be okay, I think."

Logan thought she seemed suspicious and he raised an eyebrow. He asked, "Can I speak to Danny?"

"Um, well..." her voice trailed off and she glanced behind her again, looking like she might cry.

Logan pushed the door open forcefully, causing Astrid to move away to avoid getting hit by it. Danny was nowhere to be seen and their rucksacks were gone. Logan looked under the bed, in the bathroom and flung out shelving looking for his food and water.

Astrid started crying and curled into the fetal position on the floor. It did nothing to prevent Logan from growing impatient, however. Feelings would count for nothing if they were going to starve. He said, "Where is he? Where are our bags?"

She didn't respond and kept her face in her hands, weeping uncontrollably. Logan bent down to her and asked again, his voice getting louder, "Where is he?"

"M-my dad is d-dead and he...he...he was all I had left," she sobbed.

Logan rolled his eyes and said, "I'm sorry for everything that has been going on, but if he took all of our food, we're as good as dead."

She gained control of herself, as best she could with her new tears forming new streaks on her face, and said, "H-he said he was l-leaving me. E-even called me a b-b-bitch."

"Did he say where he was going at all?"

Astrid's response was more tears.

Logan sighed and left the poor girl on the floor to cry. He opened the door and looked down into the snow. He seen several tracks, some mostly covered in the last of the snowfall, but some

194

were fresher. Only one set went northwards in the parking lot towards woodlands, and he knew it had to be Danny's.

Eve appeared. She looked tired and her hands were stained with blood, presumably Jon's. She looked down into the snow as well and said, "What're we looking at?"

"Danny's tracks," said Logan, walking forward as he tracked the younger man, "He took our food and water. Did he seem suspicious to you at all before you were able to get a vehicle going?"

"Well..." Eve said, but then went silent.

Logan looked at her, noticing the silence, and said, "Well what?"

"He hit on me some and was being creepy. That's about it," she said with a shrug.

She was hiding something. Logan knew her too well. If that bastard touched her while he and Jon were gone...

"I'm going to go find him and bring back our supplies," Logan said.

"What're you going to do with him?" Eve asked.

Logan felt his mind shifting to darkness. He looked at Eve with a sharp look and said, "What do you want me to do with him."

She gave a sudden, pleading look towards Logan and said, "Don't...do anything to him. I know Ironson would say he's a liability and Jon would call him a good for nothing pussy or something like that. But we can't...kill...our way through life.

"Bring him back and maybe we can talk to him? You're the

only able bodied man left and if those things come back you might need Danny's help. Those things are the bad guys. We have to learn to live with each other."

She was right, of course. He just hoped he could do what she wanted when, or if, he found Danny. He said, "Very well."

"Just be safe," said Eve as Logan walked past her, keeping his gaze on the footprints, "I don't want to see both the men in my life hurt in one day."

"I'll be alright. He couldn't have gone far," said Logan, adjusting the strap of the shotgun on his shoulder as he walked towards the wooded area.

Logan could have used his flashlight, but deemed the moonlight sufficient enough to track Danny's footprints in the snow. The dim light shone down through the naked, brambling tree limbs from up above.

As he trekked, further and further away from his friends, his mind was transforming. He thought back on the man he killed in anger, as much as he had tried to push it from his head, the memory remained. Part of him felt remorse for what he did, but a bigger part of him was glad he did it.

Then Omega's final words swirled into his head, "Just try to be good men from here on out." It hit him like a brick. All his life he had tried to do exactly what Omega said, but in this new world, Logan wondered if it was possible to truly be a good man. What Eve

196

had told him mirrored what Omega said in a way. Maybe she was right.

Footsteps trudging through the snow up ahead and out of view shook Logan back to reality and his task at hand. He stepped silently but quickly as he approached the source of the steps.

Through some trees up ahead, he could see Danny in his tan coat and overalls. He was laden with their bags full of food and water, comically carrying them as he high stepped through the snow.

He could end Danny so easily. His pocket knife had proven enough to do just that. Logan didn't know what happened between Danny and her when he was away, but it was enough for her to keep it from him. Eve's way could work though, so he pushed the thought from his mind. For now.

Logan continued to creep up on him, silently. He gained on the thin red head, who was clueless to the shadow following him. Once the gap was closed, Logan sprung into action.

He pulled the bags downwards, causing Danny to squeal in shock as he fell down on his back. Logan took a step over him and looked down at Danny, who was terrified. He appeared to try to say something, but his voice was caught as he stared up at the cloaked figure with wide eyes.

"Oh God, oh God," Danny choked out before trying to turn and crawl away.

Logan promptly set him back in place with a kick from his booted foot. He said to his quarry, "What were you trying to accomplish here?"

"I didn't wanna be with Astrid no more and Eve freaking hit me with a crowbar, so I made off when ya'll were gone. Didn't think you'd find me," said Danny, who looked like he was about to wet himself again.

Eve hit him with a crowbar. What did he try?

"Do you take us for idiots?" said Logan in a low, threatening tone.

"No, I-"

"We went out there to find the burrowers' nest and make the area safe. Not just for us, but for you too. Jon almost died out there, he still might. And you repay us by taking our stuff and making moves on his fiancé. Tell me, why should I let you live?"

If it were possible for Danny's eyes to go even wider than they were, they would have. He kept stuttering, unable to form sounds into complete words.

Logan took his pocket knife out and extended the blade. He leaned down until his face was inches from Danny's, close enough to see the red head's individual freckles. He held the blade of his knife between their eyes and said, "I'll be taking my supplies back now and you'll be coming back with me. If it weren't for Eve's kindliness, I would leave you out here to fend for yourself. But I promise you this, Danny, if you try to make a move on Eve again, or take any of our supplies, I will slit your throat in your sleep. Do we understand one another?"

"Y-y-yes," stuttered Danny.

Danny did as he was told and Logan took the bags. They headed back towards the truck stop only hearing the crunch of snow under their feet. Logan's mind was abuzz with mixed emotions. He'd try Eve's way for now, but he couldn't help but feel like he should leave Danny out in the wilderness.

He began counting to keep his mind busy as they hiked back.

Chapter 18 - Try to be a Good Man

"Why're you taking me back?" Danny asked.

Logan, who had counted up to 462 in his head, barely heard the red head and said, "What?"

"I don't mean nothing by it, but I think your friend would have killed me back there," said Danny, staring forwards as they walked through the moonlit snow.

Ironic.

"Jon?" said Logan, "No, he wouldn't have killed you. He would have beat the brakes off you, though."

"Ya'll sure don't seem to want me around, so why bother? I don't think I woulda taken me back."

"We're going to try to work together," said Logan, who really didn't like the red head at this point, "But remember what I said."

Danny stopped talking and they walked the rest of the way in silence. When they reached the truck stop, Eve was waiting. She breathed a sigh of relief at seeing both of them.

"I reckon I'll sleep in my own room tonight," said Danny, avoiding eye contact from either Logan and Eve. He walked off down the line of doors, trying each one until he found one that was unlocked and as far away from the others as he could get.

Eve turned to Logan and checked his bandage. "I'll need to change this before we head to bed. C'mon," she said, leading Logan to room 108. They entered the room where Jon lay injured. Sweat glistened on his face, each bead illuminated by the dim moonlight that entered the room from the window.

Logan sat down in a chair as Eve turned on her flashlight long enough to peer inside her first aid kit, before powering it off to conserve the batteries. She said, "I'm running out of supplies, so this might be the last bandage I can put on you for a while."

"It's ok, Joseph and Jon need them more," said Logan.

Eve peeled the blood-dried bandage from Logan's face and started unwrapping it off his head. As she put her nursing skills to work, Logan said, "How's he doing?" as he kept his gaze on his bearded friend.

"His heart rate is normal and he's breathing steady, but he has a fever," said Eve with worry in her voice, "I don't have the equipment to keep him hydrated intravenously, so I have to wake him up every now and then to give him water, which I'm glad you got back because I used a whole bottle already."

"I'm just glad we found him alive," said Logan, who started to stare off into space.

Eve stopped wrapping fresh bandages on Logan's head just long enough to say, "Me too..." in a trailing off voice before continuing to work. She changed the subject, "Astrid was asking about you by the way."

Logan raised an eyebrow and said, "Oh yeah? Why?"

"With Danny breaking up with her and her father dying right in front of her, I think she needs a... distraction," Eve said, grinning, "She's cute, you know."

Logan couldn't lie to himself, he found the girl attractive, but she was the last thing on his mind. "How long until Jon and Joseph are on their feet again?" Logan asked.

"Too long," said Eve, who looked disappointed at Logan's response, "I had to use quikclot to seal the wounds because I don't have any way to make stitches. Even a simple needle and thread would work at this point. Depending on how long it takes them to heal, we may be here for another week if not longer."

Logan's shoulders dipped and he cast his gaze onto the floor. "You're right, that is too long," he said in frustration, "We'll run out of supplies by then."

"Let's think on it more tomorrow," said Eve, finishing up the bandage on his face.

"Eve?" said Logan as they made eye contact.

After a moment of silence, Eve cocked her head curiously, causing her blond ponytail to wave behind her, and said, "What is it, Logan?"

He wanted to tell her about what was on his mind and the darkness that was making its way in, but he couldn't put it into words. Even with Jon, he was never good at explaining his feelings. After a moment, he said, "Keep me up to date about Jon, but get some sleep if you can. I know I'm exhausted, myself."

When Eve gave him a troubled look, he knew she wasn't convinced that was what he wanted to say. He almost start blabbering, maybe she'd make sense out of his random words and understand what was going through his head.

"I feel like I can fall asleep on my feet at this point," she said before Logan could put thoughts into words.

"I'll be in the office if you need me. Sleep well," said Logan, who exited the room and made his way up the line of room doors until he reached where the office was.

He entered into a small waiting area, surrounded by large windows. There was an old, brown couch there, which started calling Logan's name. Across the room from the entrance was the front counter and a door leading to the administration office behind it. The walls were covered in wood paneling.

He put the rucksacks behind the counter. He then sat down on the couch and stripped off his cloak, tactical vest, and his boots.

He set his pocket knife on the end table and plopped his head down onto the arm rest. His feet dangled off the opposite side, but he barely noticed in his tired state.

He covered himself in his cloak and just as he was about to fall asleep, there was a light knock on the door. He begrudgingly sat up from the comfortable couch and looked out the window.

It was Astrid. It looked as though she had cleaned her face, and brushed her long, dark hair, curling at its ends as it drifted over her shoulders. She was shivering, which prompted her to knock once more.

Logan got up and opened the door. He opened it and noticed she was wearing only a sweatshirt, pulled down to her upper thighs, and sneakers. Her bare legs shook from the cold.

"Um, hi," he said.

"Can I come in?" she asked, her green eyes staring directly into his as she looked up at him.

"Sure, yeah, sure," Logan said, backing away to let the girl in.

She stepped in and Logan shut the door behind her. As she passed by him, she stretched her arms upwards, causing the sweatshirt to show her revealing underwear. She brought her arms down and played with her fingernails before looking down as Logan asked, "Is um, everything ok?"

She met his eyes once more and said, "I just didn't want to be alone tonight."

Logan was never a ladies' man, but he knew what she was after. He couldn't stop himself from breathing heavy but he gulped down his nervousness and said, "You know what, I don't either."

Astrid pressed herself against him, wrapping her arms around his abdomen. He could feel her cold, untethered breasts against his torso as their lips met. A warmth surged through Logan's body and all of his mixed feelings faded away as he gave in to lust.

As he threw her on the couch, he could have sworn he seen a splotch of red hair through the window, but he was thinking with his other head at this point. He ignored it and joined Astrid.

The warm sun pierced through the window of the office, waking Logan up. He opened his eyes, blinking from the brightness. He hadn't slept that deeply in a while and his coupling with Astrid made him feel good, if not a little confused.

He looked around and seen that she was gone, which he couldn't blame her for; the hotel beds were probably more comfortable than the couch. He flung his cloak off him that he had used for a blanket and got dressed. His clothes were scattered around, causing him to grin as he gathered them up and put them on.

He still didn't have any feeling in a couple of his toes, which were white and scaly. With Eve tending to both Ironson and Jon, he didn't want to bother her about it. She hadn't asked about it either, but Logan knew she had her hands full.

Once he was fully clothed, he took one of the rucksacks and

went outside. It was warmer than it had been and Logan was thankful for it. The snow was turning to slush as he made his way to the closest room that was occupied by one of the group.

He opened it and seen Ironson laying in the bed, still asleep and breathing heavily. Logan opened a can of green beans with his pocket knife and left a bottle of water for him. Not wanting to disturb him, he left to go to the next room.

He knocked on room 106's door. Astrid opened it, wrapped in a blanket. She looked as if she had just woken up and brushed her dark hair from her face. When she seen it was Logan, she smiled knowingly and said, "Hey."

"Erm, hi there," said Logan with a grin, "I'm handing out food for everyone. It's not much of a breakfast, but I thought maybe we could eat together?"

Logan handed her a can of mushroom soup, which she took and said, "Thanks, but I think I might eat alone this morning."

His grin diminished as he said, "Oh. Ok, sure."

"Last night was fun though, I needed that," she said, stepping back into her room, "I'll talk to you later, ok?"

"Yeah," Logan said as she closed the door to her room. He stood there for a moment before shrugging it off and continuing to the next room.

He knocked on the door to room 108 and the door sprang open immediately. Eve said, "Come in," quickly and Logan did.

Jon looked pale and his sweating was even worse,

dampening the hotel bed he was laying on. He coughed as Logan walked in. Logan handed the pack to Eve so she could get whatever she needed out of it. She dug through it and snatched up a couple bottles of water before sitting next to her fiancé and helping him drink.

"His fever is getting worse and his wounds are getting infected," Eve said, giving Jon a bottle like a mother would an infant, "We need antibiotics, penicillin preferably."

"I'll make sure he gets them," Logan said with worried urgency, "There must be a pharmacy or something close by."

"Please hurry, Logan," Eve said, furrowing her brow in frustration, "I'd come with you, but I need to stay here with him and Ironson."

Logan shook his head and said, "Don't worry about it. I'll go."

"The keys are on the table," Eve said, concentrating on Jon, "If you can find any other medical supplies while you're out there, we definitely need them."

Logan took the keys to the technical off the table and pocketed them. There was a box of shotgun shells there as well, so he took a half dozen of them before marching off into the melting snow.

He barged into the office and started looking under the front counter for any kind of map. He was familiar with the area, but there were a lot of small towns that he didn't know about.

He turned to the door behind the counter. He opened it and entered into a small, musty room that contained a desk with drawers and had a computer sitting on top of it. A rolling chair sat at it and on both sides were filing cabinets.

After a few minutes of searching around the desk and cabinets, he found a roadmap of Missouri. He found where they wre located, at the intersection of highways 67 and 172, then started looking around at where the closest towns were. Williamsville was the closest, where Astrid and Danny were from. He folded the map and slid it into a pocket in his tactical vest then headed out in search of antibiotics.

Chapter 19 - Let the Darkness In

Logan's mind was abuzz with his internal conflict. Thrown on top of that was sleeping with Astrid the same day she and Danny had broken up. Maybe it was a one time thing? He hoped not, because he liked the distraction from everything else.

He drove the green camouflaged technical westward, down the highway towards Williamsville. He played with the radio as he carved his way through untouched, slushy snow but heard nothing but static. It reminded him of the last news he heard on the radio, about Fort Bragg and the soldiers holding out there, and he wondered if they still were.

Not a single creature had been seen by anyone since they

killed the enforcer, but he maintained his cloaked visage just in case. At this point, he felt naked without it, which he knew was irrational, but the whole world had become irrational.

The small town was only a ten minute drive down the road, which proved handy as the technical only had half of a tank of fuel left. They'd need it for the trip to St. Louis once Ironson and Jon were able to travel.

He slowed down once he entered the outskirts. Like everything else, it was a ghost town, as far as Logan could tell. Once upon a time, a few hundred people lived there. He passed by lines of snow crested houses as he drove, looking for some kind of commercial area or doctor's office.

Past the first batch of residences, he seen a gas station and a few general stores on his right. On his left were some railroad tracks and more neighborhoods beyond. He kept looking to his right for anything that would look helpful until he found a target.

Nestled on an intersection past the general stores was a small, humble building with a sign out front that named the building as LLOYD'S PHARMACY. Logan pulled the truck off the road and parked it in front of the building.

Before going further, he looked around and took in the area. Everything was eerily still and would appear no one had been there for a while, until Logan seen footsteps in the melting snow. It was difficult to tell how many there were in the slush, but he deduced it had to have been during the snow storm or after. The footsteps led across the street and towards the railroad tracks.

He shelved this information in his mind for later and walked up the small steps towards the front door of the pharmacy. He brought his shotgun at the ready as he slowly pushed the door forward with the barrel.

The inside looked ransacked, waiting chairs flung around, inspirational posters on the ground. It smelled of death in the first room and dried blood marked the tan carpet. Opposite of the front door was a glass window where people used to exchange money for prescriptions and a door leading back to the employee area. The glass was slashed, by a creature no doubt, and the door was hanging off its hinges.

Logan swung the door open to a grisly scene. Someone had tried to escape the creatures, their remains scattered all over the stock room. It may have even been more than one person, but Logan didn't look at the decaying body parts long enough to tell. When this all began, it turned his stomach, but at this point, it was as normal as breathing. He would never get used to the smell, however.

Cabinets and shelves lined the walls and stood in the middle of the small room. At one point, it probably held all the medication for the whole population of the town, but as Logan gazed upon the shelves, they were almost empty.

He began opening cabinet doors and drawers, searching for anything useful, but trying to avoid the body parts. He found some bandages, a suture kit and some painkillers, but no antibiotics or any harder medication.

After he felt like he had searched the area thoroughly, he left the pharmacy. He found some supplies but not what he was looking for, and the clock was ticking. He weighed his options: check the map and drive to the nearest town, hoping the area wouldn't be in an area of a new burrower nest, or follow the tracks and hope they had antibiotics from the pharmacy. Either way was unknowable.

He decided to follow the footprints for a ways. If he got too far and found no one, he'd make his way back and start driving.

He walked through the slush across the road and eyed the prints. There were multiple sets running along the railroad tracks. He followed them quickly, trotting along and looking down to make sure he was on the right track.

Astrid felt bad about not sharing breakfast with Logan, but he wouldn't had been able to anyways. When he rushed off in the technical, she knew something was up. Danny was nowhere to be seen when she got dressed and left her room. Good, she was done with him anyways.

What a little bitch.

With Logan's group she seen how men should act during this crisis. Before all this she never cared about how milquetoast Danny was. There wasn't drugs and alcohol for him to bribe her with anymore. After last night with how good Logan made her feel, it'd take more than that to bribe her. Danny sure couldn't make up for it sexually, he was too boring and timid.

Astrid pulled her dark hair up into a pony tail and visited Eve, who was outside to get some air. She had brought Astrid up to speed with what was going on when Logan went to go get Danny back the night before.

"How's Jon?" Astrid asked.

Eve looked like she hadn't slept in weeks. Bags had formed under her heavy eyes. She responded, "Not good. I hope Logan comes back soon with some meds."

Astrid felt for the girl, but thought maybe changing the subject would help. She said, "So you were a nurse before all this?"

"Yeah, a registered nurse," Eve responded, rubbing her eyes.

"I always wanted to get into the medical field, but I was too busy getting drunk and high," Astrid said with a sheepish grin.

Eve smiled too, although it looked forced, and said, "I've only drank socially. Everyone always seemed to get into fights if we'd go to the bar."

"Oh, I've gotten into fights before," said Astrid, who began leaning against the window sill alongside Eve, "Man or woman, I didn't care. My dad..." her voice trailed off for a moment, but she cleared her throat and continued, "He used to hate my 'tomboy attitude' as he would put it."

"I guess I was always a girly girl compared to you, then," Eve said.

"You hold yourself pretty well, though," said Astrid, who
213

was genuinely impressed with Eve, "I've never seen anyone fight those things like ya'll do."

"It's because we stick together and watch each other's backs. Now you're part of us. We all need to work together," said Eve.

Astrid was glad this group found her, even if they couldn't save her father. The moment was forever engraved into her mind, but she was doing her best to forget it. If only there was some weed around.

"What did you do before the invaders came?" Eve asked.

"I waited tables," Astrid responded, "Money was only ok, but it funded my habits."

"I guess there's no such thing as a bad habit now," Eve said, "But I need to go check on Jon. His fever has been getting worse. It was nice chatting to you."

Astrid said, "You too," as Eve went into her room.

After a ways, the snow tracks veered off towards a clump of houses on a cul-de-sac. They were all one story homes, with mostly different colored siding. The prints led to a house made of brick, the only one like it in the neighborhood.

Logan took up a cautious gate, the slush was loud to walk on. He had to assume whoever he was tracking was dangerous, even if they turned out not to be, so he stealthily moved between the homes, out of sight of the brick-walled house. Some had children's toys and play set ups, soaked in the melting snow and untouched for months.

When he was one building away, he peered out from around a corner. His hood gave his eyes protection from the beating sun as he looked for any kind of movement. He seen none so listened for voices or activity. He heard nothing, so began stepping lightly towards the building.

He put his back against the brick and began moving along the perimeter of the house. From inside he could hear footsteps, faintly clonking around. Every now and then he would hear voices and some kind of thudding noise, but only bassy baritones filtered through the walls.

There was a window that was low enough for him to peek through, so he did as cautiously as he could. It was a bedroom with no occupants. He moved on to the next window as he moved clockwise around the house and heard the thumping noise again. Another bedroom, but he seen what the thumping was. A man and a woman were having sex vigorously, each grunting with every thrust. Logan didn't linger and crept on. The voices grew louder as he moved around the corner and looked into the next window. It was the kitchen and someone was there.

It was a male, sitting at a kitchen table with his back to the window. Logan tried to size him up, but it was hard to tell from his vantage point. He wore a cut off shirt, showing his sleeves of tattoos. He appeared to be bald and was working on something at the table. This something turned out to be a handgun, as Logan seen him set it down, along with a cleaning rag, before standing up and walking away into another room.

"I'm comin', I'm comin'," he responded in a gruff manner to a barely audible voice from further inside the house, then in a tone only he could hear said, "Keep your g'damn panties on."

Logan looked around the kitchen for any sign of supplies, but the only thing useful he could see was the handgun. The voices from further inside could be heard, but no one else showed up.

He decided to try the window, but it was latched. He snuck away, ready to view inside the next window, which turned out to be a living room. The curtains were drawn, but parted just enough for him to look through. A tree in the yard cast a shadow on the window, so Logan knew it would be more difficult to see his outline through the glass.

There was a couch with a coffee table in front of it, a recliner and an entertainment center with a big, LCD television set upon it. He could make out two people sitting on the couch and a third walked up from an inside hallway. It was the bald man.

Logan's heart thumped quickly. He felt he was in over his head. He'd watch all the same since no one seemed to notice him yet. He already plotted an escape route that intertwined between the other houses on the cul-de-sac in case things went bad.

"When is it my turn?" said the smaller of the two people on the couch in a squirrely voice.

"Whenever Macon is done, Screwball, calm the fuck down," said a snaky voice, shared by a backhand into the face of the smaller one.

"What'd you want, Del?" said the bald man, impatiently.

"You and Screwball got some meds from Lloyd's, yeah?" hissed Del.

"Yup," said the bald man.

"Well where are they, Mann?"

"Yeah, we could use a fix!" shrilled Screwball.

"*I*," Del said, flashing his dagger-like eyes from under his long hair at the smaller guy, "*I* could use a fix."

"Is that what you're gonna do every time we find meds?" said Mann, even more impatiently, "Use and abuse 'em like that poor girl in there?"

Logan narrowed his eyes, but kept watching.

Del stood and moved his hands like he was giving a grand speech while he said, "We're all gonna die sooner or later, brother. I dunno why we haven't seen any of the hunters all day, but it's only a matter of time before they show up. We're on borrowed time, c'mooooon. May as well do whatever the fuck we want until the reaper shows up."

"I don't plan on dyin' anytime soon," growled Mann, before turning to walk away in a manner that reminded Logan of Jon.

Del, who was about Logan's build but perhaps scrawnier, flopped his hands down to his side and said, "You walking away from me, fucker?"

Mann stopped and, without turning around, said, "You know

217

I'll stomp your girly-headed ass on my worse day, Del. No meds, we need them."

Mann walked out of view, followed by a complaining Del. All that was left was Screwball. He was jittery, scratching his face and rubbing his crotch in preparation for his turn with the girl.

Try to be good men from here on out, thought Logan. Bullshit. "All who are not good, I'll end them all," whispered Logan to himself, before making sure his shotgun was ready to fire.

His mind had been split between what he should do, but it was far easier to let the darkness in. Let it take the reins and use his body as an instrument of justice. Destroy those who would not do good to others. Kill them.

His mind fogged.

He seen Screwball stand up, like a reanimated corpse he lurched around. "I'm gonna have a smoke, let me know when Macon is done!" he called down the hall before approaching the front door.

Logan thought of going in gun blazing, but perhaps a subtler approach would do.

Screwball flung open the front door and stepped onto the porch. Logan took out his pocket knife and flipped open the blade before hiding around the corner of the house. He used the blade as a mirror and stuck it out near the ground to watch the small man.

Screwball lit a cigarette and paced back and forth on the porch. He was mumbling to himself and furiously grabbed his crotch, causing himself to giggle.

218

The porch was about ten feet away from where Logan crouched around the corner of the house. It was elevated a foot into the air. Each round of Screwball's pacing around put his back to Logan for two seconds exactly. He appeared to be right handed, as he used it to smoke his cigarette. A hunting knife hung on his belt.

Logan weighed the variables before readying himself to attack.

Macon, the man who Logan first seen having sex with the woman, voluntarily or otherwise, left the bedroom buckling his pants. He was bare chested and his torso was covered in tattoos, some gang affiliated.

He walked into the kitchen where Del and Mann were still arguing over how to use the meds they looted. He grinned and interrupted, "Damn, that never gets old. Can't believe she lets us do whatever we want to her."

Mann shook his head and said, "You're a sick man, Macon."

"What? Like you haven't had a go with her," scoffed Macon, grabbing a warm bottle of beer from the sink.

"I haven't," said Mann, pointedly.

Del brushed his hair away from his eyes and said, "For someone who was in the pen for murder, you sure are a damn softy."

Mann flinched at the words for a split second, but turned and looked down at Del, who was a few inches shorter than him. He said, "I've done some bad shit, that's for sure, but rape isn't one of

219

them."

The woman stumbled into the kitchen, holding a sheet around her body. She was in her mid-40s and looked like she was ridden hard and put away wet even before everything went to hell. She had a black eye and a cut on her cheek.

"What the fuck are you doing out of bed?" said Macon, slapping her in the face, "Did I tell you you could get up?"

She lurched away from him as he struck her, stuttering, "I-I j-just want s-some water."

"Hey," Mann said, catching Macon's eyes with his own, "She just wants some water. I don't think she needs beat every time she doesn't have her legs open to you."

"Pfft. Fine, get your damn water then head back. Screwball wants a go with you," said Macon, letting her pass. He squeezed her backside as she walked towards a red and white cooler on the ground.

"Speaking of which, where's Screwball? I thought he was all excited about getting his turn," said Del.

"He went out for a smoke," said Mann, sitting back down at the kitchen table and picking up his handgun as if it were going to say something to him.

"I'll go tell him I'm done," said Macon before leaving the kitchen.

The woman sat at the kitchen table, next to Mann. Del punched the table and said, "Hey, didn't he tell you to get back in there?"

"Leave her be, Del. For Christ's sake, give her a moment," said Mann without looking up from his handgun.

There was a sound of something falling in the living room.

Del gave a confused look at Mann and said, "Wonder what that was."

"Go check," said Mann, "They're probably arguing about who's ne-"

The woman looked at him with sad eyes, interrupting him.

"Just go tell them to knock it off," said Mann, avoiding eye contact with the woman.

Del left the kitchen and said, "Our esteemed leader said to..."

His voice trailed off as he seen Macon laying on the blue carpeted floor of the living room, bleeding profusely from his neck. He was holding his throat and trying to speak, but it came out in gargles. The front door was open and he seen Screwball's body lying motionless on the front porch.

He brushed the hair away from his face, as if it would clear his vision from the scene he was seeing. He started to shout to Mann that there was trouble, but a hand covered his mouth and he felt his neck turn warm.

After a moment of silence, Mann placed his handgun down on the table, stood up and shouted, "What the hell are you guys doing out there, circle jerking each other?"

His answer was a swift moving shadow entering from the hallway into the kitchen, holding a semi-automatic shotgun in his direction with a stun gun taped onto it. He held his hands up as the hooded figured stood before him.

"Was only a matter of time, I suppose," said Mann, regretfully.

The figure said nothing.

The woman sat at the table, rigid with fear, or maybe it was hope.

"Well, go ahead then," said Mann, opening his arms invitingly.

"The meds you took from the pharmacy, where are they?" said the figure in a low, threatening voice.

Mann raised an eyebrow and a bead of sweat ran down his bald head. He said, "They're in the fridge."

The shadow kept the shotgun aimed at him as it moved from the entry way to the refrigerator. It opened the door, revealing several bottles of various types of medicine. The shadow snatched them all up, stowing them away from inside its cloak before backing away towards the hallway.

"You not gonna kill me?" said Mann, more curious than scared.

"No," said the shadow, "You're not like the others."

Mann almost seemed sad and said, "So... that's it then? You're leaving?"

"I got what I needed," said the shadow, "Now, it's up to you to be a better man than they were."

In an instant, the shadow was gone. Mann waited a moment in silence with the woman before getting up and finding the bodies of his fellow convicts. He walked out onto the porch where Screwball laid in a pool of blood, his hunting knife missing. He looked around but seen no indication of the direction the shadow had went.

The woman appeared behind him, hugging him around his torso, sobbing as if a great weight had been lifted off of her. He put an arm around her and said, "It's ok, no one else will hurt you from now on."

Chapter 20 - The Angel and the Dark Passenger

Eve sat on the bed where Jon lay sweating and shaking. She cradled his head hopelessly. Her fiancé was laying there, pale and in so much pain but there was nothing she could do. He had been her rock through thick and thin, even when they squabbled, she loved him more than anything else. She had never seen him in such a weak state before.

A loud, rushed knock brought her to reality and she answered the door swiftly.

Logan stood before her, his hood let down. His face was

speckled with blood, dried on the stubble of his chin and cheeks. His cloak and tactical vest were covered in blood, as if a bucket of the stuff were dumped on him.

Her face twisted in shock, causing her to drop her jaw and she said, "Are...are you ok?"

Logan stared at her as if he didn't know her and said, "I got you what you need," before pulling all of the medical supplies out from different pockets.

"Logan?" she said worriedly, "Is that your blood?"

"No."

"What the hell happened to you?"

"Just get Jon patched up," he said, thrusting the supplies into her hands.

She hastily set them down inside the hotel room and turned back to Logan, who was already walking away. She followed him and demanded, "Tell me what happened, right now."

Logan didn't respond so she grabbed him by the shoulder. He spun around and looked at her with the same, blank stare. She pointed a finger at him and said, "Don't you dare treat me like I'm some random person you don't even know. I love you like a brother and I need you now more than ever."

Logan cast his gaze down and let out a deep breath, like a demon was escaping through his mouth. He blinked and shook his head before saying, "Eve, I'm so sorry. I think...I might be going nuts."

Eve softened her eyes and said, "Dammit, Logan, I wanna give you a big hug right now, but there's no way I'm going to with all that blood on you."

Logan held his arms out and looked at all the blood on him. He said, "I didn't even notice. I barely remember the drive back."

She took him by the hand and said, "I need to get Jon his antibiotics, come with me," before leading him back to their temporary home.

Logan waited patiently for Eve to do what she needed to with Jon. He didn't get a good look at the pills he took from the convicts, but hoped they helped all the same. After a few minutes she came back out with a relieved look on her face.

"Thank you so much, Logan," she said, "Everything you found will help us all, especially the penicillin."

"Glad I got the right thing," he responded.

"I want him to rest up before I check on him again. Let's talk in the office?" she said.

Logan nodded in response and they made their way towards where he had taken occupancy. As they passed the door where Ironson was she said, "I checked on him a little bit before you came back. He's doing well and keeps trying to get up, but I told him he needs to heal before he can start moving around. He keeps looking at some kind of photo but won't tell me what it is."

"You're amazing, you know that?" Logan said, "With

everything going wrong, you still manage to keep your mind on the right track."

Eve smiled as they continued to walk and said, "I'm just doing what I did before everything went to shit."

"Still though, you're a beacon of hope in this mad world," said Logan, "Have you heard from Danny or Astrid?"

"Haven't seen Danny," said Eve, ruffling her eyebrows, "Starting to wonder if he took off again. But I did talk to Astrid while you were away. I think she likes you."

Logan mumbled, "She has a funny way of showing it."

"What's that?" Eve said, craning her neck towards Logan to hear him.

"Nothing, let's get out of the cold," he said as they reached the door to the office. He opened it and let Eve pass through before entering himself.

"If we had some running water, I'd get your clothes washed up," Eve said, looking at the blood splotches on Logan.

He took off his tactical vest and cloak and checked himself for any more blood. Eve delved into one of the packs and grabbed a bottle of water. She took a cut off piece of bandage from her pocket and wet it with the water bottle.

Logan sat down and Eve said, "It's all over your face," before wiping his chin and cheeks with the wet bandage, "Tell me what happened."

Logan explained how he searched the town before following

tracks from the pharmacy to the house, where he killed three of the convicts. "They were...using...this woman. I don't know why she stayed there, maybe because it was safer than being alone, but I could tell one of the men wasn't as bad as the others. I could have shot him then and there, but I didn't."

"What possessed you to want to...kill...them?" Eve said, busying herself with cleaning Logan's face.

"I didn't want to," he said, trying to put his feelings into words, "I wanted to go in there, grab the meds and leave. But there was something inside of me that just couldn't let them be. It was like I became a completely different person. I was so...efficient."

"There's no police anymore and we have to do what we have to to survive," said Eve, "But it doesn't mean we should start killing people."

"We needed those meds," stressed Logan, "I could have gone to a different town or something, but I didn't know how long Jon could handle being infected."

"True, we needed the meds."

"The way I seen it, it was them or Jon, even if they didn't know."

Eve finished cleaning Logan up and threw the bloodied bandage into a far corner. She sat down next to Logan and they faced each other. She said, "When you killed that man in the grocery store, I was appalled and thankful at the same time. I think you doing that broke some kind of seal. You do it once, it'll be easier to

228

do it again."

"Maybe."

"You're a good man, Logan," she went on, "I never would have thought you had it in you to take a life. Whatever is going on in your head, you need to figure out what is important."

Logan replied, "That's just it, Eve. You and Jon are what's important to me. Who knows if my family is ok back home. Right now, you two are my family and I'll do whatever it takes to keep everyone safe and alive."

Eve's expression gave away what she felt: confused. After a moment, she said, "Just do what you think is right, Logan. There are bad people, sure, but those burrower things, or demons or whatever they are, are the real threat."

"What is right or wrong anymore?" Logan asked, hoping she could say the magic words to take the darkness away from his mind.

"I don't know, Logan, I really don't. I just don't want you to get in over your head and end up getting hurt, or hurt someone else who doesn't deserve it."

"I don't think I would," said Logan, casting his gaze down at the floor, "But I never thought I'd take a life either."

She put her hand on Logan's shoulder and said, "I'm always here for you, you know that. When that other version of you starts to peep his head up, come talk to me."

"Thank you, Eve," said Logan, looking at her again, "I will."

"I'm going to go check on the injured," Eve said, getting up and opening the door to the office, "Get some rest, you deserve it."

As the door shut, Logan pondered on what was right and wrong in this new world. His pragmatic nature is what has always carried him. If he needed money, he'd get a job, for instance, but how far should pragmatism carry him. He couldn't take back the lives he took, but with Eve's help, maybe he could hold back his dark passenger.

That evening, Logan sat at the front desk of the office. He found some stationary and a pen, so he began jotting down ideas of things he could do or look for until Jon healed. While he scribbled away, the door opened and Astrid walked in.

"Talked to Eve," she said, plopping down on the couch like it was her own, "She told me what you did to get the meds."

Logan sat down the pen and sighed. He had hoped Eve would have kept that between the two of them, but she was too honest a person to withhold information. He said, "It's not something I'm proud of, even if it meant the life or death of my closest friend."

"I'm glad you did it," Astrid said, a devious flash emanating from her face as she spoke, "The world is ours now. Fuck everyone else, let's take what's ours."

"You're...glad?" Logan asked. His mind was addled from the sheer contrast of what she was saying versus what Eve said.

"Yeah, and it's sexy you'd do something like that," Astrid said.

This girl had some weird kinks.

"How is that sexy?" Logan asked, "I feel awful about it."

"You shouldn't. This is the new world, Logan," she said while standing up. She sauntered over to the desk and leaned over it, bending towards him. Her shirt hung off her neck and Logan could see her cleavage.

He fought through the distraction and said, "We need to be better, though. I don't want to do something like that unless I absolutely have to."

Astrid leaned in closer to Logan. Her nose almost touched his. Logan stared into her green eyes and he felt his chest tighten.

"I want you to fuck me over this counter, right now," she said before kissing him on the lips.

"My clothes are all dirty..." he said between kisses.

"So take them off," she said as she started undressing herself.

How she snubbed him that morning faded from Logan's mind as he pulled her over the counter and turned her around. He didn't exactly agree with what she was saying, but that feeling faded as well.

He was starting to like this girl.

Chapter 21 - January 20th

The next day, Logan decided to check in on Ironson. They were all in a hurry up and wait situation while Jon recovered, so there was plenty of time to kill. As much as he wanted to spend most of that time with Astrid, he felt responsible for the group. Eve's attention was on Jon, so Logan readied himself to take up all other duties.

Logan knocked on the door that led to Ironson's room. After a moment he heard a muffled, "Come in."

Logan entered the musty room. The sun's rays filtered in through the window. Ironson was sitting up in the bed, wearing his BDU pants and a t-shirt. Logan never noticed just how muscled the pilot was, having only seen him with his bomber jacket on.

Ironson sat a book down on the end table, his place marked by some kind of paper. When he seen Logan he said, "How're you holding up?"

Logan almost chuckled. All he had was a little cut down his nose. Ironson had been stabbed and still thought about others first. Logan replied, "Doing good, making plans for our time here. How's your wounds?"

"Eve should've been a medic with what she can do in the field," Ironson said, patting the side of his torso, "Have a seat, take a load off."

Logan plopped down in an upholstered armchair that had already been pulled up next to the bed. Presumably from Eve checking up on the Marine. Logan said, "What're you reading?"

"Some romance novel Eve found. Never was into them, but I can't really be picky right now."

"I suppose not," Logan said, picking up the book. He wasn't into romance novels either, but figured he'd give it a test read as they spoke.

"Wait-" Ironson said as his book mark slid out of the book and onto the floor.

"Oh, sorry, what page..." Logan began to say until he seen what the book mark was.

It was a polaroid of a slightly younger Ironson in civilian clothing. A woman with a huge smile was on one side of him, and a frowning young boy was on his other side. Ironson was smiling and

233

didn't look so disgruntled; his arms were wrapped tightly around the woman and child.

Logan picked up the photograph and asked, "Is this your family?"

"Was," Ironson said, looking down at his hands, "They were my family."

"I'm sorry," Logan said, setting the book back on the end table and placing the photo on top of it, "What happened?"

Ironson picked up the photo and gazed into it, as if he were transporting himself back in time. He said, "They died in a car wreck with a drunk driver while I was deployed overseas."

Logan breathed out and shook his head. He should have left the book alone.

"I'm sorry to hear that, man," Logan said, trying to sound as sympathetic as he could.

"No need to be sorry, wasn't your fault," Ironson said mechanically, "I wasn't going to tell anyone about it. Didn't want to look weak."

"How would that make you look weak?"

Ironson sat the photo face down on the end table and said, "It's the one thing that gets to me. The creatures, or whatever the hell they are, I can deal with. Other people, I can deal with. I just can't seem to deal with my family's deaths, though. I distract myself the best I can but..." his voice cracked and he stopped speaking.

Lieutenant Joseph Ironson, the most stoic man Logan had

ever met, sniffed back tears.

"G'dammit," he said as he wiped his eyes with the edge of his t-shirt.

"You're not weak for missing them," Logan said, "I don't even know how I'd feel if it happened to me, but you shouldn't beat yourself up over it."

Logan's words probably hit himself worse than it did Ironson. He felt like a hypocrite when everyone else opened up about how they were feeling, but the one thing he wanted to share, he just couldn't.

"I was a whole world away when it happened," said Ironson, "I should have been there."

"If you were, you may have died too."

"Then I would have died with them," said Ironson, a tinge of frustration coming through his words, "And I would have been ok with that."

Logan waited a moment before saying, "We can't change the past. Life hits us harder than anything else, but if we lay down and stop moving forward, then what's the point?

"A man I barely knew said try to be a good man from here on out, and I think that's what we should do. Honor your family by staying the course, and maybe some good can come out of this crazy, new world."

Ironson nodded at Logan and said, "I'll try. Thank you, Logan."

"No need to thank me. We're in this together," said Logan, who cursed himself for not being more open to everyone.

They spent most of the rest of the day talking about life, potential plans on getting to St. Louis and everything in between. Logan had broken through Ironson's rough exterior, and inside was a hurt man who just wanted to move on to something good.

Eve ate dinner with them and joined in their conversation. Jon was asleep and she said she needed company. Not long after she joined them, Astrid did too. Logan could see a distinct difference between the two girls as they spoke. They were like a yin and yang.

When it got late, Eve went back to her room to lay next to Jon. Logan told Ironson he'd check in on him the next day before he retired to the hotel office for some alone time with Astrid.

Over the course of the next week, Logan kept himself busy as Ironson and Jon healed. The first couple of days, he made excursions out from the hotel to look for supplies and food. He scoured farms and country houses, looking for anything and everything that could be useful for the group. He found a working wrist watch that he would give to Jon later.

He was glad to keep busy as it kept his mind clear, and even gave him some ideas. He found some metal plating, which kind of metal he had no idea but more than likely steel, that he sewed into their black cloaks. It made them weigh quite a bit more, but gave them some form of protection. Ironson told him that the plates would

236

stop small arms fire and perhaps glancing attacks from the creatures, but not military grade weapons.

Their supplies were dwindling, so Logan started boiling what was left of the melting snow to replenish their water. Astrid helped him in this endeavor and they grew closer, which scared the loner. The more they spoke, the more Logan realized she was an outsider just like him. He didn't agree with everything she said, however. She was a devil on his shoulder while Eve was the angel on the other. He recognized this, but her open willingness to sleep with him kept him wanting her around.

Since Logan had the larger, hunting knife he took from Screwball, he gave Eve his old pocket knife. He had it for years, a gift from his parents, and Eve gratefully accepted it. She seen it more as a kind gesture as she said she never intended to use it.

Logan had also made a trip back to the stoneworks where they fought the enforcer. It was silent and still around the town and quarry, but he managed to find Jon's Winchester shotgun half buried in the pile of sand in the large building not far from the rotting corpse of the large creature.

No one had seen Danny, but no one really cared to look for him except for Logan.

A week to the day from when Logan and Jon had taken the fight to the enforcer, the bearded man was able to get to his feet. He walked with a limp but his wounds had healed enough so he could get up and move around.

When Logan gave Jon the wrist watch and his trusty Winchester, he promptly put it on and gave Logan a bear hug. The reaction surprised Logan, but Jon praised him for keeping everything together along with Eve.

Ironson also was healed. He and Jon buried the hatchet, which surprised the Marine Corps pilot. Jon's overall demeanor surprised everyone, actually. He was kinder, especially towards Eve.

There was no sign of the creatures, but Logan wasn't convinced they were altogether gone. They were within the area of influence of the nest they had seen before, but no one could tell how far that influence reached. He deduced that there were multiple nests everywhere that had their own regions they hunted, like packs of carnivores.

With their food supplies dangerously low, the time had come to leave the truck stop. They gathered everything into the technical in preparation for the drive to St. Louis on the morning of January 20th.

As everyone gathered at the vehicle, Logan wanted to make one more sweep of the hotel to make sure they didn't miss anything. They had previously ignored the few rooms that were locked, but Logan broke the windows to gain access. He went down the line of the long building, looking for anything useful after breaking in, but finding only spare clothing.

Close to the end of the hotel, he entered through the window of one of the locked rooms. A smell immediately assaulted his senses, the same kind of smell from the cannibal's watchtower. He coughed and covered his mouth and nose with his hand.

This room looked like the others, a small table and a few chairs, the bed and a dresser with an old television set upon it. As he walked through the room towards the bathroom, the smell was fiercer.

He gazed inside the bathroom and found a body leaning against the bath tub, their head hanging down and arms spread out. The mirror over the sink was shattered and speckled with dried blood. As he got closer to the body, he seen who the body was.

It was Danny.

He had slit his wrists with the mirror shards and appeared to have been dead for a while. In his hand was a piece of paper. Logan took it and looked at it. Written in blood was the message *fuck you Logan.*

Logan hung his head in shame. He felt responsible for Danny's suicide. Danny had locked the door, slit his wrists and wrote that message in his own blood. He clearly didn't mean for anyone to find him, which made seeing the note worse.

"I'm sorry," he said, dropping the note back onto Danny's slumped over corpse.

He looked into the shattered mirror, seeing tiny reflections of himself in each, individual piece. He seen his scars on his face, one on his eyebrow and the other across his nose and cheek. He hadn't shaved this entire time, but all he had was stubble on his cheeks and chin, unlike Jon who had grown a full, epic beard in the same amount of time.

He wondered if all of the reflections were him, or if some were his dark passenger. Or maybe they all were.

He left the hotel room and didn't bother with checking the other rooms. He had seen enough.

As he approached the technical, which Jon dubbed the "Mean Green Machine," Astrid seen Logan and asked, "You find anything useful?"

Logan looked at her and almost told her he found Danny's corpse. The others looked at him as well, waiting for an answer. "Didn't find anything," he said, "It's time to get moving."

"It's gonna be a little over a two-hour drive to St. Louis. I'm driving!" said Jon as he limped to the driver's side.

"Shotgun!" Eve claimed.

"Guess we're in the back then," said Ironson towards Logan, "I meant to tell you, good job holding things together."

Logan, still distracted from what he seen in the hotel room, unhitched the back panel of the truck's bed and said, "I didn't do much."

"It may not seem like it to you, but everyone is thankful," Ironson said as he, Logan and Astrid climbed into the back of technical, "Even Jon is, but he told me not to tell you because, in his words, he didn't want to seem like a pussy."

"Sounds like Jon," said Logan.

"You ok, brother?" Ironson asked, adjusting his aviator sunglasses.

"Yeah, I'm fine. Just ready to get away from here."

Ironson said, "I think getting out of here will be good for all of us."

Inside the cab, Jon and Eve shared a quick kiss before she said, "I'm so glad you're back on your feet. I've missed you so much."

Jon grinned under his large beard and said, "Soon as we're at MEPS, we're gonna find our own room and we're not leaving for a couple days."

Eve bit her lip and said, "We're not gonna leave that room for weeks, babe."

"Hell yeah," Jon snickered as he started the truck. In a mechanical roar, the Mean Green Machine sprang to life, ready to carry its occupants to their destination.

Chapter 22 - The Dirties

For the most part, they were all hopeful as they made the drive northwards. They were all on their feet and, until they got far enough, they were free from the threat of the creatures. With each mile they rode, Logan grew more and more leery of the threat of a new nest.

He quietly kept his gaze on his surroundings. Astrid sat next to him on the wheel well, resting her head on his cloaked shoulder. He liked it, but his cautious nature prevented him from enjoying the light moment.

Ironson stood at the M240 machine gun, like a stalwart protector. His black cloak flowed behind him as the truck raced up and down the hilly road.

They were still in the Mark Twain national forest, in the Ozark Highlands. As at home Logan and his friends had previously felt in the region, they were ready for a change of scenery.

The leafless trees passed by as Jon drove the technical up the highway. Every now and then there were abandoned vehicles and signs of the creature's attacks. Some people never made it out of their vehicles, as evidenced by bloodstained, shattered windows.

The sun was a blessed source of warmth that cut through the wintery chill. Logan raised his face to soak in the warmth, closing his eyes.

Then he heard it.

He opened his eyes and looked around. He heard it again, the call of a hawk. High in the sky, it soared through the air. It was the first animal he had seen since leaving the grocery store.

Logan tapped Astrid on the knee and pointed up. "Look," he said, "A hawk."

Astrid lifted her head from his shoulder and looked at it. She pushed her beanie back from her face to get a better look and smiled as she seen it. "Wow, it's been so long since I've seen any kind of animal."

"I know," said Logan, who took it as a hopeful sign.

Ironson had noticed it as well and brought his aviators down to see it.

Inside the cab of the truck, Jon, who was busy looking at the road, had not noticed the hawk. He did see a bridge ahead, blocked by multiple vehicles parked bumper to bumper. Strangely, they were densely packed on the bridge itself, not on the road before or after it. Jon slowed to a halt before the barrier of cars and trucks.

The bridge crossed over the St. Francis River, a wide, green river that flowed into Lake Wappapello. It had a small amount of frost at the edges of the river, on its forested banks.

"How're we going to get the truck across?" Eve asked, looking around for an opening they could maybe drive through.

"We'll have to move them," said Jon, cursing to himself, "It's either that or turn around and find another way around, but we don't have near enough gas for that."

The rest of the group had noticed the blockade from the bed of the truck and they stood to look at it.

"This isn't right," said Logan.

"Why's that?" responded Ironson, "It's not uncommon for there to be abandoned cars."

"It's not that. It's how they're parked," said Logan, "They're only on the bridge."

He kneeled down and wrapped on the cab's back window with his knuckles. Jon and Eve turned to him as the driver opened the window. Jon said, "What ya think, man?"

"I think it's not good," said Logan, "They were parked there on purpose."

"Well I sure as shit ain't turning around," huffed Jon, "Maybe

244

whoever did it has left."

"Maybe..." Logan said, his voice trailing off as he looked around for any potential attackers.

Ironson leaned down from the machine gun and said to the friends, "Why don't we go check it out. We'll take our firearms and if something happens, Eve can jump on the M240."

"I don't think we have much of a choice," said Logan, "Okay, let's scout it out then get started moving the vehicles out of the way if we find nothing."

He, Jon and Ironson left the truck, shrouded in their armored cloaks and holding their shotguns at the ready. Logan took point and began walking in between the parked cars, vans and trucks. He kneeled down and looked under the vehicles to see if there was anyone waiting in ambush, or for improvised explosives.

"See anything?" Jon called to him, breaking the tense silence, once Logan had made it about halfway across the bridge.

Logan looked back and shook his head before continuing his sweep. Maybe Jon was right and whoever had done this was long gone. For all they knew, they were within a new nest's area.

When Logan was almost all the way across the bridge and at the end of the parked vehicles, he heard a noise. It sounded like a car door to his right somewhere.

Back at the technical, Eve had taken up overwatch at the mounted machine gun. She watched as the men walked the bridge,

Jon and Ironson back a little ways and flanking Logan. Astrid was unarmed and sat down in the bed where there were cases of extra 7.62mm ammo, peeking her head over the roof of the cab.

"Hello, ladies," said a voice from behind them.

The two girls spun around to see two, dirty-looking men behind the truck. One held a homemade knife and the other was pointing a .22 revolver at them. Their faces were covered in bandanas and their clothes looked like they had been unwashed for months.

"Don't go shoutin' at your boyfriends, now," said the one with the revolver, "Or I'll pop one of ya and do worse to the other."

"If they come back and see you-" Eve started as her heart began racing.

"Oh they ain't comin' back across that bridge, missy," he hissed with a disturbing grin, "But you'll be comin' with us. Now get down from that truck of yours and give your new daddy a hug."

Astrid's eyes were wide and she looked up at Eve. She had a look like she might try something. Eve looked down to her and shook her head. She said, "It's ok, Astrid, we should do as we're told."

They slowly walked off the bed and onto the road where the two, dirty men were. The one with the knife looked them up and down, then said, "Now we're gonna get off this road, here, and you're gonna watch what happens to your friends."

Logan slowly approached where he heard the car door. He looked for any kind of movement and listened for any footsteps. Jon and Ironson had almost caught up to him near the end of the bridge.

As Logan walked around a SUV, where he thought he heard the door, he was suddenly tackled to the ground from behind, losing his grip on his shotgun.

Jon noticed and shouted, "Joseph, to Logan!" before two men in dirty, old clothes hopped over the hoods of nearby cars and dashed at him. He shot one immediately square in the stomach, stopping the assailant in his tracks.

He pumped his Winchester and spun to face the other attacker but the dirty man was already on him.

Ironson ran as quick as he could towards where Logan was wrestling on the ground with someone, but he too was stopped by his own attacker. This one looked the dirtiest and held a .22 rifle on Ironson.

He had half his teeth missing and said, "Bye bye," before firing his rifle at Ironson.

Logan grappled with both his attacker and the smell of the man at the same time. He was taller than his attacker, but not as strong. He punched him in the mouth, causing the man to laugh loudly. He punched him again with little affect.

The dirty man was able to get on top of Logan and began wailing on him. Logan shielded himself as best he could. He knew he couldn't hold up to a hand to hand fight from the ground.

He grabbed the man's neck with his left hand and unsheathed his hunting knife. The man seen him go for it and tried to stop him, but Logan was quicker. He stabbed upwards, burying the knife under the man's jaw. It cut through to his mouth and he spit up blood.

Logan pushed him away and stabbed him again in the heart, letting his dark passenger and natural instinct to survive do the work.

Jon had the upper hand on his own attacker. He pummeled him over and over, breaking lose what teeth he had left and his nose. Their fight inched closer to the concrete side of the bridge. One final fist to the face sent the man into the barrier, cracking his head against the hard surface.

Jon brought his foot back and kicked the man's head into the barrier again, finishing him.

Ironson thought that was it. He was shot. But when he looked down, the bullet hadn't penetrated his cloak. He said, "Thank you, Logan," and looked at the rifle-wielding dirty.

"What the-" was all the attacker could say before Ironson's shotgun ended him.

Jon felt a pain in his head, as he was hit from behind with a makeshift club. He stumbled and his unseen attacker hit him again in his shoulder, where he was wounded from the enforcer. He growled in pain as another strike hit him in his side.

He turned in time to see his third attacker raise their club. Behind him, Logan leapt from the top of a van onto the clubber. Logan stabbed him over and over in his torso as they fell to the ground. By the time they hit the asphalt pavement, Logan had stabbed him enough times to make sure he bled out.

Logan offered a hand and helped Jon up. Ironson came running up to them and said, "Is that all of them?"

"Not sure," said Logan, breathing heavily.

"Those motherfuckers," said Jon through clenched teeth, "Why didn't Eve say anything?"

Logan looked over to where the technical was and seen it was unoccupied. He narrowed his eyes and said, "There may be more trouble."

The two men, with Eve and Astrid in tow, had been watching the scene unfold from within the woods not far off the road. Their jaws were dropped at seeing their fellow gang members fall.

"Holy hellfire," said the homemade knife wielder.

"I thought the cloaks were just for show or somethin'," said the one with the revolver, "Whatever, we got these two."

"Please, just let us go," said Astrid, who was held at gunpoint with Eve.

Her answer was a backhand by the knife wielder. She fell to the ground.

Eve was starting to feel like she knew how Logan felt. It was impossible to be good in a world full of bad.

"Don't do that again," Eve said, her normally beautiful face contorting in anger.

The two men taunted her in mock fear. The one with the revolver said, "We're so scared, missy, so scared. Get her up and come with us."

"Yeah, we should git goin'," said the other dirty.

"No," said Eve, planting herself in between Astrid and the two men.

"No?" responded the dirty with the gun, who held it up in Eve's direction, "I don't think we offered you a choice."

"Gus, we need to go, they'll figure out where we are," said the knife wielder, who was visibly uneasy as Logan, Jon and Ironson made their way back to the technical.

Gus looked at his friend, distracted, and said, "What the hell did I say about not using names?"

Eve grabbed the revolver and it fired over her shoulder. She had surprise on her side and managed to wrench it out of the man's hand. She backed up and pointed it at his head. She thumbed the hammer down, readying it to fire.

Gus brought his hands up and the other dirty sprinted off into the woods. "Whoa, now, pretty lady, we can talk this through."

Eve shook her head and said, "People like you make me sick. No balls."

"Hey, I got balls."

"Shut up!" Eve shouted as an angry tear formed at the corner of her eye, "I spent my whole life trying to save people. To heal them! I wanted to make a difference in the world. Even when the

250

creatures came, I tried my best to do what's right, but fucking people like you keep popping up."

A shadow moved next to her. It was Logan. He said, "If you do this, you'll do it again."

Eve hesitated. She wanted to pull the trigger, but her nature prevented her from doing it. Logan held his hand out and Eve pushed the revolver into his hand.

With no hesitation, Logan took aim at Gus's head, fired the gun, recocked the hammer back and fired again.

Gus fell, bleeding from his face.

"I...I couldn't," Eve said, a tear forming in her other eye.

"I'm glad you didn't," Logan replied.

Astrid hugged Logan. "I would've shot them dead," she said.

"There was another," said Eve, pointing deeper into the woods, "He ran off that way."

By this time, Jon and Ironson had caught up. Jon said, "Let him go, he isn't a threat now."

"There could be more of them," said Ironson, "By the way Logan, your mods to the cloaks saved my ass back there."

Logan nodded in response and said, "We can't let him leave."

"Haven't enough of them died?" said Eve.

"Go get him," said Astrid as the corner of her lip curled into a grin.

Logan said, "Keeping all of us safe is more important than anything. If he is part of a bigger group, we can't risk him getting

251

back to them."

The lone, dirty survivor sprinted his ass off through the woods. He had dropped his shiv somewhere behind him, but the only thing on his mind was getting away from the group that killed some of his fellow gang members.

"Gotta get back, gotta get back," he chanted to himself as he ran.

It wasn't long before a shadow picked up his trail. Within minutes, the shadow found the dirty. It sprinted faster than the running man and knocked him down to the ground.

The man gazed up at the cloaked one and said, "Who the hell are you?"

From under the hooded cloak, a low voice said, "Omega."

"O-Omega?"

"It means I am your end."

A hunting knife flashed from under the cloak. It was the last thing the dirty man would ever see.

Chapter 23 - The Commune of After

Logan emerged from the woods near the bridge after chasing down the last of the dirty men. Astrid and Eve were huddled together talking, leaning against the back of the truck. It looked like they were having a deep discussion, so Logan turned his attention elsewhere. Jon sat with his legs dangling on the front hood. He was sipping on a bottle of water.

"You're doing a great job, buddy," Jon called out to Ironson, who was in the process of moving a line of vehicles, one by one, out of the way so they could pass.

Ironson set one of them to neutral and began pushing the car from the driver side. He yelled over his shoulder, "Is there a reason you're not helping, Kilroy?"

Jon shrugged sheepishly and said, "Hey, doctor's orders, man. I'm not supposed to be on my feet."

Logan grinned and shook his head. That's the Jon he remembered. The jaunty atmosphere was welcomed after the nasty business of defending themselves from the strange attackers. It helped him flip the switch back to his normal self.

Logan walked up to Jon and said, "Never took you for a foreman."

"Hey, if things were different, I could get used to sitting around shouting out orders," Jon said, smiling under his large beard.

"When're you going to shave that?" Logan asked, motioning around his own chin.

Jon scoffed and said, "I love this big, manly beard. I'll shave it when Eve tells me to, though," he lowered his voice and leaned down towards Logan, "I bet Astrid likes the stubble, eh?"

Logan scratched his neck nervously and said, "She hasn't really said."

"Haven't talked much, nice. Been busy doing other stuff," said Jon, punching Logan in the shoulder, "Good on ya, man. I don't think she's all that cute, but good for you."

Logan raised an eyebrow and said, "Thanks, I think?"

Jon put his attention towards Ironson and said, "Hey Joseph, you need me to come over there and show you how to move those? I thought a military man would have it done by now."

Ironson stopped in his tracks and cast a stupid look to Jon.

He said, "Really?"

Logan shouted out to the Marine Corps pilot, "I'll help you."

Once enough of the vehicles were out of the way, the group was ready to carry on. Logan thought he'd try his luck and said, "Shotgun," while opening the passenger door.

Before he could enter, Eve dashed in and sat in the seat. She said, "Sorry, I have automatic shotgun."

"How do you have automatic shotgun?" Logan asked, folding his arms.

"Because Jon is driving. Duh," she said, curling her lips into a mischievous grin.

"Alright, alright, fine," said Logan, closing the door for her. He bowed down to her before taking up his not so comfortable seat on the wheel well of the truck, in the back.

She watched through binoculars from her vantage point in the woods on the north side of the river. The technical drove through the barrier her slaves had put up when God set the beasts upon the Earth. Or so she preached.

Her face was hardened but hid an extraordinary intelligence and charisma. It was how she brainwashed the members of her congregation to do anything she wanted them to.

She had an AR-15 slung on her back with two bandoliers full of pockets for excess magazines crisscrossing her chest. She was fit, muscular for a woman, although it would be difficult to tell with the layers of clothes she had on to combat the cold. Her long, red hair was braided down to her waist and slowly swayed in the chilly breeze.

This was the first time people had been able to fight through Gus's squad. The green camouflaged truck drove into her lands. Her blessed lands that she was in control of. And she was furious about it.

One of the dirty men, malnourished and garbed in ragged clothing, approached her. He walked with a hunch and an uneven gate. He fell to the ground out of respect for his messiah. Through a toothless mouth he said, "M'lady," while looking at the ground.

Keeping her binoculars trained on the technical, she said in pointed frustration, "What is it, Rat."

"Did Gus git the sacrifices?" he said, cringing from her response.

"No. Gus is dead."

Rat looked up at her with his good eye. The other eye looked off to his right. "Dead?" he said in sorrow.

"Yes. Your friend is dead. He fell by the hands of the heathens that are currently trespassing on our territory," she said, lowering her binoculars to reveal a furrowed brow and grey eyes.

"Those heathens!" Rat shouted, pumping his fists into a nearby tree.

"Radio ahead, Rat. Tell the soldiers that there will be

company and to bolster our defenses. Stop these pests, but do not kill them, not yet. These infidels will regret treading on our ground."

"It'll be done, m'lady," said Rat, scurrying off to relay the orders.

As the technical drove out of view, she smiled confidently. Whoever these people were seemed capable enough, but they had no idea what she had planned for them, or of the resources she had at her disposal.

Jon drove like the devil was chasing them. He played it cool and joked around, but he knew they were lucky they didn't get hurt from the dirty men's attack. His shoulder felt like it was being stung by a hundred bees, but he kept it under wraps to appease his fiancé.

"Geeze, Jon, think you can slow down?" said Eve, getting thrown around her seat each time Jon drove the technical around a curve in the highway.

"St. Louis is our goal and I'm getting there come hell or high water," said Jon, growling away his pain.

In the bed of the truck, Logan and Astrid had nothing to hold onto and they were rolling around from side to side. Ironson had the mounted machine gun to keep him steady and laughed hard at the sight of the two struggling to stay still.

"C'mon, babe, you're gonna kill Logan and Astrid," Eve said, holding the dashboard in front of her.

"Bah, they'll be alright. It's not like-shit!"

Jon slammed on the brakes as he rounded a rather sharp curve. On the right side of the road was a sign that said they were entering Greenville. Spray painted over this sign were the words COMMUNE OF AFTER.

In front of them, on the road, were makeshift fortifications. The wall, made of wood and repurposed metals, stretched from the tree line on their left and beyond the road sign on their right. An effigy was set in the road in front of the rickety wall. It was in the shape of a cross, but made up of human remains. Mainly legs and arms. The top of the cross was a skull.

"What the fuck is that," said Jon as he grasped the steering wheel so tight it turned his knuckles white.

Ironson kept the machine gun at the ready, sweeping the area with his eyes for threats. Logan told Astrid to stay down and stood next to the pilot, resting the stock of his Benelli shotgun on the roof of the truck.

Finally, they heard a woman's voice call out from behind the fortifications, "You tread upon the holy ground of the Commune of After! You shall pay for your trespass!"

"Jon, get us out of here," said Logan quickly, looking for the source of the voice.

Jon put the technical in reverse and started backing up. Out of the woods on each side emerged more of the dirty men, wielding clubs. There had to be at least thirty of them.

They rushed the truck, like mindless drones, shouting things like "For the Mother!" and "Sacrifice them to the Angels!"

Ironson opened fire on the freaks, mowing down half of them before they were able to make it to the truck.

Jon spun the truck around in a three point turn to get away. A few of the dirty men were hit by the side fender of the truck and run over. Through the commotion, Jon shouted, "These guys are nuts!"

As he turned the truck to backtrack to where they came from, the dirty men were upon the truck. Logan took a few out with his shotgun, but they were too close for Ironson to use the mounted machine gun. He slung his SPAS-12 shotgun from off his back and joined Logan in the close arms fire.

More and more of their assailants emerged from the woods. Some threw themselves in front of the truck, only to be crushed by the reinforced wheels. It slowed the vehicle down enough for them to swarm it and they started climbing into the bed.

Astrid, to her credit, held her own in fighting them off her. Like an animal backed into a corner, she kicked and hammer fisted them away from her. Ironson and Logan used the butts of their shotguns as clubs, but it wasn't enough. There were just too many of them.

Jon seen what was happening and floored the accelerator just as his window was bashed open and arms reached in at him. They pulled and yanked on his cloak and tactical vest, making him twist the steering wheel and sending the vehicle into a donut spin.

In the bed, Ironson and Logan were getting swarmed. Each

of their appendages had hands on them and they were getting pulled out of the bed of the truck.

Logan hit the road, getting kicked and punched. He tried to get up but he was pushed down again. One of the dirty men brought a club down onto his head, knocking him out. Jon fought the best he could, letting his survival instincts take hold. It wouldn't be enough, for he found himself bludgeoned in the head as well. Everything went dark.

Chapter 24 – Derailed

Logan awoke with his chin pressed against his chest. Try as he could, he could only open one eye. The other was swollen shut. Dried blood covered his face from a dozen cuts and impact wounds. His head was pounding like a jackhammer and he attempted to bring his hands up to feel his head.

They didn't move.

His hands were bound behind him so tight they were cutting off circulation. He tugged and struggled but to no avail. Panic began to set in as he realized he couldn't move at all save for his head. He brought his one-eyed gaze up. He had to squint to prevent himself from being blinded from a single, bright light above him. The sun?

No, a hanging light.

The rest of his immediate vicinity was cast in shadow. No movement, but he could hear breathing. Multiple people. At least he hoped it was people and not the burrowers.

He struggled again, his heart racing. It thumped as hard against his chest as his hurting brain did against his skull.

"Oh, you can struggle all you like," came a female's voice from beyond the light, "But you will find no comfort here, sinner!"

"Where...am I?" Logan asked. His own voice didn't help the migraine level of pain he was feeling.

"Be silent unless asked to speak!" said the voice, followed by something hitting Logan in the back of the head. His head jerked forward from the blow, but the rest of his body didn't budge an inch.

A shadow came into the light, but Logan couldn't make it out through his now blurred eye. It bent down towards him and caressed his cheek. "I suppose it isn't your fault that you're a sinner. It's bred into you. Part of you," she said in an eerily soft tone.

Logan had questions, but he kept his lips shut.

"Why have you come into our lands?" she said, standing to her full height.

"We...are just...trying to...go home," Logan squeaked out.

She scoffed and said, "There is only one home for someone like you. Hell is your only destination. I seen the way you slaughtered my people. Tell me, have you killed before?"

"Yes."

"So you are a murderer!" she screamed as she backhanded him in the face with a surprising amount of force.

"You will be cleansed, then you will join the others. You will suffer, but you won't die. Not yet. We will break the sins from your flesh and perhaps in time, you will be judged before the Angels."

She left the light of the hanging bulb and for a moment, Logan could just see a door open and close. Two other figures took her place and they threw Logan backwards in his chair, knocking the wind out of him as he landed.

His face was covered by some kind of cloth and he heard another woman's voice, higher than the previous one, say, "It is time to be cleansed."

Logan couldn't see anything and he was completely helpless. When he felt the cloth on his face grow damp, he knew what it was, seen it in movies before. It was some kind of water torture.

Even knowing what it was, it did nothing to prepare him for the agony it caused him. He held his breath as long as he could, but couldn't take it. With every breath it felt like he was sucking in water, causing him to choke. No matter how much he moved his head from side to side, the cloth wouldn't move. It was stuck to him somehow.

It could have been minutes or hours, he couldn't tell. He tried to keep his mind on his friends and hoped they weren't going through what he was.

But maybe he deserved it. Was this his karma? Was he

actually being judged? His mind raced back and forth between these thoughts and his friends for what seemed like an eternity of torture until he finally passed out from pain and helplessness.

When Logan opened his eyes, the one not swollen shut anymore, it was pitch black save for a few torches hanging on a rock wall. He was in some kind of large, windowless room as far as he could tell. All he could make out were other people laying on makeshift beds.

His tactical vest was gone. His hunting knife and shotgun were nowhere to be seen. His cloak was taken, which made him feel naked. He had only taken it off to sleep up until now. All he had were his boots, long underwear, jeans and sweatshirt.

He tried to stand, but as soon as he did, he felt the pain on the top of his head where he was struck by clubs. He cringed and held his head. The torches on the wall multiplied as his vision doubled. He closed his eyes and fell back down onto the hay-padded covers.

What happened? Was the torture a dream?

While trying to center himself, Logan heard a squeaky door open somewhere in the darkness. He looked in the direction of the sound and seen two robed figures enter. They were holding torches, the same kind as on the wall.

One of the figures held up a piece of paper. Apparently it was a woman and she read from her notes, "Number three, where are you?"

"Here!" said a male in the darkness, enthusiastically.

"Reproduction time."

"Blessed be the Mother!" the same man said before running to the robed figures and dropping to his knees at their feet.

"Stand, number three, and come with us," she said before turning and exiting the room with Number 3.

Logan had no idea what was going on, and almost in answer, a voice next to him said, "Welcome to the Commune of After, such as it is."

"What was all that about?" Logan asked the unseen stranger as he held his head and shut his eyes. He couldn't see much of anything anyways.

"You're in the breeding den. A step up from the sacrificial den, I must say," the man said, "A select few get stuck here and used as studs."

"Like sex slaves?" Logan asked.

"I suppose you could call us that," the man said with a chuckle, "Except they believe in a more of a one and done doctrine. You go in, put your baby in one of the women, then they sacrifice you to, who they call, the Angels. If you were in the sacrificial dens, you just get sacrificed without the coitus."

"Angels?"

"The creatures that birthed this sham of a cult. Delilah calls them Angels."

Logan shook his head in disbelief. "How did I get myself

into this situation," he said, half laughing at the ridiculousness of his situation.

"A question I often ask myself," said the man, "Name's Benjamin Perez."

"I'm Logan Foster. I was with some friends; you see them?"

"They only dragged you in here, from what I seen," said Benjamin, "Your friends could have been taken to either the sacrificial den or the work camp. Unless any of them were female, then they're probably getting brainwashed right now."

"Why did that man gladly go with those people when he knew he was going to die?" Logan asked, trying to wrap his head around everything.

"Delilah has a way with people. Most of the men here are like you until they meet her a few times. She has many means to get her tendrils into your brain. Torture for some, sex for others. Then they'd do anything for her, including allowing themselves to be killed."

"So we're just waiting here to die. Great," said Logan.

"That's about the long and short of it. I've been in here for a month now and they still never call my name," said Benjamin with a sigh, "When the world went to hell, people just lost their minds. They needed something to latch onto, someone to tell them it'll be ok. At first, we were a community, but then Delilah went mad with power. Now, I don't even know what you would call the Commune."

The realization of his situation made Logan's head hurt more.

Apparently Benjamin noticed this and said, "Get some sleep, Mr. Foster. I believe tomorrow you will be meeting my wife, Delilah."

"Your wife?" Logan asked.

"Yup. A story for another time, if either of us survive tomorrow," said Benjamin. Logan heard him shift on the padding on his sleeping spot.

He didn't ask any more questions. He shifted into as comfortable position as possible and wrapped his arms around his pounding head. He wouldn't find sleep for a few hours as his mind raced with all the information he just found out.

"This is fucking bullshit!" Jon shouted, slamming his fist into the rock wall, making a nearby torch shake in its holder. He was in the same kind of room that Logan had found himself in.

The calm attitude Jon had taken up after his brush with death took a back seat to anger. He hated not being in control of at least himself, and he was in no way in control of this situation. Not knowing where Eve was didn't help matters.

"Getting pissed off isn't going to help anything or anyone," said Ironson, leaning against the wall on the opposite side of the torch.

"It'll help me!" Jon said through gritted teeth. Both he and the pilot were wearing sweat pants, sweat shirts and old slippers. All of their clothing were falling apart, dirty and shredded.

"I checked the door," Ironson explained, "There's armed

guards outside and that door won't move even if everyone in this cave tried to move it."

"One way in, one way out," said Jon, frowning under his beard, "You happen to see where they took Eve?"

"Couldn't see much through the bag over my head," said Ironson, "They must have drugged us, because I don't remember my clothes getting changed or coming in here."

"Hey, go to sleep!" said someone in the darkness.

"Blow me!" Jon yelled, "I'll keep everyone up if I g'damn want to."

"We probably should try to get some sleep, for now," Ironson said, sitting down with his back against the rock, "Not much we can do right now. Can't see shit, can't do shit."

Jon huffed and said, "I'll try, but no promises." He paced back and forth for almost an hour before finally laying down in an unoccupied sleeping spot.

The effects of whatever the cult members had injected Eve with wore off. She opened her eyes to a fancy bedroom that looked untouched by the ravages of time. Her bed had gold encrusted foot and headboards. To one side of it was a large, mahogany dresser. On the other was a hutch with a mirror on it. A padded stool sat tucked under it. The walls were whitewashed with paintings of ships hanging on each side of the heavy, wooden door that led out to a hallway.

Eve's belongings were also taken and she was wearing a long, brown robe. The bed was comfortable, but she was ready to find out what the hell happened. Last thing she remembered was being pulled out of the technical. She had no idea how much time had gone by, but looking out the second story window she could tell it was night.

Her body hurt as she hopped off the tall, heavy bed. She looked in the hutch mirror and seen nicks and cuts all over her face. Her long blonde hair, normally pulled up in a ponytail or bun, had been washed and brushed. She could smell lavender as her hair swung delicately on each side of her face.

She could feel herself start to panic, but controlled her breathing. She inhaled and exhaled slowly as she started tearing through the hutch and dresser for anything that could be of use. All she found was an extra robe and spare bedding.

She opened the heavy door and stepped into an equally as extravagant, long hallway. There were more paintings of ships on the walls and a half dozen doors that presumably led to bedrooms like hers. Two ceiling lights lit the white walls and the Victorian-inspired carpet.

At the end of the hallway she could see the top of a staircase. She began walking towards it, faster and faster for each step she took towards it. When she was at the top of the stairs, a door opened behind her. She didn't wait to see who it was and ran down the staircase.   Down below was a large foyer with marbled floors.

Doorways led to other rooms of the mansion on the ground story. A gold, electric chandelier hung down in the center of the foyer. A large, doubled door was her exit.

The footsteps of whoever was behind her were getting louder as they approached the staircase.

She ran to the front doors and tried to open it. Locked, from the outside?

Someone was walking down the stairs.

She ran through the closest doorway into an unlit dining room. A long table, able to sit twenty people, with matching chairs filled the whole room. She ducked behind the furthest, end chair and controlled her breathing.

She looked under the table to see who was pursuing her. The person emerged into view, but she could only see them from the thighs down. They appeared to be wearing the same kind of robe she had on.

"Come, dear, let us speak," a female voice said softly, "You cannot leave the mansion unless the Mother wills it, which she will, depending on what you do next."

Eve remained silent.

The woman began walking, slowly, around the table and chairs towards where Eve was at. She said, "Don't think of yourself as a prisoner. In truth, you are a guest here amongst the Mother's disciples, but as I am sure you can relate to, we don't know you and must be cautious."

Eve started to crawl on her hands and knees in the darkness towards another doorway that led to the kitchen. Her foot bumped one of the chairs, causing her pursuer to stop and say, still softly, "Please don't run, child."

Knowing her cover was blown, Eve stoop up and sprinted into the kitchen. It looked like a full crew could cook a meal for hundreds of people with how large it was. It had multiple islands with stoves and cutting areas. Pots and pans hung from the ceiling above fryers and stoves.

There were three ways out from the kitchen: the doorway she just ran through, that led to the dining room, another doorway that went into some kind of living room and a door that exited into a garage. She tried her luck with the door, but it too wouldn't budge. So she ran to the doorway towards the living room.

She was met by another robed woman. Her face was soft and she smiled as Eve skidded to a halt in front of her. The first woman who was pursuing her caught up to them.

"My name is Abigail," said the woman who had been talking to her, "This is Lisa. Why don't we make some tea?"

Eve spun towards Abigail and said, "To hell with your tea! Where is my fiancé? Where's Jon?"

The two women exchanged knowing glances before Lisa said, "We will tell you everything we can tomorrow, but for now, perhaps some tea and get back to bed?"

Eve turned to Lisa with a wild look in her eyes and said, "I don't want any tea. I want to leave."

"I'm afraid that is very much out of the question," said Abigail, "But I can understand your desire for information. When I first came here, I was just like you, now I wouldn't want to be anywhere else. God has saved us."

"What the hell are you talking about?" said Eve, confused as much as she was scared and angry. She turned back towards Abigail, feeling trapped between these two women.

"I think it is time we all went back to bed," said Abigail, who gave a quick nod towards Lisa.

Eve felt a small prick in her neck. She stumbled away as she tried to run, but she quickly lost consciousness.

Chapter 25 – Delilah

The next morning, Lisa and Abigail brought Eve to the dining room for breakfast. Other women, donned in brown robes, congregated in the room. Some of them had small, pregnant bellies that pushed against the loose robes. They all looked immaculate, with makeup and almost perfect hair. Eve seen Astrid for the first time since they were attacked and motioned for her to sit next to her, which she quickly did.

The morning sun shone through the thin, embroidered drapes as everyone spoke amongst themselves. Astrid and Eve leaned in to each other. Eve said, "We need to find a way out of here."

Astrid looked equally pissed and frustrated as she whispered, "This is fucked. Maybe we can fight our way out of here?"

"Not a good idea," Eve said, looking around to see if anyone was listening, "We need to keep our heads. I'll find a way. I think we're safe at the moment, so for now we just need to play along."

"I hate these robes," Astrid said, tugging at the itchy cloth.

"Me too," said Eve, who had already thought them uncomfortable.

"Wonder how the guys are doing," said Astrid.

Eve had been wondering that same thing. She knew they could take care of themselves, but from the looks of things they were up against an army. She said, "We're on our own for now."

Their conversation was interrupted by Lisa saying, loudly enough for everyone in the room to hear, "The Mother comes."

Delilah had just walked down the staircase into the foyer. Her robe was much fancier than the others. It was white with gold lining. It was the first time Eve and Astrid had seen Delilah, but it wasn't the first time she had seen them.

Her hard face looked odd as she smiled, opened her arms and said, "Good morning, sisters. God's Angels have blessed us with another day."

The women cheered with some shouting "Hallelujah!" and "We are blessed!"

Delilah walked into the dining room with a confidant and strong gate. She stood before the end chair and waited. In answer, Rat scurried from the kitchen. He looked half the size of Delilah when he was hunched over, which he always was.

He pulled the chair out for Delilah to sit down. He then, carefully, took her long, red, braided hair and placed it over her shoulder. Then he wobbled off without a word.

Everyone else sat down once Delilah was settled. She said, "I would like to welcome two new additions to the Commune," as she stretched her hands in Eve and Astrid's direction.

They all applauded.

"They came here on the wings of devils, but we shall save them, sisters."

Applause and knowing smiles.

"My newest sisters, please, tell us your names."

It went silent as everyone's attention was on Eve and Astrid. Finally, Eve said, "My name is Eve Parker."

"Welcome, Eve Parker!" Delilah said enthusiastically, "And your friend?"

Astrid grimaced but Eve kicked her foot under the table. She then said, "I'm Astrid."

"And welcome Astrid! You'll have to forgive our cautious nature last night, but I assure you, you will love it here," said Delilah with a devious smile, "We will speak in private later on. But for now, let us eat. Rat!"

Rat scurried in and bowed, his head almost touching his knees. He said, "Breakfast is ready, my lady. Today we will be serving wheat pancakes."

"Oh, I love pancakes," said one of the women.

Four dirty men emerged from the kitchen carrying covered pans. Where the women were clean and smelled nice, the men stank and looked like they never changed their clothes. They served each female pancakes and placed several pitchers of water in the middle of the table. As soon as everything was served, they disappeared back into the kitchen.

Delilah said, "Before we begin, let us pray."

Everyone grasped hands with the person next to them. Eve and Astrid were reluctant, but they did the same and they all bowed their heads.

Delilah began her prayer, "We thank God for another day amongst the Angels. We thank Him for this food. We thank Him for our sisterhood and we thank Him for our new additions. Amen."

"Amen," they all said, with the exception of Eve and Astrid, who gave each other unsettled looks.

Logan woke up to a loud ringing, like that of a school bell notifying students to change classes. His head hurt, but his vision was back to normal. He was still exhausted from the torture that seemed to last all of the day before. Sunlight shone through the small, barred up porthole in the heavy door.

There were a dozen dirty men in the cavern, and they all lined up in front of the door. Logan stood and watched as they all seemed to wait enthusiastically.

"Morning mass, if you can call it that," said a voice beside

276

Logan, "I started this tradition."

Logan got his first look at Benjamin. He was once well built before his malnourishment and had a long, dark beard speckled with grey. He had long, ragged hair to match. He looked like a broken man, who had once had life figured out.

The two of them took their places in the back of the line. Benjamin spoke as they waited to be let out, "I used to be in the Navy, ya know. Got ordained as a priest afterwards. These morning talks were supposed to be a way to keep hope up in people. Now...well, you'll see."

"So this all used to be something else?" asked Logan, not having anything else better to do.

"Oh yeah. Some of us were religious, but others weren't. It didn't matter back then, but my wife took her zealous beliefs too far. Now the Commune is more of a cult."

"Why are you still here? Why didn't she kill you?" asked Logan.

Benjamin shrugged and said, "I guess somewhere in her fortified heart, she still loved me enough to keep me around. Who knows anymore. Haven't really talked to her for a while."

The door creaked open. A chilled breeze filtered into the cavern as they started walking outside. Logan wished he had his cloak to keep him warm and to potentially keep himself from getting marked. They were further north from the nest they took out and he was sure they had to be in an area influenced by another.

They marched out of the cavern, one of two carved out of a tall, bedrock cliff once cut out from a long gone stream. Atop the cliff were trees and foliage hanging down over the layered rock. Three sisters of the Commune stood guard with rifles as the men were let out of their cells.

Outside the cliff was an open, muddy area, surrounded by more of the makeshift walls. Beyond those the forest expanded out for miles. The walls rounded around the clearing and led to a single gate with a guardhouse. Another armed sister stood guard there. Further out from the gate the second story of a white house peeked over the walls from on top of its hill.

Just inside this gate was a rickety, elevated podium where stood Delilah. She waited for her subjects and was flanked by Abigail and Lisa, both armed with ARs.

Logan counted a hundred men, but there were more as he got lost in a sea of mud and broken males. Some looked like they had their souls sucked out, while others lit up at seeing their leader.

Amongst the murmur of the crowd, Logan felt a large hand on his shoulder. He turned to see Jon and Ironson. Their faces were just as cut and bruised as Logan's was from the assault on the technical. Ironson's trademark bomber jacket and aviators were gone, making him look like the rest of them. Logan noticed their ragged clothing.

"We're fucked, man," Jon said with wide eyes, "I say we rush the gate right here and now."

Ironson rolled his eyes and said, "Be my guest."

"We need to wait for an opportunity," Logan said, "They have shooters on top of the cliff, one at the guard house and two more with, I presume, Delilah."

Jon looked up at the cliff, seeing the armed sisters that he had not noticed before and cursed under his breath.

Benjamin leaned in with the group and said, "If you're going to try to make a break for it, I'd highly suggest you don't."

"I ain't gonna just let them imprison me," Jon said, furling his brow, "I worked at a prison before and let me tell you, I never thought I'd be on this side of the fence."

"This is Benjamin Perez, their leader's husband," Logan explained.

"If this is how she treats her husband, I'd hate to see how she treats the rest of us," said Ironson with a grim look on his face.

"Others have tried to escape before. They either go in the Hole or are sacrificed," said Benjamin, "But none have been able to get very far. Delilah's henchwomen make sure of that."

A whistle brought all of the men's attention to the podium. Delilah stretched her hands out and spoke loudly, "My dear, dear subjects. Today is a special day. A blessed day!"

Cheers rang out within the walled courtyard from the more persuaded cult members.

"God has tested us by bringing devils into our sacred lands, but we rose triumphant. Some of us passed into Heaven in order to fight them, but they will be remembered as we sacrifice one of the devils to the Angels!"

Cheers again, mixed with raspy laughs.

Delilah pointed in Logan, Jon and Ironson's direction and said, "Bring these menaces to me."

The dirty men Logan and company were standing amongst immediately turned on them before they could react. Multiple hands held them by their arms, legs and heads as they carried, or in Jon's case dragged, them up to the podium.

"Get the hell off me!" Jon shouted as they were all let go.

"Kneel," commanded Delilah with a fiery look in her eyes that matched her red hair.

"I kneel to no one," said Logan, his sharp look matching hers.

"I said KNEEL!" she shouted, spittle flinging from her mouth as she pounded her fist on the podium.

The dirty men hit the three behind their knees and the back of their heads, making them collapse to the ground.

"Only I command here," said Delilah, baring her teeth, "What hope do you have to try bravery against the truth that is my rule?"

"I thought God commanded everything," said Logan, "I was never the religious type, but I seem to remember the Bible saying specifically what happens to those who think themselves akin to God."

"Oh, He guides me, don't mistake that," Delilah said, seemingly coming unhinged, "He seen what men did to this world when the Angels came to test our faith. Now the future is in the matriarchy, given to me by holy power."

"You're one fucked up chick," said Jon, shaking his head.

A foot to the back of his head was his answer as the dirty men boo'd and shouted things like, "Sacrifice them!"

Delilah stepped proudly off her podium and began pacing in front of the three. She said, "One of you will be sacrificed tonight. Would you like to pick, or shall I?"

They exchanged worried glances but remained silent.

"Very well, devils. I will decide for you. You, loud one!" she said, pointing towards Jon.

"Oh, go fu-" he started to say before Delilah backhanded him with a strong hand.

"Tonight, the Angels shall feed upon your flesh. What is left shall be made into a cross giving thanks for your death. You will die, and your friends will die each night after. This is your penance for trespassing into the Commune of After!"

Logan stood and Delilah flashed daggers from her eyes at him. He said, "Let me go in his stead."

"Logan, don't," growled Jon.

"I am a killer and I deserve it more than anyone here," Logan said, "My sins are greater and it is I who should die, not them."

Delilah's face changed from agitation to glee and she said,

"Very well, killer," before climbing back up to her podium to begin her prayers and blessings.

Benjamin approached Logan and said, "You're mad. You realize there's no coming back from this?"

"I know," said Logan, who felt the full weight of the situation, "You said you were a priest, right?"

"I am, yes," Benjamin replied.

"Before my time is done, I'd like to confess."

"I think you just did, from the sound of it."

Logan stepped closer to Benjamin and in a whisper, said, "There is something I need to confess that happened before the collapse."

Chapter 26 - The Confession

Slaves from the work camp were Delilah's most trusted minions. Rat was in charge of them and he was her link to the goings on with the dirty men. It was they that served slop to those stuck in the courtyard.

Logan stared at his bowl of gooey whatever it was, contemplating what exactly he would say to Benjamin. He was hungry, but he couldn't eat. He sat in a circle with Jon, Ironson and Benjamin. They were offered no chairs so their asses were cold and getting even more dirty.

"So what's this confession you mentioned?" Jon asked, slurping slop from the bowl in disgust at the taste.

Logan looked up at his friend. He had known him for years but never told him his secret. He couldn't find the words so he cast his gaze back down to the bowl.

"Ok then..." Jon said with a betrayed look, "So you can tell this priest guy you've known for two seconds, but you can't tell me?"

Ironson said, "Leave him alone, Kilroy, if it's that big of a deal it'd make more sense for him to tell a priest."

"Yeah, sure ok. Are you even really a priest?" Jon said, turning his ire towards Benjamin.

"I was for several years. Now, I don't know what I am," Benjamin replied with a sigh, "Maybe I can talk to Delilah."

"Don't bother," said Logan, "If it's not me, it'd be one of you. We still don't know if the girls are safe, so I don't want to ruin their chances. Besides, I deserve this."

Jon seemed to calm down and he said, "Logan, I've known you for years. What could you have really done to make you feel like you deserve death? Sure, you were depressed for a while, but c'mon man."

Logan said, "Just find a way out, get Astrid and Eve safe."

"I hope they're ok," said Ironson.

Jon turned his gaze towards the mansion and said, "Yeah, me too."

Jon couldn't tell, but he had met eyes with Eve through a window in the mansion's top story. Her and Astrid were plotting when they happened to look out the window and down into the courtyard. They counted through hundreds of men before finding Logan and company sitting in a circle by themselves.

"I see them," Eve said quite loud before looking around to make sure her and Astrid were alone in one of the bedrooms.

"Are they ok?" Astrid asked, wringing her hands together.

"From what I can tell, yeah, but I don't know for how long."

"I don't know how much longer I can stand staying here," said Astrid, her expression giving away her feelings of worry and anger.

"Same," said Eve while taking a deep breath before continuing, "I think tonight we'll break into that walled in area and try to get them out."

"How do we do that?" asked Astrid.

"We play along, make it seem like we want to be here. They take the men in and out sometimes. We go in and say we need that group for Delilah or something, then make a break for it once they're out."

"Will that work?"

"I hope so."

They heard footsteps in the hallway. They left the window and exited the room. They were met by one of the women they hadn't really met yet.

She smiled to them and said, "Praise be God and the Mother."

Astrid and Eve exchanged a quick glance before replying in unison, "Praise God."

When the sun was starting to tease the horizon, the two groups of men were ushered back into their respective caverns. Jon tried to say something to Logan but the guards kept them separated.

Logan and Benjamin found a quiet corner in the dark cavern to speak. Benjamin said, "Normally this would be done in a confessional booth, but this will have to do."

"It's good enough," said Logan, who had been thinking of what to say all day since he was sentenced to be sacrificed.

"Tell me what troubles you, child," said Benjamin, switching gears from friendly to priest.

"I'm not entirely sure where to start, to be honest," said Logan.

"Well we have maybe an hour before they come get you, so start from the beginning."

Logan took a deep breath and said, "Ok, here goes...My family, the Fosters, were a hard working family. Everyone had factory or physical careers. I was one of the few who went to college. We had somewhat of a rivalry with the Fox family, who were prominent in our hometown. They were rich, had positions in the city government and generally controlled everything.

"It never really turned violent until my brother got entangled with a Fox girl. I don't know why, but at this point in his life, he had already turned to drugs and had a reputation as an abuser of women. He and I weren't close.

"One day, Edward Fox, who was my age, found out about my brother hitting his cousin. He called the police and my brother was arrested. This only caused more tension between our two families. My parents never believed my brother was truly as bad as he was, but I knew the truth.

"He eventually got out of prison, but it didn't do him much good. He went back to drugs and got himself a new girlfriend in the trailer park."

Logan paused, staring into the darkness of the cavern, which prompted Benjamin to say, "It's ok, continue whenever you are comfortable."

"He beat the hell out of her, Benjamin. He went back to prison for a couple years and when he came back, he tried to get money out of my parents. At this point, they were as done with him as I was.

"He needed a ride back to the trailer park, where I guess he was going to stay with a friend. So I took him, but I drove out in the country so I could talk to him. I figured I'd try to talk to him one last time. I didn't want to give up completely on him.

"I parked the car and we started talking, but it went bad real quick. It was like he was a different person. He wasn't my brother anymore.

"He got out of the car, so I did too to tell him I'm done with him. He attacked me and we tumbled down into the ditch, off the road. He started hitting me over and over. At first, I just tried to block his blows, but something overtook my senses. So I fought back."

Logan hesitated again before saying, "I didn't just fight back. I killed him. I got him to the ground and I stomped his skull until he wasn't moving anymore.

"Anger gave way to fear. I was so scared. I would be locked up longer than he was. So I threw him in the trunk of my car and drove out into the boonies. I buried him out in the woods."

Logan heard Benjamin breath out heavily before he continued, "I thought for sure I would get caught anyways. Maybe a satellite was watching me and seen what I did. Maybe the person I was driving him to would report him missing and that he never got there that night. Maybe someone else seen what I did.

"But nothing ever happened. My parents questioned me after they hadn't heard from him in a while, but I just said I didn't know where he was. The police were under the Foxs' thumbs and hey never investigated anything. No one cared and no one knew what happened to him except me.

"When friends would ask about him, I'd just say he was in prison. It wasn't so farfetched because he was in prison a couple times before. A year later, Jon, Eve and I decided to go out on a long hike to clear our heads. Maybe being out in nature would help me forget what happened.

"Then the creatures came, and I really did forget about it for a while, until I killed again in defense of Eve. Then I killed again when Jon needed medicine." Logan felt his voice start to quiver and a tear formed at the corner of his eye. He stammered, "I'm such a horrible person, Benjamin. I don't know who I am anymore."

"This would be the point where I would tell someone to turn themselves in," said Benjamin in the darkness, "I would tell you that it would release you of your guilt and that God blah blah blah.

"The priest in me wants to say those things, but seeing as how the world is now, I'd say you were ready for it before anyone else was."

"What do you mean?" asked Logan, sniffing back his tears.

"What happened before doesn't really matter anymore. You killed your brother. It happened. It goes against God's commands, but no one is truly good anymore. As long as you're honest with yourself, you can only be as good a man as you can."

Those words again. Be a good man. Logan said, "I don't think I can be a good man anymore."

Benjamin chuckled and said, "Well, you're being sacrificed tonight, so I don't think you'll have much of a chance to try." He cleared his throat and got serious again, "All you can do now is forgive yourself for what you did. Try to find some semblance of inner peace before you go into the unknown."

"Benjamin?" said Logan.

"Yes, my son."

289

"You're a terrible priest."

They shared a laugh before Benjamin said, "Yeah, well, maybe you're right."

"But I appreciate you listening to me. I already feel better just telling someone," said Logan, "Whatever happens tonight, I do think I will be at peace with myself now."

They fell into silence as the light slowly vanished from outside. Clouds moved in and, as if they were stabbed by a needle, they burst. Rain started to fall violently outside and lightning streaked across the sky.

Chapter 27 – Sacrifice

Rain pelted the robed women, who held their hoods against the wind, as they passed through the gate to the muddy courtyard. Rat followed closely behind Delilah, Abigail and Lisa. He had no protection from the storm and tried to block the sideways rain by scurrying behind the sacrificial detail.

Delilah grinned in triumph. Logan would be the first to go, then the loud one, then the pilot. She was hoping Eve and Astrid would come around. They were playing along and she knew it.

They stopped before the door that led to the breeders and Abigail unlocked the door. They entered into the dark cavern and shook the water from their ARs.

Logan was already waiting at the door. He was leaning

against the rock wall with his arms folded. Delilah started to open her mouth to speak, but Logan interrupted, "I'm ready. Let's go."

Delilah frowned at being stopped at giving a speech but she said, "Fine, come then, devil."

Lisa took a hood out from inside her robe and threw it over Logan's head. She then tied a rope around his neck to keep the hood in place and to make sure he couldn't see.

They turned to leave but were stopped by someone saying, "Delilah, dear."

Delilah recognized the voice, but hadn't heard it in what felt like forever. She turned to see the shell of her husband and said, "What is it, Ben."

He took a step towards her and said, "You don't have to do this. He may have done some bad things, but he can be forgiven. Everyone can."

"He is a killer and invaded our lands. He killed some of my followers. I don't care who he is, he deserves this," she replied with a stone cold glare.

"I miss you, hun," said Benjamin, "Why can't things be how they were?"

Delilah hesitated but dared not change her glare. She finally said, "I am the chosen leader of the Commune. Things can't be how they were," before turning violently away from Benjamin and leaving the cavern.

Eve was surprised the front door was unlocked this night. She stood before it with Astrid next to her. Maybe their acts were starting to work? Either way, it was time to go.

They opened the fancy door and stepped into the dark, howling storm. A Sister stood outside, lit up by the porch light. The covered area stretched the entire length of the white house.

She turned and said, "Hello, new sisters. You should stay inside, for God is angry tonight."

Eve put her hands together as if in prayer and said, "The Mother wants us to help in the sacrificial detail. Uh, just in case there's trouble."

The Sister cocked her hooded head to the side, her face hidden from sight. She said, "Oh? I was given no such orders."

"It's...part of our initiation, she said. We need to witness the sacrifice," said Eve, hoping it'd make sense.

The Sister looked at the girls for a moment before saying, "Ok, go on. Be blessed."

"God bless you, sister," said Eve with a bow.

Her and Astrid quickly stepped away from the porch and made their way down the hill towards the gate that led into the courtyard. To the side of the gate was a guardhouse that had a view of each side of the wall.

As they approached, the Sister standing guard in the guardhouse said, "Hello, sisters. Come in out of the rain. What brings you out into the storm?"

They walked into the small room that was the guardhouse. Eve shook the rain from her robes and said, "We are to help with the sacrificial detail."

"Ah, well you are too late," said the guard, "The Mother has already taken the devil to the sacrificial grounds."

Eve and Astrid exchanged worried glances before Eve spoke again, "How long ago was this?"

"Just a few minutes ago."

Astrid blurted out, "Do you know which one they took?"

The guard said, "The killer. Maybe you should head back to the house."

Eve and Astrid again looked at each other, then nodded in unison.

The guard was at ease and not ready. Eve rushed her and wrestled the assault rifle away from her. Astrid tackled her to the ground and began laying into her with fist after fist. Eve pulled Astrid away from the guard and put the barrel of the AR into the now bloodied woman.

"Which way to the sacrificial grounds?" she asked, hurriedly.

"Sacrilege!" the guard shouted, "How dare you strike one of the Mother's disciples!"

Eve said, "We don't have time for this," and turned the rifle around. She hit the woman in the jaw with the rifle, knocking her out. She turned to Astrid and said, "We get Jon and Joseph, quickly as we can. Then we go get Logan and get the hell out of here."

"Let's do it," Astrid said, bouncing with energy.

On a shelf was a rung of keys, which Astrid took while Eve scanned around to see if anyone had noticed them. They left the guardhouse and approached the first cavern door.

Eve looked up to see if she could find the guards up top. She couldn't see them, so she hoped they couldn't see her and Astrid either. She quickly pulled her gaze away as the rain began stinging her eyes.

It took a few tries to find the correct key for the door, but they finally managed to open it. They entered into the torch-lit cavern. Most of the men were already asleep.

"Jon? Joseph?" Eve called out.

Some of the men stirred, but only one approached them out of the darkness. He had long hair and a ragged beard. He said to them, "You must be the newcomers' loved ones. They are in the other cavern."

Eve and Astrid turned to leave before the man said, "Let me come with you. You are suicidal if you are planning an escape, but I could be of use."

"We don't need anyone else," said Eve, dismissing the man.

"I know these grounds just as well as Delilah. You won't know where they took Logan. He and I spoke a great deal in his short internment here. I would like to help him."

Astrid said, "Let him come, he's right. We don't know where they took Logan."

295

"Fine, c'mon then," said Eve. They left with the bearded man and didn't bother locking the door back up.

They hurried over to the other door, unlocked it and entered. There were many more men in this room, but it was just as dimly lit.

"Jon!?" Eve called out.

She heard someone say, "Holy shit, Eve?" before Jon and Ironson ran up into the light of the torch. They were dirty and looked like prisoners, but Eve didn't complain when Jon bear hugged her and gave her a sloppy kiss.

"You brought the priest with you?" Ironson asked.

"Yeah," said Astrid, as Eve was momentarily distracted, "He said he can take us to Logan."

Jon let go of his fiancé and said, "Well, what're we waiting for."

Logan couldn't see anything from under the bag on his head. He had to rely on Rat guiding him to make sure he didn't run into anything. All he knew is they had been walking for the last ten or so minutes on some path.

Lightning cracked up above and he could hear the epitomic two-toned howl of the creatures far away. The hairs stood up on the back of his neck as he had not heard or seen the creatures for a week.

"How have you survived from the burrowers?" Logan asked aloud to anyone listening.

"We give them sacrifices and they leave us alone," said

Delilah, as if it were as common as breathing, "We have a wall that spans the entirety of the compound and they have never tried to breach it. It is God's promise to us."

Lightning cracked again and the rain shifted directions. Logan was freezing, but he barely noticed his shivers from being drenched.

"You should really try working things out with your husband. He's not so bad," Logan said.

His answer was an unseen backhanded strike to his temple. He nearly toppled over, but Rat kept him steady.

"No more words, devil. Your forked tongue will not poison me," Delilah said.

They stopped and Logan heard the sound of metal on metal. They walked forward a few steps before the screeching sound came again; then they were on their way. Some kind of gate.

They walked nearly ten minutes more before stopping. He was thrust against a post and his hands were tied behind his back around it. He felt the tight grip of the rope on his neck be released and the hood came off.

They were in a large clearing. The edges were hidden through the rain and darkness. The only light was from the occasional lightning and a torch held by Abigail.

Delilah stood eye to eye in front of Logan. Her eyes looked like they were on fire from the reflection of the torch. She smirked before backing up and shouting into the howling wind with her hands extended towards Heaven, "We give you this gift, Angels! Let it be a mark of our continued love and compassion! Slay this demon in His name!"

A creature's call came from somewhere on the edge of the clearing. This prompted the sacrificial detail to run off in the direction they had just come.

Logan was alone, for the moment. All he could hear was the howling of the storm and creatures coming nearer.

His mind flashed the faces of everyone he had killed. He seen the faces of the dirty men he had put down. Then he seen the convicts' faces and asked them for forgiveness. He seen the face of Danny, whom he had not killed, but felt responsible for. He asked him for forgiveness. He seen Michael from the grocery store and asked him. Finally, he seen the face of his brother, what he could remember of him, and tears mixed with the rain.

"I'm so sorry," he said, aloud, "Please forgive me before I die."

Lightning cracked and very briefly he could see multiple creatures prowling from the edge of the large clearing, about a football field away. When it was dark again he could barely see the blue orbs of their eyes floating towards him.

Benjamin led the reunited group through the woods and storm. They jogged as quick as they could through the brush and between trees. He knew they didn't fully trust him, but he didn't care at this point. His wife was truly gone to him and he had nothing left. Perhaps helping Logan out would give him some semblance of purpose.

Benjamin stopped and motioned for everyone to get down. Up ahead he could see a torch, but he knew it was his wife. He purposefully led the friends off the path so they could pass by Delilah unseen.

As they passed, a walkie talkie chirped and Delilah pulled it from out of her robes. He could hear her say, "What is it?"

The answer was barely discernable over the rain, "Newcomers....doors open...out in the courtyard."

"Dammit all," Delilah hissed, "Abigail, Lisa, double-time!"

They rushed off past the group hiding amongst the trees. Once they were out of earshot, Benjamin turned to everyone else and said, "We need to hurry. They know we're gone, I do believe."

"How much further is it?" Jon asked, impatiently.

"Not far now. The gate to the outer wall should be just up here. If we run as fast as we can, we can get to him in a few minutes."

Logan tugged at the ropes that restrained his hands to the pole. Part of him was ready to die for the bad things he had done, but with the creatures coming ever nearer his instincts were kicking in. Maybe if he survived, he could turn things around. Maybe he could be better than he was.

It was no use, though, the ropes were tied tight. Just as they had been when he was tortured.

Logan tried rocking the post back and forth, but it was futile. It barely budged half an inch in each direction. It felt like every time he moved, the bindings on his wrists dug deeper into his skin.

There was nothing he could do, and the creatures were fifty yards away from him. He couldn't tell how many of them there were, but counted at least five. It didn't matter, one would have been enough.

He started to panic, even with his wrists bleeding. He twisted and lurched around, trying to find some way off the damn post.

Then he heard a gunshot from behind him. It was loud and made his ears ring. The creatures stopped their trek and huddled down in surprise, howling in Logan's direction.

He seen several shapes before him and, as the lightning cracked, seen it was Jon and Eve. Ironson ran by them with an AR and opened fire into the clearing. He aimed at anything that moved, but no one could tell if he was hitting anything in the darkness.

"Time to get you out of here, buddy," Jon said as he started untying the ropes.

"We'll never make it," Logan said, "You shouldn't have come for me. The burrowers are out there."

The bindings fell off of Logan's hands and he started to fall forward. He had not realized how much energy he had used trying to escape. Jon caught him before he hit the ground and helped him walk away from the post.

"Let's move!" shouted Ironson, backing up with them, popping a shot off at the howling creatures.

Astrid ran up and put Logan's other arm around her shoulders to help him. "I'm so glad we found you," she said.

"Me too," he answered.

They moved in a unit, but Benjamin remained rooted in place. "You'll be safe if you make it to the gate," he said.

"What're you doing?" Logan said, "Come with us."

"One rifle won't keep those things from getting you. I'd rather die out here than in those caverns. I've made my peace," he said, grimly, "If you meet Delilah again, do whatever you have to do, but tell her what I did here."

Jon and Astrid kept dragging Logan away, even when he started shouting, "No, wait!"

Eve and Ironson followed them as they ran away, leaving Benjamin behind. They left into the darkness as Benjamin leaned against the sacrificial post.

"Goodbye, my love," he said, as the creatures surrounded him. The group heard him scream for a while as they ran back to the Commune's outer wall.

Chapter 28 – Trapped

The group took a moment to catch their breath on the inside of the Commune's sprawling wall. They were drenched, head to toe. Logan was slowly getting his energy back again, but was more dumbfounded by Benjamin's suicide-by-creatures.

"They'll have heard the gunfire," Ironson said, "We can't keep this position for long."

Jon was pacing around and replied, "Yeah, sure as shit. What do we do now?"

"We can't go back out there," said Eve.

"And we can't go back to the compound," Astrid said.

"We could walk along the perimeter until we find a safe way out," said Ironson as he scanned the darkness for movement.

"Who knows how big the wall is, though," said Jon.

"And there might be cameras," said Eve, "They had power in the mansion."

"They already know there's trouble. They might already be heading this way," said Astrid.

Logan finally joined in and said, "Why would Benjamin let himself die like that?"

The group had been so focused on what to do next, the question took them all by surprise. They looked in Logan's direction.

"Who knows, man, all these people are fucking nuts," said Jon.

"He wasn't though," said Logan, "And he said to tell Delilah what he did. Maybe he thought his death would snap her out of it or something?"

"No offence, but we need to focus on how we get our supplies and leave," said Ironson.

"That's what I'm thinking about too," said Logan, "Maybe we don't need to fight our way out. Maybe I can talk to Delilah."

Jon raised and eyebrow and said, "You, of all people, want to talk?"

Logan replied, "We have one assault rifle between the five of us. She has an army we lost to when we were armed to the teeth. If we fight them, we'll definitely lose.

"We need to remain hidden and move silently. The storm will be our ally. Eve, you were in the mansion. Do you have any

303

idea where they took our supplies?"

Eve shook her head and said, "I have no idea. There was a door to a big garage I couldn't get into. The truck might be in there, but no idea if our stuff is there."

"One of the keys might open it up," said Astrid, who had stowed the keyring into her robes.

"You two should check out the garage. Keep your hoods up and hopefully you'll blend in until they realize who you are," said Logan, finding the beginnings of a plan, "Benjamin mentioned a work camp. From what I've seen and heard, that's where the more trusted guys are. Jon, you and Ironson check it out there. Try not to kill anyone and stay hidden. We'll meet behind the mansion afterwards."

"Worth a shot," said Ironson.

Jon furrowed his brow and said, "And what are you going to do? Get yourself in trouble and make us risk our lives to save you again?"

"Not this time," said Logan with razor sharp focus, "I'm going to pay Delilah a visit."

When the mansion was in view, the group separated. Jon and Ironson, still wielding the AR, headed in the direction of the work camp. Eve and Astrid snuck towards the mansion. Logan would sneak around and try to pinpoint where Delilah was, which didn't take long.

The compound was on high alert. Armed Sisters patrolled the grounds in groups of two and three. Logan headed towards the commotion of the walled courtyard. He couldn't see what was going on from the outside of the wall, but he heard shouting and the sound of hundreds of confused men.

He heard Delilah shouting, so he waited behind a tree for her to come out.

The creatures' howls drew closer.

The work camp was down the hill from the mansion and the courtyard. A path led right to it, but Jon and Ironson kept to the darkness of the surrounding woods. Several patrols passed by them on the path. The night and raging storm kept the two men hidden as they crept.

Here and there were powered LED lights illuminating the path down the hill. After a few minutes, they found themselves on the outside of what Jon presumed was the work camp. There were multiple tents and one room cabins, placed in a senseless manner all around a large area amongst the trees.

Ironson motioned for Jon to go one direction while he would go another. They split up and kept low as they systematically checked each domicile.

Most had sleeping, dirty men in them with various carpentry tools hung up on the walls of the cabins. The tents were large enough for two people to sleep in and generally contained nothing else.

Jon peeked through an open window of one of the cabins and seen a Sister standing guard in front of three locked cabinets. Inside he could see multiple firearms, but one caught his attention. His trusty Winchester.

"Well hello there," he whispered to himself as he started to figure out how he was going to get in there unnoticed.

On the other side of the work camp, Ironson had found nothing so far but guards patrolling. He stayed behind tents and cabins to keep out of sight as he looked for supplies.

One particular tent housed a dirty man that just couldn't get to sleep. It was Rat. He tossed and turned on his cot before finally getting up. He rubbed his eyes and stepped out of the tent.

As he did, he met eyes with the marine pilot who had been sneaking by. "HEATHEN!" he shouted without hesitation.

Ironson hit him with the stock of the AR, knocking him out cold.

A nearby patrol heard Rat shout and immediately ran to his location. They seen him sprawled out on the wet, muddy ground but no sign of his attacker.

The Sister who had been standing guard at the makeshift armory also heard the shout. She took a key from out of her robe and unlocked one of the cabinets. She pulled a rifle out, but immediately

306

dropped it as a strong arm wrapped around her neck.

She struggled, but she was no match for Jon's strength. She finally passed out from lack of oxygen and Jon set her gently down on the ground. He checked to make sure she was still alive before taking her key and unlocking all the cabinets.

He snatched up his Winchester shotgun and held it up as if he had just found Excalibur. He found the rest of the group's shotguns and more. 9mm pistols, several AR-15s, a slew of .22 hunting rifles (which he left) and ammo for everything. Some of the stun gun cartridges were there, about a dozen.

He was barely able to carry everything out, using his sweat shirt as a sort of carrier to hold all the ammo for everything.

He snuck out of the work camp and met up with Ironson, who had already been waiting amongst some trees. As they huddled down, Ironson took up some of the load and said, "G'damn, you found our shotguns and some."

"Hell yeah, I did," said Jon with a huge grin on his face, "Let's get back to the mansion and hope everyone else hasn't gotten themselves killed."

Eve and Astrid kept their hoods pulled low as they approached the porch of the mansion. There were two Sisters standing guard as they approached. When the friends walked up the steps, the guards stepped forward.

"Hello, sisters," said one, "Do you have anything to report?"

Eve said, "Yes, we seen the devils climb the walls and head towards the gate to the sacrificial area."

"Damn, we just missed them," said the other guard.

"Go inside and get dry," said the first guard as she pulled a walkie talkie from out of her robe.

The two walked into the mansion, their hearts racing. It was empty inside, thankfully, so they rushed into the kitchen where the locked door to the garage was.

Eve kept a look out while Astrid tried several of the keys before finally being able to open it. They entered the garage and shut the door behind them.

It was a three-car garage and was lit up by a single bulb hanging in the very center. The Mean Green Machine sat inside, as if it had been waiting for them. All of its fenders were dented in from the assault when they first came into the Commune's lands. A second vehicle sat there as well, an old, all-terrain jeep. Hanging on the wall were tactical vests and the four, black cloaks they had worn for so long.

Eve approached the cloaks and said, "At least we know where these are. Now how do we get the truck out of here without anyone noticing."

She was answered by silence, so she looked back around to Astrid, who stood frozen. Behind her was Abigail with a hefty revolver pointed at the back of Astrid's head. The door was open.

"Oh, my dear, dear sisters," Abigail said, "You should have

run while you could."

"Eve?" Astrid said, shaking in fright.

"We were only-" Eve started to say, but she was cut off by Abigail firing her revolver at Astrid's head. Blood shot out from the back of the girl's dark hair, and she fell into a heap on the ground.

Eve's eyes went wide and she yelled, "You bitch!"

She ran at Abigail, who fired her revolver at Eve, hitting her in the arm. It didn't stop her, though, and she tackled her into the doorway. They both fell and Abigail's revolver spun away from her. Eve used her unwounded, left arm to punch Abigail in her face.

She managed to get up and slammed the door into Abigail's head, over and over, until she didn't move. There was shouting from the foyer of the mansion, so Eve pulled Abigail's body out of the way, then shut and locked the door.

"To hell with not killing anyone," Eve said, picking up the revolver. She bent over Astrid and checked her pulse. Nothing.

Delilah was finally able to get order back to the men in the courtyard. Her Sisters were finally able to herd all the men back into the caverns. She left the courtyard with Lisa just in time to hear two gunshots from the mansion.

The shadow that was following her also heard the shots, and he knew something went wrong.

Delilah and Lisa sprinted the short distance to the mansion, with Logan following behind. He darted between trees and high grass to stay hidden.

Then the red eyes and howls came. Logan ducked as creatures started running around the mansion. Delilah and her crony were barely able to make it to the front porch before they came.

"Give your lives for your Mother, sisters!" Delilah screamed.

The two guards and Lisa rushed towards the creatures, firing their weapons. They put in a good effort, but without experience in fighting the uncannily quick things, they weren't able to get any critical hits off. Delilah ran inside and shut the door as the three women were torn to shreds and eaten.

Logan seen a terrace that led up to a high window on a dark side of the mansion. He snuck across the yard to it, hoping the creatures would be distracted enough not to notice him. He started climbing.

Jon and Ironson heard the howls over the storm and gave up trying to sneak. Ironson took his modified SPAS shotgun and Jon loaded his Winchester. They hid the rest of the firearms under a root in the woods. Ironson took some of the stun gun cartridges and pocketed them.

"It's go time," said Ironson as he loaded the last slug into his weapon.

"And here I was thinking tonight wasn't gonna be exciting," said Jon, pumping his shotgun.

Chapter 29 - Containing the Darkness

Jon and Ironson ran up the path to the mansion. The scene before them was one of chaos. Half bodies laid around the house, some still being eaten by the creatures. Others were climbing around the large house and breaking into the front door.

"Dammit, no way to tell where Eve is," Jon said, glancing around at all the bodies to see if he could recognize them. No one important that he could see.

"We can only hope for the best. She's gotta be in there somewhere," said Ironson, "Let's go, single column and keep your head on a swivel."

"Sir, yes, sir," Jon said, sarcastically. No time to argue.

They were able to speed past some of the feasting creatures without being noticed. When they made it up to the porch, they heard screams and howls coming from inside.

Jon, already worried Eve was in danger, was of one mind at this point. He had to get to her.

They ran in, weapons at the ready. The chandelier had fallen into pieces in the foyer. Claw marks and blood were everywhere, shattering the once ornate nature of the mansion.

A creature was prowling up the staircase. Ironson stunned it and like clockwork, Jon ran up on it and blasted it in the back of its head. The slug exploded the back of the thing's head into a fountain of black goo.

They heard a shout and gunfire come from the direction of the kitchen and Jon said, "That sounds like Eve!"

They raced to the kitchen and seen the door leading towards the garage had been crushed. They entered and seen Eve on top of the technical, firing the revolver down at two creatures who were about to pounce on her.

Ironson stunned one creature and Jon unloaded his Winchester into the other, but wasn't able to get a head shot. It started darting around, only suffering glancing wounds, even with the slugs.

Ironson finished off the stunned creature and Eve dropped down to the still loaded, mounted machine gun. She shouted, "Get down!" and spun it around at the other menace, who was only a few feet away from the barrel.

Jon dove out of the way and Eve squeezed the trigger. The men had to cover their ears as the rat-tat-tat of the machine gun was deafening. The force of the attack sent the creature into the wall of the garage. It tried to get away, but it was riddled with bullets in a matter of seconds.

When it fell dead, Eve jumped down off the back of the truck and hugged Jon. She started crying and blurted out, "Astrid is dead."

Jon looked over her shoulder at Astrid's corpse and closed his eyes, silently cursing their dilemma.

Ironson hung his head and said, "It's unfortunate, but we need to keep going. There's nothing to be done for her, now."

"As much as I hate it, he's right," said Jon as he released his fiancé. He looked into her eyes and said, "We need to find Logan and get the fuck out of here."

Delilah's bedroom was more of a safe room than an actual bedroom. The door was lined with heavy, metal plating and she had her personal weapons hanging on a wall. There were a few ARs, a machete and homemade pipe bombs.

As she closed the door behind her and locked it, the power was cut. She was bathed in darkness and became aware of her open window. A streak of lightning illuminated the room for a moment as rain poured in.

She marched over and shut the window, locking it. She then pulled a metal grate down to cover the window. She then went over to an oil lantern and started rummaging around a dresser for a way to light it.

As lightning flashed again, she heard a low voice from somewhere in the room say, "Need a light?"

Delilah spun around, darting her eyes around the dark room. She said, "Who's there?"

"The man you sent away to die," Logan said.

"Devil!"

"Maybe. If I am, I've made peace with it. I just thought I'd let you know that Benjamin Perez is dead."

Something bubbled up in Delilah that she hadn't felt since she took over power over the Commune of After. She said through gritted teeth, "You killed him, didn't you?"

Logan's voice came from a different side of the room, making Delilah back up towards the gated window. He said, "No. He sacrificed himself so that my friends and I could escape. He was a good man, but there was nothing I could do."

"That damned fool," Delilah hissed, "Everything was fine until you came around!"

"Imprisoning your husband is fine? Brainwashing people and twisting a religion is fine?"

"I just did what God wanted me to do!" Delilah shouted, becoming more and more nervous. She had never been in such a weak position.

"You called me a devil without even knowing who I was. Who knows how many others you and your people have killed. All in the name of God? Because He, in all his omniscient wisdom, told you to kill strangers and sacrifice them to your Angels?"

"I...I thought that..." Delilah started.

But Logan didn't let her finish, "Your husband thought that you two could build a community. A safe haven for those in need. Even if God sent the burrowers to the world, don't you think humanity is worth fighting for? Did you even love Ben?"

Delilah couldn't keep up the act anymore. Her solid, charismatic facade fell as she went into the fetal position. She said through tears, "I loved him with all my heart. I... just didn't know what to do. I've been so confused and lost."

Lightning cracked and for a split second, Delilah could make out the figure of Logan standing over her. She said, "Just kill me and get it over with."

There was a howl out in the hallway and the sound of clawing.

"You were right to call me a killer before," said Logan as he looked down at the broken woman, "But that part of me is contained now. I guess I should thank you and your husband for giving me clarity. I had never been tortured before, but I found wisdom in it. You only made me stronger.

"I'm not going to kill you, even though I probably should. I think you're already defeated. I'm going to get my friends, our stuff and food and we're leaving this place."

Delilah hugged her knees closer to herself and she said, "Where is there even to go anymore?"

As Logan unhooked one of the ARs from the wall and injected a magazine into it, he said, "I'm going home."

Jon led the way up the stairs, his Winchester outstretched before him and ready to respond to any threat that would come their way. Eve followed directly behind him with the revolver at the ready. Bringing up the rear and marching backwards to cover their tracks was Ironson.

They heard gunfire in the hallway above them. Jon halted their advance and laid on the stairs to get a view of what was going on. His eyes had adjusted to the darkness after the power was cut. He stuck out the littlest of his head he could behind the cover of the banister.

He seen Logan standing over a freshly killed corpse of a creature that was prowling the hallway. He held an AR, which still had its barrel smoking.

"It's Logan," Jon said, climbing the rest of the way up the steps and meeting his friend in the hallway. Eve and Ironson followed closely behind.

Logan was glad to see his friends, but noticed there was one missing. He said, "Where's Astrid?" but he feared he already knew the answer.

Jon put his hand on his friend's shoulder and said, "I'm sorry, man. She's gone."

Eve pushed past Jon and hugged Logan. She said, "I was there, but there was nothing I could do. I'm so sorry."

"It wasn't your fault," said Logan, even though he didn't know what had happened, "This room is fortified. It should keep us somewhat safe until morning."

They entered Delilah's bedroom, but she was no longer in there. Ironson shut the door behind them and Jon looked out the open window, searching for any threats. Logan sat on the bed, processing the death of Astrid and Eve sat next to him.

"I didn't know her for long, but I liked her," Logan said.

"I know," said Eve, "She liked you too. She didn't deserve what happened to her."

Eve proceeded to tell Logan what happened and how they found the technical and cloaks. Logan then told them all his conversation with Delilah. He had let her escape through the window as he left the safe room to search for them.

"Surprised you let her go," Jon said.

"Not everyone needs to die by human hands," said Logan, "Sometimes it'll be unavoidable in this new world, but there's something to say about staying your hand."

"Suppose you're right," said Jon with a long sigh, "Just we'd be in St. Louis by now if it wasn't for her."

Logan said, "Speaking of which, I think we should go back home to Arborsville."

Ironson said, "But what about the plan? What about MEPS?"

"I know I don't speak for everyone, but I, for one, will join you to MEPS and make sure you get there alright. After that, I'm going home," said Logan in a conviction that no one questioned, "I do want to see if Eve's family is safe before heading into Illinois, though."

Eve looked towards Jon and said, "What do you want to do, babe?"

Logan could see the gears in Jon's head were churning. After a moment of thinking, the bearded man finally said, "Well, we're a team. If Logan's going to Arborsville, then we should too. If we find your family, they can come with us. That's how I see things, anyways. What do you think?"

"I really don't know," Eve said, "I'll decide after we find out about my mom and dad."

"So I guess we'll be parting ways soon," said Ironson. His tone was saddened, but he didn't let it show too much.

"Why are you so gung-ho about going back to Arborsville, anyways?" Jon asked.

Logan sighed and said, "I'm also worried about my family, but I think we would have a better chance of surviving in a smaller town where we might still know people."

Jon said, "Fine, fine. At any rate, we should get some sleep in shifts. I don't know about you guys, but I'm fucking tired."

Chapter 30 - Man's New Best Friend

Another restless night sleep. Exhaustion helped Eve rest, but the creatures' howls outside kept her on edge. Every now and then she would hear someone scream, but at some point in the night it became apparent that the creatures had breached the cavern doors down in the courtyard. She didn't need, or want, to see what happened, as the sounds of the fiends feasting at their human smorgasbord was all she needed to know what happened.

The rain stopped and the clouds parted by morning. The sun rose upon the Commune's grounds, once full of living people. The rays shone through the metal grating on the window of the bedroom.

Ironson had been keeping guard, so was awake already. The others awoke one by one. They were all sneezing as they rose. Jon and Eve had taken the bed. Logan slept on the floor.

"Think I got a cold," said Eve as she stepped out of the bed.

"Running around in the cold and rain didn't help nothin'," said Jon, immediately sneezing as he stretched.

Eve shook Logan to wake him up. He blinked as he came out of his slumber. Yesterday felt like it didn't happen, but the memories of everything that had happened flooded to him.

Once everyone was up and lucid, Ironson said, "We have free reign of the house. I scouted around and everyone is either gone or dead. There's still running water. I suggest we get ourselves cleaned up, find what we can and get the hell out of here."

"Sounds good to me," said Jon.

Eve scratched Jon's bearded chin and said, "You're shaving that, then."

Jon's shoulders slumped and he said, "Aw, but I like it."

Logan felt the fuzz on his cheeks and chin and wondered if Astrid would have wanted him to shave. As he said, he hadn't known her for long, but he couldn't help but think about her.

The upstairs bathroom was grand and unscathed from the creatures' attack from the night before. Jon had just finished showering up and shaving when it was Logan's turn.

Logan seen his clean shaven friend. Aside from the nicks and marks that scarred his face, he looked like he used to from way back when. Logan said to him, "You look younger without the beard."

Jon ran his rough hand against his now smooth face and said, "Yeah, I suppose it doesn't look half bad."

"I got some clothes together," said Logan as they passed by each other in the bathroom doorway, "I found some of our clothes from before, but not everything. It's all in the safe room."

"Alright, thanks, man," said Jon, "You ok, by the way?"

"As good as I can be, I suppose."

"Just with everything, we haven't had much time to just stop and talk much," said Jon.

"Haven't really had the time," said Logan with a shrug, "Maybe when we get home we can settle down and shoot the shit, as it were."

"That'd be nice. Well, shower up while you can. God knows when the next time we'll be able to will be," said Jon with a wave before turning down the long hallway.

Logan undressed and looked at himself in the body-size mirror. His face looked like he lost a fight with a lawn mower. Cuts and marks from the dirty men's attack covered his body.

He started the water of the shower and stepped in through the steam. As he let the water run down his body, he leaned against the marbled wall and closed his eyes. He let himself have a moment of peace while he could.

Once everyone had cleaned themselves up and got dressed

with various sweaters, jeans or sweat pants, they took note of all the supplies they had gathered through the morning.

There were the black, hooded cloaks and tactical vests for everyone. Logan took the one with dried blood on it, knowing it was his by the stains. When Logan slung his cloak over his shoulders and clasped it, it felt like he was saying hello to an old friend.

Logan took a 9mm pistol and holstered it into his tactical vest, along with several magazines for it. There were enough AR-15s and ammo for everyone, along with their individual, modified shotguns. They all pocketed stun gun cartridges, enough for ten per person. Eve had found the pocket knife Logan gave her before and pocketed it. The watch Logan had given Jon was nowhere to be seen.

Food-wise, they found a mix of the canned goods they had previously along with oats and stale bread. There was some dried meat in a store room, but they left it as they did not know what kind of meat it was. They found some of the bottles of water that was theirs, but also found some canteens. They filled those up with water from the tap. Whatever they couldn't carry in their backpacks they threw into the cab of the technical.

Logan looked for Omega's journal, but couldn't find it anywhere. He even enlisted the help of Eve, but after a while they gave up.

Cleaned, armed and ready to go with enough provisions to last them a couple weeks, they were finally ready to leave the

Commune's grounds. They gathered beside the technical and Logan noticed Astrid's body was no longer there.

"Where's Astrid?" Logan asked the group.

"I took her out into the woods and covered her with stones," said Eve, "I would have buried her, but I couldn't find a shovel. I just couldn't leave her laying on the floor."

"You did a good thing, Eve," said Logan, "She deserved some kind of burial."

"Everyone ready?" said Ironson, taking up his position at the mounted machine gun.

"Time to get the hell out of here," said Jon, jumping into the driver's seat.

Logan opened the garage door, letting the warm sun in, before jumping into the back of the truck and sitting on the wheel well. Eve jumped into the passenger seat of the cab and shut the door.

Jon fired up the engine and it roared to life. He pulled it out of the garage and they left the shattered Commune of After.

It was midday before they finally made their way out of the Commune's compound and back onto highway 67. They didn't see another living being the whole time, but stayed on guard just in case.

Eve's mind was on her parents. She had no way to contact them and didn't know if they would even be home. She tried to stay positive, but their journey had been the opposite up to this point.

They emerged onto the highway just north of Greenville. They drove a bit up the forested road before Jon pulled over and opened the back window to talk to everyone.

"We'll be in Farmington in about an hour, maybe a little less," he said, "You want to stop now and eat? Who the hell knows how the city will be once we get there."

"I could eat something," said Eve, who was growing more and more anxious the closer they got to her former home.

"Sounds like a plan," said Ironson, "We may not get another chance."

They built a small fire on the side of the road and boiled some water to use for oatmeal. They sat in a circle, feeling relatively safe since they had their cloaks back.

Between spoonfuls, Jon said, "Should we still try to use the metro to get close to MEPS?"

"I'm not so sure anymore," said Logan, "Those things burrow into the ground. The metro systems will probably be swarmed with them."

"It is a good idea to weigh our options now," said Ironson, "The roads will probably be blocked by abandoned vehicles, so driving all the way there is potentially out of the question."

Eve said, "So we go on foot, out in the open?"

Logan replied, "With our cloaks, we'd be safe from getting marked by the burrowers, but be fish in a barrel for other threats."

"Your family lived in Chesterfield, right?" Ironson said,

turning towards Eve.

"Yeah, it's the western part of St. Louis," she said.

"We could go the long way around," Ironson suggested.

"That's a big negative, buddy," said Jon, brushing oatmeal off his now clean shaven face, "We only have so much fuel and I want to drive as far as we can before we have to give up the Mean Green Machine."

"We'd still avoid the main city if we drive directly to Chesterfield. It's once we're in the main metropolitan area we'll need to be overly cautious," said Logan.

Ironson said, "I guess we'll just have to see how things are once we get there."

The continued their meal. Eve hadn't had oatmeal since she was a kid, never liked it much. Her parents had forced her to eat it. She had always complained, but looking back she felt foolish for complaining about something so petty.

When they were finishing up, Logan heard the screech of a hawk. He looked up and at first didn't see anything. Another screech led Logan's eyes to some tree limbs, where he seen the hawk.

The others had noticed it too. Eve said, "I didn't think I'd ever see another animal again."

"I wonder if that's the same hawk I seen a few days ago, before we got attacked," said Logan.

The hawk leapt off the tree limb and, not so gracefully,

fluttered down to the ground near the group. It looked at the others curiously as it kept one of its brown-feathered wings slightly extended.

"Aw, it looks hurt," said Eve.

"That thing will peck your eyes out if you get close," said Jon.

"We have to try, though," said Logan, who stood up and began slowly approaching the raptor with his arms out. He kept his bowl that had a few oats left.

The hawk screeched at him, but didn't move. Logan said, "It's ok, girl, I'm not going to hurt you."

When he was within a few feet of the hawk, he hunkered down and held out his bowl. The hawk looked in it and pecked around, but didn't eat anything out of it. It looked up at Logan and cocked its head.

"Seems like its wing is hurt," said Logan, "It can probably only fly short distances, now. We have any cans of food that have meat in it?"

Jon rolled his eyes and said, "Oh, c'mon, are you really gonna waste-"

Eve cut him off, "Yes, we are. This is the only animal we've seen since those things came. We have to do something."

Jon put his hands up in defeat and said, "Alright, alright, do what you gotta do then we should get going. I don't want to get caught out in the dark when we're in the city."

Eve rummaged through a pack and found a can of beef stew. She opened it with her pocket knife and gave it to him. Logan emptied the can into the bowl and stepped back.

The hawk pecked through it, but it gobbled up the bits of beef that were in it. As it ate, Logan said, "I'm sure it'd rather hunt, but if it's hungry enough, it'll take anything. Just not oatmeal, I guess."

They packed everything back up and snuffed out the fire. They got back into the truck and, as Jon started the engine, Logan heard the hawk screech again. He looked down from the back of the truck and seen the hawk looking up at him.

He said to it, "You're welcome, buddy, but we have to go now."

The hawk fluttered up to the truck and perched along the side of the bed. When the truck started moving, it hopped down at Logan's feet.

Ironson had been watching and said, "Looks like you have a new friend."

"It would appear so," said Logan, grinning at the aspect of having a pet hawk, "You can come with us for as long as you want, my friend."

Chapter 31 - Close Yet Far

The forest grew less dense the further north they drove. They would be leaving the Mark Twain National Forest soon, as nature began to give way to civilization. They passed by a few smaller towns, nestled alongside US-67.

The hawk had its injured wing up, plucking at its feathers with its beak. Logan had been watching it and said up to Ironson, "I think I'll name her Habrok."

Ironson had his gaze on the road ahead and barely heard Logan. He blinked back to reality, turned and said, "Habrok, eh? What's that mean?"

"It's something from Norse mythology," Logan replied, "I just don't remember what it means."

"Fair enough. How random is it that the only animal we've seen alive is in our truck with us now," said Ironson with a chuckle.

"Random, indeed," said Logan, who thought maybe it wasn't so random, but wasn't in the mood to talk about spirituality.

In the cab of the truck, Jon and Eve had been driving in silence. Eve was playing with the pockets on her tactical vest. She looked deep in thought as she looked down at her hands.

"You ok, babe?" said Jon, keeping his eyes on the road. He had to swerve around abandoned vehicles more and more the further north they went.

"Yeah," Eve said, distantly.

Jon gave her a sidelong glance and said, "I know that tone. What's wrong."

Eve plopped her hands down into her lap and looked out at the road. After a moment she said, "Who are we, now?"

"I'm Jon, you're Eve, and back there we have Joseph and Logan," said Jon.

"No, I mean...who have we become?" she asked, "The closer we get to home and hopefully finding my parents, I can't help but think who will my mom and dad see when they look at me."

"We've taken our licks, that's for sure," Jon said, "Look at Logan, dude has scars all over his face now. You got little ones all over you, too. That doesn't change who you are. When I look at you,

I still see Eve Parker. The girl I've loved since I can remember."

Eve's mouth spread into a wide grin and she said, "I love you too, babe."

Jon held his free hand out and took hers. He said, "Your parents will think the same thing, I'm sure."

Her smile faded a bit and she said, "If they're even still there..."

"Well, we'll be finding out before too long," he replied.

Roughly an hour after they left the Commune's grounds, they started driving through Farmington. Forests were giving way to farmland and then to a commercial area along the highway.

At an intersection with a traffic light that hadn't been on for months, the group looked at all the fast food restaurants around them. Logan could feel himself salivating as he thought back on the last time he had a big, greasy hamburger.

"What I wouldn't give for a double cheeseburger," said Ironson.

"I know what you mean," said Logan as they passed by the buildings. They kept their eyes on the various logos even after they were out of view.

They passed by some hotels, large shopping centers and even more fast food restaurants. Jon hadn't really noticed them as he was focused on driving as far as he could. Eve, however, was mesmerized.

"I'd gladly blow someone for some cheese fries," she said.

Jon laughed and shook his head before he said, "Yeah, sure."

She shot a cheeky look at her fiancé and grinned.

Twenty minutes after passing Farmington, the Mean Green Machine started to rattle. The engine churned and heaved before it stopped working entirely. Habrok fluttered around in the bed of the truck as the whole vehicle shook.

Jon looked down at the meters and seen the fuel gauge fall to empty. "Oh, what the fuck," he said as he slammed his hands into the steering wheel.

They coasted for half a mile before the technical came to a complete halt.

"G'da-" Jon started to say before being interrupted by a violent sneeze. He blew his nose on the edge of his cloak before throwing open the door.

Everyone got out of the truck. Logan noticed there was a dark streak in the road that came from under the truck. He said, "A gas leak?"

Jon seen the streak too and got on his knees to look under the vehicle. Sure enough, the last of the fuel dripped from a broken line in the undercarriage. He slammed his fist into the asphalt and sneezed.

"Looks like we're hoofing it from here," said Ironson.

"Can we fix it?" Eve asked as Jon got to his feet.

332

"Even if we could, we don't have any gas left," said Jon, rubbing his cleanly shaven chin.

"We take what we can, then walk to Chesterfield," said Logan, "Maybe we'll get lucky and find another vehicle along the way."

"Doesn't look like we have a choice," Jon replied.

They packed all of their food, water and miscellaneous supplies into the rucksacks and shouldered them, along with a canteen for each person. Eve took any medical supplies she could stuff into her own pack, including some antibiotics, cold medicine, bandages, alcohol and sutures. They slung their individual, modified shotguns on their shoulders and snatched up an AR-15 each.

Habrok hopped up onto the top of the truck and screeched. Logan said to the hawk, "End of the road, friend."

The hawk fluttered up into a tree and screeched down at him.

Jon took one last look at the Mean Green Machine before sighing and turning away. They began walking alongside the road, keeping their eyes and ears open for threats.

Every now and then one of them would cough or sneeze. Logan and Eve was starting to feel better and Ironson didn't seem too affected. Jon, however, seemed to get worse as he walked along in his uneven gate.

Logan had been calculating how long it would take to walk to Chesterfield. They were 80 miles away from the city, which would have only been an hour and a half drive. He shook his head as he figured up how long it would take them to walk it.

"I hate to be the bearer of bad news, but if we walk ten hours a day, it's going to be three days before we get to Chesterfield," he said, grimly.

"Are you serious?" Jon said, sniffing away the drainage from his sinuses.

"I'm afraid so. That means we're going to need to find safe places to camp during the night. We're more than likely in the circle of influence of a new burrower nest," Logan said.

"Let's keep up the pace, then, people," said Ironson, "We got a hike ahead of us."

They walked north up highway 67 until it was nearly nightfall. They passed by a few small towns along the way and they chit chatted about anything but their predicament, to distract themselves. Eve was quiet along the way, as she was too preoccupied with thoughts of her parents to be distracted.

As the sky turned purple, they seen an exit sign that said DE SOTO OLYMPIAN VILLAGE with an arrow. With the last bit of energy they had, they jogged up to the exit ramp and made a left towards a lone gas station.

They passed by abandoned vehicles, some with segmented, decaying corpse bits scattered around them. The blood dried dark into the asphalted road.

Habrok had been keeping up with them. She would fly ahead
334

a ways before stopping to rest in a tree or on a roadsign. She'd wait until the group got ahead of her, then repeat the process.

Ironson had been keeping point and he held his fist up, indicating for the others to stop. They took cover behind a former soccer mom's van in the road just outside the gas station.

"You see anything?" asked Logan, quietly.

"No, but I don't want to be taken by surprise," he said, "We should approach it in two different directions. Logan, you come with me along the south side of the building. Jon, you and Eve come at it from the north."

"Got it," sneezed Jon.

They separated into their two groups. Logan and Ironson dipped into a ditch alongside Athena School Road and cut through some brush towards the south side of the building. Jon and Eve ran across the road towards the fuel pumps and ducked behind a car.

Jon held up his AR and kept it ready as he gazed into the gas station's windows from across the parking lot. He didn't see any movement, so he and Eve pushed up to the building. They poked their heads up and looked through the dusty windows.

Jon tested the door and it opened right up.

As they entered the front doors, they seen Ironson and Logan enter the sales floor from a door that led to the back. "Looks like we're ok," Jon said.

"Looks like it," responded Ironson, safetying his AR, "Never can be too cautious, though."

"I guess this is home for tonight," Eve said.

"Let's get some food ready, I'm starving," said Jon as they all took their packs off to get ready to settle down for the night.

Chapter 32 - Silent Watchers

The shelving units had long since been ransacked. Molding hotdogs sat in a rotisserie machine on the front desk. The coolers' glass doors were smashed up and were completely devoid of drinks, except one can of Coca Cola that Logan found lying underneath a shelf.

The four didn't want to risk having a fire, so they settled on canned cocktail fruit. They sat on the front counter as they passed a couple cans of food around. It wasn't enough to fill their bellies completely, and their forms were starting to show how much weight they've lost.

After the cans of fruit were eaten up, Logan said, "I found something, thought it'd be a nice treat," as he pulled out the can of soda.

"Coca Cola?" Jon said before shrugging, "Why not."

Logan opened the can, expecting to be greeted by a hiss of carbonation. Instead, there was no noise and he took a sip.

"It's a bit flat," said Logan, passing it on to Jon.

"A Coke is a Coke," Eve said.

They took turns drinking the Coca Cola until it was empty. It was enough to raise their spirits ahead of their oncoming journey. It even helped Eve's sullen mood.

With it being completely dark, it was time to bed down for the night. Jon and Eve took up residence in the office for some privacy before actually going to sleep. Ironson used some old boxes as a bed in the back stock room. Logan slept on the sales floor, propping himself up by his pack.

He slept light that night, expecting there to be trouble. He could hear the howls of distance creatures, which kept him up. He finally let sleep take him once he didn't hear the fiends.

Logan was woken up by the sun shining on his face. Its warmth made him want to lay there longer as if he were snoozing an alarm clock. When he seen everyone else start to stir, he finally got up.

Jon and Eve seemed to be in a good mood as they gathered their things. Logan was glad for the gas station's thick walls as he re-equipped his gear and joined everyone else at the front doors.

Ironson asked, "Do we want to stick to highways, or walk as the bird flies directly to Chesterfield?"

"There are still some forested areas between here and there," Logan responded, "It'd still be quicker to keep to roads."

"We're not far from Festus," said Eve.

"Yeah, then we can take 55 up from there," Jon said, "Made the drive enough times when going on float trips, so I know where we're going, more or less. Once we get to Festus, we can start heading northwest towards Chesterfield."

"Let's get to it then," said Ironson, "We're burning daylight."

Jon saluted the pilot and said, "Sir, yes, sir."

Ironson rolled his eyes and took point exiting the building. Logan made sure his hood was pulled tightly around his head. This was mainly for protection from the creatures' gaze, but there was a bite to the wind that morning, as well.

He heard Habrok call from a nearby road sign, as if it were ready to travel. A bit of gore from an unknown corpse hung from her beak as she watched the group leave the gas station and cross back over to the highway.

She flapped from sign to sign as they travelled, as she didn't seem able to fly yet. Logan made sure he knew where she was as he walked with the group. He had a dog back home, but had no hope for it still being there by the time he got back. Habrok gave him a sort of a pet, even if she did her own thing, having her close gave him something to cling to.

339

There was a steady line of abandoned vehicles facing south, away from St. Louis. The group started to check them for any supplies, or to see if they were drivable. They gave up after a while, as they found nothing and checking every vehicle was slowing them down.

After a couple hours they walked into Festus, Missouri. There was a clump of trees in the middle of a cloverleaf interchange, where highway 67 met with I-55. They decided to stop there to eat something while they got their bearings.

Habrok hopped up into a lower tree limb as the group huddled together amongst the densely packed trees. They ate out of a can of baked beans, cold as they didn't want to stop long enough to build a fire.

As they finished eating, Habrok started screeching nonstop, fluttering her wings as she hopped back and forth on the tree limb.

"Shut up, already, we're goin'," Jon said as he got his pack ready.

"I think she's trying to warn us," Logan said.

"How do you know that?" said Jon.

"I don't, but I haven't seen her act like that yet," said Logan as he crept over to a tree on the outskirts of the little grove.

He peered out and immediately seen what got Habrok excited. Up on an overpass, which is where they needed to go to get onto I-55, he seen a group of creatures peering down at his location. They were perched on the concrete wall, like unmoving gargoyles.

340

"Burrowers," Logan said, getting his modified shotgun ready. Jon, Ironson and Eve didn't question him and got all their weapons ready in response.

"How many?" Ironson asked, stepping behind a nearby tree to get a look.

"I see three, but they're right where we need to go," said Logan.

"Fuck em," said Jon, cocking his trusty Winchester, "Let's just walk on up and say hello."

"I second that," said Ironson.

"What're they doing?" asked Eve as Logan pointed to where they were at for her, "They're creeping me the hell out."

"They're just...watching us," said Logan.

"Let's go up the exit ramp to get onto the interstate. If they give us trouble, we'll put them down. If they don't, I don't see a reason to waste ammo on them," said Ironson.

Jon groaned and said, "Fine, but I'll warn ya, my trigger finger is feeling mighty itchy right about now."

"Stay frosty, move as a unit, and call out anything if they move or you see more," said Ironson, "Logan, you take point. I'll bring up the rear. Jon, Eve, you two walk side by side between us. We'll approach in a diamond so we have all sides covered in case there's more."

They left the grove and moved as Ironson suggested. They walked up the exit ramp that was furthest from the overpass. Their

cloaks, torn and dirty, fluttered in the chill wind as they made their
way up to I-55.

They again found lines of cars, trucks, vans and semis in the
southbound lanes. Remnants of people who were trying to flee the
city. Corpses littered the roads and smashed in windows. It appeared
the creatures had once feasted heavily on the escapees here.

The group kept to the northbound lane, as the amount of
vehicles there were far less and it gave them more visual space.
Eventually, the creatures on the overpass were out of view.

They passed by Festus's commercial district, full of
restaurants and chain stores. The distraction of fast food that they
had before was gone, as they were worried about the creatures.

Once they passed through this area and into a residential
area, Ironson finally spoke, "I don't see them anymore."

Eve breathed out a heavy sigh of relief and said, "Thank
Christ, I think I was holding my breath the whole time."

Habrok fluttered onto a mile marker and squawked at the
group. Her wing was still injured and she seemed tired. Logan seen
her struggling to keep up and walked up to the hawk. He didn't think
she would respond, but he held his arm out anyways.

"Tired, buddy?" he said, "C'mon, it's ok."

Habrok cocked her head at the cloaked man and held her
beak open. When she felt like she wasn't threatened, she hopped
onto his arm. Logan felt her sharp talons dig into his layered
clothing, pinching his skin. She moved up onto his shoulder, where

342

they were both more comfortable, before he started walking again.

"Well, ain't that some shit," said Jon, impressed.

"Aw," said Eve, "Wish I had a camera."

Even Logan was galvanized by the hawk's gesture and he said, "Can't say I ever had a bird on my shoulder."

Ironson nodded his head in approval, and said, "That is cool, actually, but stay ready."

They passed by lines of houses on each side of the interstate. The only sound they could hear was the sound of their boots on the road's pavement. The chill air was still and even Habrok was silent, twisting her head around.

Ironson heard skittering amongst the houses to his right and shot his gaze over to the sound. He held his weapon at the ready, pointed towards the homes. He seen nothing but kept at the ready.

Up ahead, Logan seen a disruption in the interstate, as if the road had been upturned by a bomb. He was too far away to make out exactly what it was, but they were walking directly towards it.

The skittering sounds on each side of the interstate grew more intense the further north they walked. No one seen anything but all four survivors were spooked each time.

"What're those sounds?" Eve asked, her voice quivering either from anxiety or the cold.

"I think the burrowers are following us," said Ironson.

They approached what Logan had seen in the road. Both sides of the interstate were upturned into a ovular pit. Cars hung off the edges of each side and there was shrapnel buried in the dirt. Everything surrounded a dark hole in the very center of the pit.

The group stopped at the edge of the crater, taking in the sight. Ironson said, "Must have been from the military."

"I don't like this," said Eve, standing close to Jon.

From the hole a mighty roar erupted, shaking the very ground the humans were standing on. Jon and Logan recognized the sound and exchanged uneasy glances.

"What the hell was that?" asked Ironson.

"I think we've just stumbled into a burrower's nest," said Logan, "That roar came from an Enforcer, one of their leaders."

"Which means we're going to have trouble," said Jon.

Chapter 33 - Concerning I-55

Before Ironson had met with the three, his encounter with a nest ended in disaster. The Marines, as brave and ready as they thought they were, simply had no idea how to fight the creatures. These civilians had taken down an Enforcer with nothing but regular firearms. This feat was extraordinary, but it did nothing to keep the pilot from on edge as they started at the nest's entrance.

"Fight or leave, we have to decide now!" exclaimed Ironson as the sounds of hundreds of two-tone howls came out from the hole.

"I say we stand at the hole and blast anything that comes up," said Jon, puffing his chest out bravely.

"There'll be too many of them, we'll run out of ammo before

we kill them all," said Logan, looking around for options.

"Wish we had the machine gun right about now," said Eve, shifting her weight from one foot to the other.

"I've seen what a nest of those things can do to Marines, we have no chance if we fight, but there's no way we can outrun them," said Ironson, his face contorted in anger. The memories of seeing his fellow servicemen mercilessly cut down swam to his mind.

There was a van leaning halfway off the edge of the road. It was tipped down into the crater. Behind it were more vehicles lined up for miles upon miles, which they had seen before. Logan had been staring at it before he said, "We can try blocking up the hole with that van. It might slow them down enough to get away. It's still daytime, so they may not be so ravenous."

"I dunno, they seem pretty damn hungry," replied Jon, having to talk over the howls, "But seems like a solid plan, we gotta do something."

"Jon, get in the driver seat and try to steer it towards the hole. Everyone else, get ready to push," said Logan.

The group ran up to the van. Habrok, who had been comfortable on Logan's shoulder, fluttered away as they ran. Jon opened the driver's side door and plopped down in the seat. He threw the van in neutral as the other three members took up position behind the motor vehicle. All at once, they pushed with all their strength. The van listed and its front wheels touched the dirt, while its back wheels went up in the air.

Ironson heard the sound of movement amongst houses on either side of the road, but did not see anything. Whatever it was wasn't attacking them, so he ignored it.

"Keep pushing!" said Jon, thrusting the steering wheel towards the hole. He kept his eyes on the entrance. He seen a claw emerge from the hole, followed by the head of one of the creatures. "They're starting to come out!"

"On it!" shouted Ironson, "Eve, Logan, you better push that damn van down in there."

Ironson jumped off the edge of the crater and slid down into the dirt. The creature was halfway out of the hole when the pilot came to a stop. He raised his modified shotgun and pulled the trigger. The slug penetrated the creature's chest. It screamed in pain as Ironson got to his feet, ran up to point blank range and shot the thing in its eye. Black goo flew up from its neck as its head exploded in gore. Ironson shielded his face as the goo was flung onto his cloak.

Logan and Eve pushed with all their might. They barely gained an inch as the dead creature slumped over in the hole. It was closely followed by another creature, which Ironson put down with uncanny precision as soon as it shown its head.

"Feeling kinda useless here!" said Jon, watching Ironson battle anything that came out of the nest's entrance.

"Oh, for fuck's sake, Jon, switch me places," Eve blurted.

Jon jumped out of the van and ran to the back as Eve jumped

into the driver seat. Jon said, "Ok, Logan, on the count of three, you push like your life depends on it. Got it?"

"My life does depend on it, Jon," said Logan, impatiently.

Jon counted, "One, two, three!" and they pushed the van again. It fell forward and began slowly rolling.

Jon and Logan nearly fell over the edge of the crater as they watched the van roll towards the hole. Eve kept it steered in the right direction. Ironson finished off the fourth creature to emerge from the nest before he noticed the van rolling towards him.

As the pilot leapt out of the way, the van tipped down into the hole. Eve jumped out of the open door and tumbled in the dirt as the van fell downwards. They didn't realize how deep the hole was as only the back of the van was still visible as it crunched down into the earth below.

"Another, just for good measure," said Logan.

They ran to the opposite side of the crater as the van shook from the creature's confused attacks. The group repeated the process with a large truck, tipping it over the edge and stopping it as its tires ran over the van, forming a vehicular T in the hole.

"It'll buy us some time," said Logan, "But we should move while we can."

He turned to say something else, but everyone else had already kicked rocks. Without hesitation, he sprinted after them on the interstate. He caught up to them quickly, even with the quick pace everyone stayed at.

348

They ran and ran. The creatures' howls soared through the air after them, giving them the motivation they needed to run. They didn't look back as they hoofed it up the interstate.

They didn't stop until they were out of Festus and they could no longer hear the howls. In the rush to leave, Logan lost track of Habrok, which saddened him. Yet, he knew staying would mean certain death.

"They may still hunt us," said Logan while they caught their breath.

"We're a threat to their nest and those vehicles won't have held them," said Eve, looking back from whence they came.

"We should keep going, then," said Ironson, "We have about three hours of daylight left, so we should find somewhere defensible when the time comes."

Eve said, "I think we can make it to Arnold before we have to stop for the night."

"Arnold it is, then," said Ironson.

No casualties, no panicking. Just getting the job done. That's what Ironson was used to and he was impressed with how far the three had come after he first met them.

They headed north up I-55, not daring to stop for breaks. They soon passed by the exit for Herculaneum. This would be the last stretch of road where there were large swathes of forest. Parts of the interstate were carved through hills, revealing layers of rock on each side of the road. The friends had driven through this area many times before and the rock walls were normally an afterthought. Something to see while driving to their destination.

They passed through Barnhart, then Imperial as the sun readied itself to be taken over by night. They entered the outskirts of Arnold when they began to hear the hunting calls of the creatures.

The group quickened the pace off the interstate and onto a side road. Just off the interstate was a V shaped strip mall that had once provided various services. It was a brick building with smaller, house-like windows. There was a general store in the center of the V, flanked by a motorsports store and a chiropractor. The very end departments were empty with FOR RENT signs in the windows.

"Well, we can take our pick for the night," said Jon.

"The motorsports store might be interesting," said Logan, "Might find something useful."

Ironson shook his head and said, "This close to the city, I doubt it, but we should get inside and out of view while we can."

They carefully entered the store and were met by cold, stale air and darkness. They flipped on their flashlights and cleared the sales floor. It was one of the larger departments in the strip mall, mainly consisting of an open area with various sports vehicles. There were ATVs, dirt bikes, side by sides and golf carts on display. There were spots for many more, but they must have been taken. On the back side of the store was a heavy, metal garage door.

When they knew the area was safe, Jon and Eve began

350

getting a meal ready. Potted meat and green beans would be their feast for the night. With no way to cook anything, they prepared themselves mentally to eat cold meat.

While the couple got food ready, Ironson and Logan looked around for fuel. They checked every nook and cranny. It would be in vain, however, as there was nothing else of use in the store.

"Think we'll be safe here for tonight?" Logan asked after they completed their search.

"Safe as anyone can be," said Ironson with a shrug, "But I think we'll be alright. The garage door looks thick and the burrowers didn't see us enter as far as I know."

Logan was silent, prompting Ironson to say, "What's on your mind, friend?"

"I've just been thinking. Are we cursed?" Logan said, half lost in thought.

"Cursed? I'm not one for superstition. What do you mean?"

"Back when everything first went down and we first met you, that grocery store was relatively safe. Then people died or fled. Then the cannibals died. Omega was dying when we found him. Astrid and her father survived until we met them. Eric died and so did she not too long after. I killed a group of convicts just to get medicine. Everyone at the Commune, deranged as they may have been, died, with exception to maybe Delilah. Everyone we meet seems to die."

Ironson took in what Logan said and sighed. He replied, "It's survival of the fittest, Logan. Some of those people didn't deserve what happened to them, but, mentally, some people can't take this strong of a turn in their lives.

"It used to be if you got fired from your job, that was enough to send someone into a depression. Look at how things are now. Those that couldn't take getting fired can't make it in how this world is now."

Logan said, "Yeah, but what if we never met some of those people. They might still be alive or had a better chance."

Ironson defaulted to his commanding voice as he said, "I don't play around with hypotheticals, Logan. Shit happens. You're not going soft on me, are you?"

Logan shot the pilot a look and said, "No."

Eve walked up to them and said, "When you two are done jerking each other off, we have food ready."

Logan couldn't help but grin and shake his head. Ironson patted Logan's shoulder and said, "C'mon, let's eat."

The survivors choked down their cold food and drank some water. Jon was particularly disgusted by the look on his face, but he was too hungry to complain. Logan could hear the creatures' hunting calls outside, but he was so used to the sound, he barely noticed.

After they were done eating, they bedded down for the night. There weren't too many choices as far as comfortable spots, so they slept on the cold, hard floor. Logan felt a pain in his toes, but ignored it as he was exhausted. He let sleep take him, as they needed as much rest as they could get for the continuation of their journey the next day.

Chapter 34 - The Marauders

Three pairs of blue orbs watched the strip mall throughout the night. These fiends kept watch on the cloaked ones, and they had done so ever since they first made the trek onto I-55. They were not there to attack, but to scout.

A fourth creature had been watching, but had already left. It ran, tirelessly, towards its own nest. Through field and street, it ran. What would be a couple days walk for a normal human to reach St. Louis, this creature made within a few hours.

It ran through the dilapidated city streets, where the U.S. military had valiantly fought and lost. Signs of the battle were throughout the entirety of the city. Buildings were caved in from artillery strikes. Streets were upturned by tank tracks. Decaying, half-eaten bodies laid everywhere. A snack for later, perhaps, as no human had been seen in the city proper for months.

Finally, it reached its destination. The St. Louis Arch. Once a beacon of hope and the gateway to the west, it gave a home to one of the largest creature nests the military had tried to fight. This is where the watching creatures made their home.

Several holes burrowed deep into the Earth under the Arch. This creature passed by its more elite brethren, who stood watch at the entrances. They snarled in passing as the scout descending into the darkness of its home.

Through miles of winding tunnels and caverns, which were ever expanding, the creature passed by multiple Enforcers, giving orders to hundreds of the fiends. Unbeknownst to it, most nests were led by just one of the larger, but slower, Enforcers. This nest was special, however.

It ran into a large cavern, at this point underneath the Mississippi River, where several Enforcers stood guard where their leader laid. One of these gargantuan monsters was scarred with myriads signs of battle. In a reverence only seen in subjects of the Middle Ages, the creature bowed before the thing that even dwarfed the Enforcers.

It then relayed information about the cloaked ones. These dangerous humans, whom they could not track with their normal way of marking, had already destroyed a nest. And they were traveling closer to the Arch.

A clawed hand, as large as the creature's torso, stretched out from the darkness and touched the creature on the head, gently. It purred as it did not previously know if it would be reprimanded or praised based on the information.

It left the chamber, knowing its Queen was pleased.

Logan awoke before anyone else, having to take a piss. The sun was just barely beginning to filter in through the small windows. When he stood, the tingling he felt in his toes was gone. In fact, all feeling in a few of his toes was altogether gone. He tried wiggling them, but a few did not move.

He moved into the light of one of the windows and sat in a side-by-side. He removed his boot and sock. Two of his middle toes were white. He poked one and it was hard to the touch, but he did not feel it. The skin bulged up where he pressed his finger.

He knew something was wrong, but didn't understand exactly what. He put his sock and boot back on and went outside to urinate, making sure his dirtied and cut up cloak was pulled tight around him. Partially to keep himself from being marked, but also because the morning air was chilling him to the bone.

As he relieved himself, he heard a skittering down the road. He squinted to try to get a good look, but the area had not yet flooded with the sun's glory. He kept a mental note of it and turned to go back into the motorsports store.

A squawk above him scared him out of his skin. He looked up at the edge of the flat-roofed building to see Habrok feasting on a mouse. Logan said, "Jesus, Habrok. I'm not used to seeing animals around anymore. Glad you found something to eat."

The hawk chirped at him and fluttered its wings.

Logan said, "Your wing feeling better? Good. We'll be leaving soon, so eat up."

Logan entered back into the store, where his friends were starting to stir. Jon and Eve shared a morning kiss before searching for cans for a proper breakfast. Ironson had begun cleaning their modified shotguns, Jon's Winchester, and ARs with a rag, checking the chambers and making sure they were in working order.

Logan approached Eve and said, "Hey, can I show you something?"

"Better not be your dick," said Jon, smirking as he opened some cans of sweet corn with a knife.

Logan rolled his eyes and said, "No, it's my toes."

Jon raised an eyebrow and said, "You got some weird fetishes, man."

Eve smacked Jon in the chest and said, "Oh will you just shut up," she turned to Logan with a softer look and said, "What's up?"

Logan showed her his toes and she went into nurse mode. She looked all around his foot for a moment before saying, "They never got better? We have to warm your toes up, or you might lose them. I won't lie to you, though, it might be too late."

"I don't want to lose my toes," said Logan, looking down at his foot.

"If we get some warm water and you let them soak, they might be ok. Normally, I'd say not to walk on it for a day or so, but..." she looked over at Jon, who had been groaning, "We really do need to keep moving."

"It's fine," said Logan, "I'll get a fire going and-"

He was cut off by the sound of an engine outside. He pulled the 9mm Beretta from his tactical vest's holster and crept towards a window. Ironson had already loaded an AR and trained its sights on the door.

Logan peeked out and seen a group of people exit a heavily modified SUV. It was black with white skulls painted all over it. There were metal shutters on the windshield and windows. Spikes had been welded into every fender. The front bumper had an array of twisted barbed and razor wire.

The men themselves looked much like their vehicle. They were wearing hockey, or football masks and patched together metal and leather armor. As far as Logan could tell, there were six of them, and they were all armed with some kind of firearm.

Logan looked back at his friends, pointed at his eyes and held up six fingers before making the shape of a gun with his hand. This prompted them all to grab a weapon. Ironson and Eve kept an AR ready, while Jon grabbed his Winchester. Logan unsafetied his pistol and waited.

"Tell me again why we need a motorcycle?" said one of the post-apocalyptic looking men.

"Because, the Marauders are plannin' to go to Fort Bragg. It's safe there, yo," said another.

Another said, "Yeah, I'm tired of hiding out in the outskirts of the city."

"Well, let's get it then get goin'" said the first Marauder as they approached the door of the motorsports store.

Logan reached over to the door and locked the deadbolt right before one of the strangers tried to open it. The door didn't budge, so the Marauder shoulder checked it, but to no avail.

"It's fuckin' locked," he called back to his group.

"Well, bust it down, ya pussy," said another.

"No," said someone in a commanding voice who had just opened the driver side door of the SUV, "Wait."

The Marauders turned to the driver, who was much more armored than them. He looked like a modern day knight as he was covered from head to toe with segmented, plated armor, albeit somewhat rusted. Spikes were welded into his pauldrons and there were twenty hatch marks carved into his helm. Most likely they were kill counts, but for creatures or humans?

"You two," he said while pointing, "Go around the back."

"What's up, boss?" said a confused Marauder.

Logan could swear he had heard that voice before. The helmet muffled it but it sounded so familiar.

"Barging your way into every building without a plan is a good way to get your asses handed to you real quick. Especially with a store like this, someone might be using it as a shelter, or got the same idea we did," said the armored one.

Logan definitely recognized that voice. He turned to his friends again and said, "Do you all trust me?"

"What?" whispered Jon.

"You have to trust me on this," Logan whispered, holstering his 9mm.

"I trust you," said Ironson, "But I'm not putting my weapon away."

"Good, keep it trained on the door just in case," whispered Logan before taking in a huge breath.

He knocked on the window, causing the Marauders to turn with their weapons at the building.

The armored one put up his hand and said, "Wait," before stepping closer to the store in a fearless manner. He said through the window, "Someone in there?"

"Yes," said Logan, elevating his voice so he could be heard, "Tell me, what happened to the woman you were with?"

The armored one stood straight up as if he had been tazed and said, "Hold on a minute, who are you?"

"We met before, and I let you live. Will you show myself and mine the same courtesy I showed you?" said Logan.

The armored one shook his head and chuckled. He said,

"You mean the same courtesy you showed Del? Macon? Screwball?"

One of the other Marauders said, "Holy shit, Mann, is that the guy?"

"What guy?" said someone else.

"This dude went all assassin on some cons that Mann was with, but he let him go."

"Sounds like we need to take care of him, then," said a gung-ho Marauder.

Mann raised an armored hand and said, "Don't even think about it. The only reason we're still standing here is because he is letting us. Keep your g'damn weapons down," he turned back to the window, "Ok, you let me go and I owe you for that. So you have my word that we will not harm you."

Logan said, "And you have my word that we will not harm you, so long as your friends stay cool."

"I'll kill 'em myself if they try anything," said Mann. He took his helmet off, revealing his intense gaze and bald head. An eye patch covered his left eye.

"What the fuck just happened?" said Jon.

"He's the guy that Logan took the antibiotics from when you were dying," said Eve.

"The con?" said Jon, scrunching his nose in anger, "I've seen plenty of 'em to know you can't trust 'em."

"Keep your weapons ready, but don't do anything stupid,"

361

said Logan, "Let's get our stuff ready and go out there."

"I hope you're right about this," said Ironson with a worried look, "We're walking through a choke point with a well-armed contingent on the other side."

"I'll go first if it makes you feel any better," said Logan.

"You comin' out or what?" Mann said from outside.

The group got their packs and weapons together and lined up single file at the door. Logan unlocked the deadbolt and opened the door. As he exited the motorsports store, the other Marauders silently took him in.

"Never got your name," said Mann, extending a hand out.

Logan cautiously grasped hands with him and said, "I'm Logan Foster."

They shook hands as Mann said, "Lance Mann."

"What's up with the knight in shiny armor get up?" Jon asked, sarcastically.

Mann smirked and said, "This armor has saved my life more than once. You all look like a tough group. Why don't you join us? We're heading to Fort Bragg. Apparently it's safe there. They have a community and everything."

"Thanks for the offer, but we have our own road," said Logan, "Do you know anything about St. Louis or Chesterfield?"

Mann's face went from friendly to grim and he said, "I know that it's suicide to go any closer to the city than we are now. The hunters there are...strange."

"Strange, how?" said Logan.

Mann explained, "Normally the hunters will track you during the day and hunt you at night, right? I'm sure you know that g'damn much since you're all still alive. These ones though. They'll watch you for days and never attack. Instead you'll wake up one day and find someone missing. No blood, no sign of a struggle. They're just gone."

"That's creepy," said Eve, who got chills in the already chilly weather.

"These ones are smart," Mann continued, "They don't howl like the others. Instead it sounds like..."

He trailed off, which prompted Logan to say, "Sounds like what?"

"It's ok boss, we've heard them too," said one of the Marauders.

Mann looked Logan square in the eyes and said, "They talk to each other. Can't understand them, but they...they talk to each other."

Jon started to laugh, thinking it was some kind of weird joke. However, he noticed he was the only one laughing, so he stopped and said, "Are you serious? They use actual language?"

Mann nodded and said, "I'm dead fucking serious. How fucking creepy is it to walk around during the day and hear something that sounds like people talking in a foreign language just one or two houses over. You go to investigate and don't see a g'damn thing. You only hear the talking a few more houses down again. You look back to say something to your friend, but they're gone. Taken."

Logan and company exchanged uneasy looks before he addressed Mann again, "We're going to Chesterfield to check to see if Eve's parents are still there. Then we're going back home to Illinois."

"You're as good as dead, then," said Mann with no emotion, "You asked how that woman was, right?"

"I did," said Logan, raising an eyebrow.

Man raised his arms in a shrug, clanking the metal of his armor together, and said, "Couldn't tell ya, because she was taken by those g'damn, creepy-ass, fucking hunters. She's probably dead."

"I have to know," said Eve, "We've all lost so much, I just need to know if my parents are safe or...or not."

Mann sighed and looked Logan's group up and down. Before it was too awkward of a silence, he looked at Logan and said, "Well, if I'm not a g'damn sucker for family reunions. I'll take you to Chesterfield, but I'm not going through St. Louis."

"You loco, boss?" said a random Marauder.

"Probably," Mann said while scratching his bald head, "Deacon, you and Miles come with me. The rest of you stay here and get as many vehicles going as you can with what fuel we have."

Lance Mann re-equipped his helm and said, "After this, you'll owe me one instead."

"Deal," said Logan.

Chapter 35 – Chesterfield

Taking the most ideal route from Arnold to Chesterfield would have been a half hour drive. Mann was not going close to the city if he could help it, however, so he took a more roundabout way to their destination. This way was more scenic as they could see the rocky hills that they were used to as they drove on Route 141 towards Fenton.

Logan sat in the front while Mann drove the customized SUV. Jon and Eve sat in bucket seats behind them, while Ironson, Deacon and Miles sat in the very back. Logan had noticed that Habrok was flying around the SUV, keeping up with them. He was glad the hawk had full use of her wings back.

"What happened after the last time we met?" Logan asked.

Mann responded, "More like, what didn't happen. After you left Elaine and I, I spent a little while shitting myself, thinking you were gonna come back and finish what you started. Those idiots deserved what they got, by the way. Poor Elaine, though...

"Anyways, we wandered for a few days until we fell in with the self proclaimed Marauders. Their previous leader tried to kill me, but all he got was my eye. It was tribal-like shit, Logan. I killed their leader and they started to follow me. Gotta earn alpha status. I didn't want to be a leader but turns out I'm damn good at it."

"You sure are, boss!" said Miles from the back.

Mann shook his head and said, "Stop kissing my ass, already. Jesus."

"How'd you get that armor?" Logan asked.

"It was their last leader's, but I welded the spikes into it and segmented parts so I could move easier in it," Mann said, keeping his eyes on the road.

"Where'd you learn to weld?" said an untrusting Jon, "At the prison work camp?"

Mann flashed a look in the rear view mirror at Jon before saying, "I used to be a union welder before I went to the pen."

"What were you in for, anyways?" Jon asked.

Mann winced at the question but answered all the same, "Murder. And that's all I'm gonna say about that part."

"Jon, be nice, he's taking me to my parents house. I don't want to be dropped off the side of the road," said Eve with a stern

366

look at her fiancé.

"Fine, fine," said Jon, but keeping his eyes on Mann and the Marauders in the back.

Ironson leaned in from the back and asked, "Has anyone heard anything about MEPS?"

Mann said, "There were some military types holed up there for a while. The Marauders told me they even spoke to them on the radio, but eventually the calls stopped."

Deacon pushed up his hockey goalie helmet and said, "They either left or they were overrun. Had a cousin that was there. Was going to go stay there with him but he said it was too dangerous to go into the city. Who knows what happened."

Ironson flopped back into the seat, looking defeated, and said, "Roger that."

Mann asked, "So what's up with the cloaks besides to look like some kinda fantasy group?"

"They keep the creatures from marking us. I put some metal plating into them to stop small caliber bullets, too," said Logan.

Mann nodded and said, "Impressive. How'd you figure out how to counter the creature marks?"

"We didn't exactly figure it out ourselves. Another group did that we ran across," said Logan, not wanting to go into too much detail about the cannibals.

"Well, you're here and they aren't, so I'd take credit for it if I were you," said Mann, "I'd check your weapons now, we'll be going through Fenton and Manchester before we get to Chesterfield."

The rocky hills gave way to a flatter region as they drove by a shopping center just outside Fenton. There were dozens of abandoned stores and restaurants that they paid little heed to as they sped past them. The highway then cut through a residential area, some of which was hidden behind a wall with vines growing all over it.

This region was different than further south, in that towns and cities were nestled right next to each other rather than being miles apart. It was a reminder that they were close to St. Louis, as tens of thousands of people used to live in this area.

141 passed through Fenton and into Twin Oaks, a smaller city compared to its neighbors. They were heading north at this point as the highway cut into Manchester, again mainly residential areas in this area.

Mann slowed down as they were nearing the border of Manchester and Chesterfield. He looked at Eve in his rearview mirror and asked, "Where abouts is your parents' house?"

Eve, who had been chewing on her finger nails the last few miles, looked up as if she had just been shaken awake. She said, "They live on Brook Hill Drive, just off of Schoettler Road."

"You're going to have to direct me, not sure where that's at," said Mann.

"If you make a left on Milldale Drive, I can guide you there. It should be just up here," said Eve, looking around at her surroundings.

It had been a while since Eve and Jon had last visited this area, but she knew exactly where she was. She lived in Chesterfield when she was younger, before moving to Arborsville to attend a smaller university when she decided to go into the medical field.

Mann turned onto Hilldale Drive and Eve guided him through the maze of suburbs. This area was not designed in a grid, like in a smaller city. Instead roads snaked around each other and sometimes ended in a cul-de-sac. If it wasn't for Eve, they would have gotten lost.

The houses there were nice, or at least they used to be. They mainly consisted of brick homes with small front yards and large back yards. Expensive looking vehicles were parked outside some of the homes, while others were boarded up when people tried to hold out in the beginning of the collapse.

Eve told Mann when to turn left or right and they found themselves on Schoettler Road. Her directions became more hurried the closer to her childhood home they got. They turned onto Brook Hill Drive and Eve guided Mann down a cul-de-sac that had five homes around it. All five houses were two story and made of brick. The house Eve pointed to was the very middle one.

Mann drove around the circular drive and parked the SUV in front of the house Eve said was hers. Before he had even come to a complete stop, Eve was opening the door and running towards her house.

"Eve, wait!" Jon shouted, following her.

"Should we go with them?" Mann asked.

Logan said, "Let them be. If there's trouble, we'll hear it."

Eve ran up to the dark stained, wood door. A claw mark in the form of three jagged lines was scratched across the expensive entrance.

Eve's heart was racing as she shouted, "Mom? Dad?"

There was no response so she pushed open the door. It fell off its top hinges, slamming into her. Jon pushed the door off her and said, "Be careful, ok?"

She barely noticed as she walked into the living room. There was Mom and Dad's couch that they had since she was a kid. The TV was new, though. Empty tin cans and blankets were on the hardwood floor.

"Mom?" shouted Eve once again, her voice beginning to tremble as she investigated the house. Jon followed behind her, quietly.

They swept the kitchen, den, bathroom and downstairs bedroom. They headed upstairs where there was a half-bath, another bedroom and a master bedroom. All along the walls and floors, there were claw marks and punctures. At the end of the upstairs hallway was a pull-down staircase that led to the attic.

"They have to be up there," Eve said as she started to climb the attic stairs.

Jon put a hand on her arm to stop her and said, "Do you want me to go up first, babe?"

Eve hesitated for a moment before simply saying, "No."

She climbed into the attic and Jon followed behind her. Boxes of her childhood toys were scattered around and in disarray. She recognized a teddy bear she used to have to sleep with every night. Cobwebs were everywhere, but she ignored them as she searched.

Then she found them.

For Eve, time froze as she looked down at her parent's decaying bodies. They were huddled together and their skin was stretched taught against their skeletons. Even through the completely decayed skin, Eve could tell they had slash marks on their torsos. Her father's skull was caved in where a claw had punctured it. The circular, attic window above them was broken, where their fiendish attacker had most likely left through.

Jon said nothing as he gently put his arm around Eve's waist. She didn't move or flinch as tears fell down her face.

Everyone else had exited the SUV, but stayed outside while they waited. Ten minutes had gone by since Jon and Eve entered the house. Deacon and Miles were looking around at the other houses while Mann paced around. His armor clanked each time he turned around. Logan leaned against the mail box alongside the road with his arms folded. Ironson walked along the cul-de-sac with his AR drawn, searching for threats.

"What's taking so damn long," said Mann, "They should have found something by now."

"Patience, sir knight," said Logan in a fake, noble voice.

"Hardy fuckin' har," said Mann before continuing his pacing.

The engaged couple emerged from the house, their faces distant. Eve was wiping her eyes. Logan knew immediately that the news would be bad. Seeing the girl he considered a sister looking so distraught hurt him. He had met her parents a few times and they seemed decent people. It made him wonder if he would find his family the same way.

Mann said, impatiently, "Well?"

Eve said nothing as she walked up to the SUV, sat in her seat and closed the door.

Jon walked up to Mann and said, "What do you think?" before taking his own seat and holding Eve's hand.

Logan approached Mann and said, "Give her some time."

"How much g'damn time is she going to need?" asked Mann, impatiently.

Logan furrowed his brow and said, "As long as she needs."

"I need to get back with the others sometime, ya know," Mann said, "I'll give her a few minutes, but I'll need to get going soon."

As they fell silent, Logan heard whispers. He looked around and thought he almost seen something looking at him from behind a house, but it disappeared as soon as he looked.

"You hear that?" Logan asked.

Mann nodded and stayed still.

Ironson, who was in the middle of the cul-de-sac, heard the whispers as well. He backed towards the SUV while trying to find where the sounds were coming from. It sounded like it was all around them.

Mann said, "Where are Deacon and Miles?"

Logan looked at the other houses where he had last seen them, but found no trace of them. He said, "Taken?"

"Shit, we gotta go," said Mann before rushing towards the SUV. Logan and Ironson did the same. They clambered in and shut the doors.

Mann started the SUV and swung it around the cul-de-sac and back onto the road. He raced down Schoettler Road and went back whence they came. When he reached 141, he laid on the brakes, causing everyone to jerk forward.

"What the hell?" asked Jon, who had been comforting Eve.

Mann said nothing, but looked at the highway in the direction he was about to go. Logan too was looking there, unblinking. Jon looked out his window and seen what they were looking at.

Hundreds of creatures blocked the road southwards. They weren't snarling like their more rabid brethren that Logan and company had grown used to. They stood unmoving, as if they had been disciplined. Two Enforcers stood before the army, towering over everything. One held Deacon in its arms, and the other held Miles. The two Marauders squirmed futilely as one of the Enforcers' arms was as long as they were tall.

As the survivors watched on, the two Enforcers held the Marauders out by their waists. Simultaneously, they effortlessly ripped the two men in half. They screamed in pain for a moment before falling limp as their guts fell onto the pavement.

"Go north," said Logan without looking away from the scene.

"What the hell are those..." said Mann.

"Enforcers," explained Logan, "They lead the other burrowers. Go north."

"They just...ripped them..." said Mann, stunned at what he just seen.

"Go fucking NORTH!" Jon screamed at the ex-con.

Mann blinked back to reality and turned the SUV north up 141. The Enforcers didn't move save for pointing at the vehicle with razor-tipped claws. The burrowers started sprinting on all fours after them.

Ironson looked out the back window. Even with Mann pressing the peddle to the floor, the creatures were gaining on them. The pilot shouted up to the front, "Can this thing go any faster?"

"I'm pushing her as fast as I g'damn can," said Mann, focusing on driving and avoiding the odd, abandoned vehicle.

Ironson used the butt of his AR and smashed the back

window, which was still covered by metal shutters. He poked the barrel of his firearm through these shutters and opened fire.

Chapter 36 - Mann on the Run

Jon and Logan had joined Ironson in opening fire against their pursuers. They used ammo as sparingly as possible, only firing their weapons when a creature ran too close to the SUV. Eve looked comatose, staring at the back of the driver seat.

Mann sped up 141, nearing 100 miles per hour. The creatures kept up with them, but the Enforcers were nowhere to be seen.

Mann said, "Logan, there's a walkie talkie in the glovebox, grab it."

Logan set his AR on his lap and opened the glovebox. Sure enough, there was a walkie talkie in it. Mann held his armored hand out and took it. He powered it on, switched it to a different channel, then took his helmet off.

"This is Lance Mann, calling out to all Marauders," he said through the walkie talkie, "We are being chased up Route 141."

The walkie talkie chirped, "*Why are you so close to St. Louis!? You're crazy, dude.*"

"Thank you Captain Obvious. I need help. A distraction, anything."

Another voice said through the walkie talkie, "*We can rendezvous with you, maybe further east?*"

The SUV was coming up on the 141 and 64 junction. Up on the overpass were more creatures waiting for them, complete with an Enforcer behind them. They began leaping off the overpass onto the road in front of the vehicle.

Mann slowed as much as he could, as he was going at such a speed, and sped onto the on-ramp eastwards. The SUV nearly tipped as he curved around the narrow road. The two groups of creatures joined together into a larger group as they chased them eastbound.

"I'm on 64 now, how far east can you meet me?" Mann said through the walkie talkie.

After a moment, the walkie talkie chirped up again, "*We can meet you in Brentwood in twenty minutes.*"

"*Yeah, Brentwood will do, but that's so close to St. Louis...*"

"*It's the boss, we gotta help him!*"

Mann said, "The way I'm driving I'll be there before twenty minutes. Every Marauder that's not a pussy, meet me there and get ready for a fight!"

"*I'm ready for a fight, my group is ready.*"

"*I... I guess so, we'll be there.*"

"*We'll be armed and ready by the time you get there, but I hope you know what you're doing.*"

Logan had been listening to the conversation in between popping off shots at the creatures. He turned to Mann and asked, "How many of there are you?"

Mann smirked at him and said, "A lot. Pretty much everyone in this area who survived is a Marauder. We're all over St. Louis County, except for in the city of course. We can't take this many of those fucking things though. There's hundreds of 'em behind us, now."

"Sorry to get you caught up in this," said Logan.

Mann shrugged and said, "This was inevitable. We were testing fate by staying this close to the city. At least we'll go out with a bang, eh?"

Logan responded, "Hopefully we don't go out at all..."

Eve came back to reality, her fists balled up and shaking. She was murmuring something, but Jon couldn't quite understand what she said. He brought his Winchester back inside to reload it and said, "What's up, babe?"

She turned to her fiancé and gave him a fiery look. Through the cuts and scars on her once beautiful face shown a deep and angry determination. She said, "I'm going to kill every fucking one of them."

"That's my girl," said Jon, turning back to his window to look for threats.

Eve rolled her window down and began firing an AR through the metal shutters at creatures that were unfortunate enough to feel her wrath.

For the most part, they were only managing to wound the creatures. Ones that ran too close to the SUV were met with a shotgun slug or bullet. Some were critical hits, mainly by Ironson, making the creatures go head over heels as they were running at an incredible speed. Others were only slowed down and they would back off, only to be replaced by another.

As the SUV approached Frontenac, the walkie talkie chirped again, "*Lance, we see you. Get ready for a bang!*"

"That was Brent," Mann said, "If he's talking about what I think he's talking about, it'll be a huge fucking help."

They were driving through the 64-270 junction when a semi, complete with a trailer, drove up next to them from an on-ramp. It had creatures chasing it as well, but not nearly as many. The semi-truck was spiked up like the SUV and had a large scoop on its front bumper. Its trailer had openings on each side, much like an eighteenth century battleship. In these openings were men and women firing at the creatures with turreted machine guns.

"Holy shit," said Jon, who was on the side where the semi drove next to them, "It's like something from a freaking movie."

"That's Brent for ya. He had been working on that thing since everything first went down," said Mann.

A Marauder pointed an RPG out of one of the trailer openings and fired it behind Mann's SUV. The rocket hit the dense group of creatures and exploded. Their limbs flew every direction, mixed with the road's asphalt and black goo. The opening was quickly filled with more creatures, but they were being riddled with the mounted guns.

"How'd you find all that firepower?" Ironson called back after the rocket blast.

Mann said back to the pilot, "There were a few places where the military battled the monsters. There was shit laying everywhere. Machine guns, grenades, RPGs, you name it. Not that much ammo leftover from their fights, but still enough to help us."

"*Boss, we're in trouble! We aren't going to make it to Bre-*" a voice screamed over the walkie talkie.

Mann frowned and said, "We're already losing some of my people."

"What's our endgame here?" Logan asked, trying to figure out a way to get out of their predicament, "You said going into the city is suicide, but we're going straight there."

Mann said, "We can't slow down. If we do, we die. So right now our best bet is to cut right through the city and hope 64 isn't blocked. We're going to the g'damn river and hopefully enough Marauders meet us at Brentwood to help keep the creatures at bay until we cross."

Up ahead and on their left-hand side they seen taller buildings past some blocking trees. It was the St. Louis Galleria and Clayton was past it, further north. Logan knew they were passing through Brentwood at that point.

Half a dozen Marauders on motorcycles joined Mann and the semi from an off-road. They had sidecars where people fired their automatic weapons from. They were faster than the SUV and semi, and more maneuverable. They dipped in and around the two larger vehicles, providing covering fire towards any creatures that got too close.

Mann pumped his fist and said, "That's Sherry's group. Now that's a woman, I'll tell ya."

On an overpass that they were about to pass under, were several cars parked alongside the road. Marauders were standing at the edges with recoilless guns. They fired them behind the convoy, eliminating any creatures that were caught in the blast. Craters and creature body parts remained in the road as the dust lifted.

They got back in their cars as the convoy passed beneath them, but they were swarmed by a fresh set of creatures. They were ripped out from their vehicles and, although they put up a fight, they were savagely torn apart and eaten. This new group of creatures jumped off the overpass and joined the horde after they were done feasting.

"Godspeed," Mann said upon seeing his Marauders die in the side mirror, "And thank you."

The convoy drove on, but the gunfire lessened. Everyone was running out of ammunition. There were so many creatures following the vehicles that it didn't even seem like they made a dent. Even the machine gun fire from the semi and small arms from the motorcycles had all but ceased.

Ironson flopped down in his seat and said, "I'm out."

"Me too," said Jon, dropping his Winchester and AR down at his feet.

"I've only got a few left," Eve said, checking her weapon's magazine.

"Same," said Logan.

"All we can do is run, now," said Mann, before picking up his walkie talkie, "Any Marauders out there who are not with me right now, stay away from the city. Get out and get safe. I'm going to the river."

"Stay safe, boss."

"We'll meet you on the other side, if we can."

They passed by the St. Louis Zoo, then the Science Center. It was devoid of life, save for another horde of creatures that emerged from it as the convoy drove by. Their numbers seemed endless.

They could finally see St. Louis's skyline on the horizon. The buildings rose out of the ground, lasting reminders of humanity's once great empire on the Earth. Beyond the buildings the Arch could be seen. Logan was beginning to feel hopeful that they might actually make it, even if they had no more ammo.

The natural world of Missouri was past, as the group were in the concrete jungle of the city. Roads twisted above and below them as they drove onwards. Multiple story apartment buildings rose on each side of them, along with multitudes of long closed businesses.

The further into the city they drove, the more dense the abandoned vehicles were. The Marauders on motorcycles had no troubles navigating the mazes of cars, trucks and semis, but Mann had to let Brent and his semi go in front of them. He used the semi's front scoop to plow his way through any vehicles in the center lane. It slowed them down, but fortunately it also slowed the creatures down as well. They had to run around or clamber over these vehicles.

They began passing through Midtown. Union Station loomed off to their left. Next to it was Enterprise Center. Then they drove by what was once their destination. St. Louis MEPS. It was a brick building, just over ten stories tall, nestled between the Red Lion Hotel and an office building.

As they passed by, Ironson looked at it and noticed many of its windows were busted out. Long dead bodies hung out of it or laid inside its dark interior. He said, "So much for going to MEPS."

Jon looked back at him and said, "Yeah, I think that ship has sailed."

The convoy passed by MEPS and several other buildings when they heard a loud screech. Logan looked up and seen Habrok flying high in the sky. She screech again and again.

Then they heard a much louder call. Like a banshee, something wailed. Logan had to cover his ears that were already hurting from all the gunfire.

As they were about to pass by Busch Stadium, the road in front of them looked like it had been hit by a large explosion, as rubble and asphalt exploded into chunks. A few Marauders on motorcycles got caught in the blast and were sent flying over the side rails of the road.

The convoy had no choice but to hit the brakes.

The creatures behind them also came to a halt, standing like soldiers at attention.

A head poked out of where the road used to lead to. It was huge, larger than an Enforcer's. It looked like a female's head, with smooth skin segmented like armored plating. She had a mohawk, much like the other creatures, that sat on top of her head. Horns grew from just behind her red, pupiless eyes, giving a look like she had a crown.

She scowled and wailed again before jumping all the way up onto the elevated road. Her figure was slimmer than the Enforcers, very feminine for a creature. Yet still, she stood over two stories tall. If it wasn't for her skin looking armored, she would've looked more human than any of the other fiends the group had seen up until now.

"What the fuck is that!?" Mann shouted.

Logan couldn't answer, as he had no clue. He could only look on as this new threat bent down and picked up the front of the SUV

384

as if it were a toy. She brought it up to her face and she peered in through the shuttered windshield.

She wailed again and pushed the SUV towards Busch Stadium. She flipped it over the guard rail, sending it crashing into one of the long, outer windows of the stadium.

Chapter 37 - Pugna Autem Gladiatores

Habrok soared through the sky, observing what had just transpired. The people who had fed her were out of sight, after being tossed like a toy into the side of the stadium. The semi was making a good go of it trying to escape, but it was swarmed.

The hawk seen thousands of creatures crawling into and on Busch Stadium. The bigger one, the Queen, had hopped off the elevated road and was making her way around the side of the stadium.

The creatures were up to something, but all Habrok wanted to know was where her friend was.

Logan opened his eyes. His head was ringing and he could feel blood dripping down the side of his face. His left arm felt like it had been twisted like a drill and he couldn't feel some of his toes.

He looked from side to side and only then noticed the SUV was sideways. Mann was gone. Eve and Jon were in a heap, laying on a door. They weren't moving. Ironson was stirring, but he had hit his head as well.

Still in a daze, Logan said, "J-Joseph?"

Ironson looked over at him, one of his eyes was closed and covered in blood. He said, "You ok?"

"Not really," said Logan, who stumbled around to find his feet.

Even though he felt as though he would pass out, he crawled over the seat to check on his friends. He rolled Eve over off of Jon. Her forearm was bent at a ninety-degree angle, but she was breathing.

"We have to get them out of here," Logan said.

"You get Eve, I'll grab Kilroy," Ironson said, brushing the blood off his face with his cloak.

It took a few minutes, even with the wailing of the approaching Queen putting them on edge, but they managed to drag Jon and Eve out of the SUV. Jon had a bruise forming on his face and his eye was swollen from an impact.

The large man awoke in a violent shake, as if he had been

woken from a bad dream. He looked around for a moment before holding his head and growling. He glanced over to Eve with his good eye and said, "Is she..."

"She's breathing," Logan said as his dizziness slowly faded, "But her arm is broken."

"Where's the con?"

"No idea, he was already gone when I got up," said Logan looking around for a way to escape.

They were on a second story walkway. The large area below them was filled with abandoned tents, sleeping bags and trash. Various baseball memorabilia were scattered around. Logan deduced that this was once a sanctuary for hundreds of people, but they had all been taken, killed or forced to flee by this point.

The last time Logan visited Busch Stadium, he was with his grandfather and just a child. He always watched Cardinal games on television, but never managed to see a game live after his grandparents passed away. He never could have imagined he would come back under these circumstances.

"We were so close," Jon said as he checked on his fiancé.

Logan replied, solemnly, "I could see the bridge over the Mississippi."

The sounds of claws on brick put Ironson in go-mode. He said, "We need to move."

Like a reanimated marionette, Jon rose to his feet. He picked up Eve and threw her over his shoulder. They walked as fast as their injured bodies could take them. They passed by escalators and more makeshift living areas.

The sudden appearance of creatures down their pathway forced them to stop. They stood watching them, while also blocking their path. The injured group turned and seen more creatures up one of the escalators.

They had no choice but to go downstairs to the ground level. As they made their way down the staircase, Logan said, "I don't think we were being chased."

"What do you mean?" asked Ironson.

"They aren't attacking us, and they made few attempts to attack us on the road. I think we were funneled here to the stadium. To the large female burrower."

"But they were killing the Marauders?" questioned Jon as they got to the bottom of the staircase.

"Think about it," said Logan, "They can't mark us with our cloaks and these burrowers seem smarter than others we've run across. It's possible they're more curious than anything."

"Well they can take their curiosity some other damn place," growled Jon as they made their way through shredded tents on the main walkway.

They seen the multi-door entrance of the stadium. Its windows had long been busted out. More creatures watched them there. They were leaning towards each other, whispering their odd language. Behind them, they seen they were being followed by more creatures. Silently stepping behind them.

"They're boxing us in," said Ironson.

The group turned towards an entrance that led to seats just behind home plate. While inside this hallway, Eve groaned. Jon gently leaned her against the wall. As she regained consciousness, she yelped in pain and held her arm.

"Where are we?" asked Eve through gritted teeth.

"We're in Busch Stadium," Jon said, "Not exactly how I seen us coming back here, but here we are."

Eve grabbed her broken arm and said, "Y-You need to s-set my arm back in place."

Jon hesitantly grabbed her broken forearm and said, "It's gonna hurt like a bitch."

"I-it already hurts. Just do it," she stammered.

Jon took a deep breath and snapped the two pieces of her forearm back into place. Eve shrieked in pain as the bones were put back where they should be. Jon took a bandage roll from out of her first aid kit and wrapped her arm up tight. He then took off his belt and made a sling for her with it.

Logan could've sworn he heard laughter from him.

"You ok, babe?" Jon asked.

Tears were coming down Eve's face as she said, "No. My parents are dead and my arm is broken."

"I'm still here for you," said Jon, in an uncharacteristically soft tone.

"We all are," said Logan, bending down to his friend giving her a consoling look, "But right now we have to keep moving. Can you walk?"

"Think so," she said, rising to her feet and putting her injured hand into a strap on her tactical vest to give her arm more support.

The way they came was blocked by a whispering creature. The four friends walked out to the stadium proper. It was large enough to hold more than 45,000 people. There were no people in the seats at this time. Instead, they were filled with the creatures. There were thousands of them, watching the cloaked ones enter.

"This isn't good," said Ironson as the survivors looked around the stadium in awe.

The creatures following them were closer in the hallway, forcing the group to move on. To their left and right the creatures stood watching them in the premium seats. They were mere feet away from them, but didn't attack.

Logan led the group towards the field. It was unkempt and there were more tents along its edges. The dirt, which was normally even during games, was scattered around and only barely resembled the old diamond. Standing at the pitching mound was Mann, hunched over and holding his side.

All along the fencing were bodies propped or tied up. There were probably a couple hundred. Those who had been taken, perhaps?

The group crawled over the low fence behind home plate and

stepped onto the uncut grass. They walked over to Mann, who was rotating around, looking at the filled seats.

He noticed the four approaching them and said, "I always wanted to stand on the pitching mound."

"Can mark it off your bucket list, now," said Logan.

"Thanks for leaving us, by the way," said Jon, narrowing his eyes.

Mann shrugged and said, "Say what you will. Doesn't look like it fucking matters, now."

Logan heard Habrok screech from up above and seen her fly down to him. He stretched his arm out and she landed on him before fluttering to his shoulder. "Hello, again, friend," he said.

"What're they waiting for?" said Ironson, "We're defenseless."

His answer was the Queen's wail. She walked over the seats at left field. Her gate was confident and powerful. The creatures parted for her as she passed, looking as if they were bowing. Even from across the field, she looked gargantuan.

She stopped at the outfield wall and stretched her arms out. She wailed once more and the creatures all around the stadium began shouting. Not the two-tone howl that Logan and company were used to, but more like the sound of a crowd after the Cardinals had just scored a homerun.

From out of the sea of shouting creatures, an Enforcer stepped out near its Queen. It was the largest Logan had ever seen. It stood ten feet over the humans and had scars and old bullet wounds all over its body.

The Enforcer hopped onto the field and slammed the ground with its mighty fist, quaking the ground and shattering the earth under it. This sent the watching creatures into a frenzy. They hopped up and cheered.

The Queen stretched her arms out again. Everything went silent. She pointed at the humans, then at the Enforcer.

"What the fuck is going on?" Jon growled.

Logan responded, "I think she wants us to fight the Enforcer."

"What, are we some kind of gladiators for them?" said Jon.

"I think that's exactly what we are," said Logan, pulling his hunting knife out, "She wants to test us, I think. The bodies all along the field are probably those who failed the test."

"These burrowers are too smart," said Eve, "I think I prefer the crazy ones we fought before."

The Queen reached down and picked up something from behind the wall. She then threw the items at the humans. They rained down near second base, flipping around as they landed. They were various weapons, including a woodcutter's axe, a bolo longknife, a sledgehammer and a trench axe.

"We have to fight," said Logan.

Jon said, "Eve's got a broken arm. I can't see out of one fucking eye. You and Ironson look like your heads are leaking and

Mann is a pussy. How are we supposed to take that thing on?"

"Who're you calling a pussy?" said Mann, puffing his armored chest out.

"Oh don't even, con," said Jon, "Go practice falling down, I'll be there in a second."

"Stop," said Logan, turning to the group, "The only way we win is by working together. The Enforcers are too strong to brute force our way to a win, but they're not very quick. We can surround it, try to take out its legs."

"I unloaded I don't know how many bullets from that machine gun into one of those," said Eve, "And it only barely killed it. How are we going to kill one with knives and axes?"

The Queen wailed at the Enforcer, who stared to lumber towards the group, shaking the ground with each step. The stadium erupted into cheers and shouts from the surrounding creatures.

"We have to be smart and quick," said Ironson, who picked up the trench axe, "We have no other choice but to execute Logan's plan. Surround it, take out its legs."

Logan took the bolo longknife and grasped his hunting knife in his offhand. Mann took up the sledgehammer and Jon took the two-handed woodcutter's axe. Eve unpocketed the knife Logan had given her.

"Stay back, babe," said Jon, "I ain't gonna risk you getting more hurt than you are."

"I'm going to help where I can," she said, "But it won't be
394

much with this arm. I'll call out who it looks like he is about to attack."

"That'll help," said Logan, "Whoever has his attention should back up so the rest can attack. Rinse and repeat."

The Enforcer was nearly upon them. Ironson said, "Ok, spread out and get ready!"

None of them were able to move as quick as normal after the wreck, but adrenaline kept them alert. Jon and Mann flanked to the left while Logan and Ironson flanked right. They kept their distance, waiting for an opening. Habrok flew off Logan's shoulders and circled the fight, giving her an elevated view.

The Enforcer lunged towards Mann, who stumbled out of the way, narrowly dodging the crushing claw that flung up dirt and grass. From his knees, Mann brought the sledgehammer down on the Enforcer's hand. It growled but otherwise was unaffected.

Seeing an opportunity, Logan dashed forward as quick as his injured body could and swiped at the Enforcer's ankle with the bolo. It scratched the skin, barely a tickle.

"On you, Logan!" shouted Eve from the backlines, who was keeping a meticulous watch on the fight.

Logan ran back as the Enforcer turned towards him. This allowed Jon to hack away at the back of its legs, taking small chunks of skin out with each swipe. He backed away as Eve called to him.

Mann did not hear the call as he brought the sledgehammer down on the Enforcer's taloned foot. The blow broke one of the talons at its base, but the armored convict was not able to move away from the Enforcer's counter.

In a wide swing, the Enforcer slashed Mann's torso, ripping the breastplate off. The claws dug into his ribcage, splitting his chest open. The critical hit brought Mann to his knees as he clutched his chest.

Ironson and Logan furiously cut away at the back of the Enforcer's legs, but weren't able to distract the large beast. It hammer-fisted the top of Mann's head, flattening him out in the grass and breaking every bone in his body. The dooming hit rang out in a disgusting crunch.

The melee continued on as the watching creatures hollered in their unknown language, rooting for their champion. The Queen watched with an almost gleeful look on her face.

With Mann out of action, the others had to dodge and dive away from the Enforcer's attacks more quickly. Eve's calls were effective at giving the men instructions on where and when to move.

The Enforcer charged at Logan, who had just dodged away from an attack and was not fully on his feet yet. As the great monster growled at the cloaked man, it seen a fluttering in its vision. Habrok had descended and was pecking at its eye. Before the Enforcer could grab the hawk, she had already flew away.

Black stuff began oozing out of its eye socket. It closed its injured eye and looked back to where Logan was, but he was no longer there. All while Ironson and Jon were hacking at the back of its knees.

It turned towards the axe-wielders and swiped at them, narrowly missing Jon, but Ironson was hit in his side. The pilot was sent flying away from the battle, his cloak fluttering like a flag in the wind. He landed inside the dugout and out of view.

It kicked backwards at Logan, who was behind him slicing into tendons. Its foot hit the man's leg, sending him into a backwards somersault. Logan landed on his back with a shattered kneecap. It knocked the wind out of him and he couldn't move.

With everyone else knocked away or out of action, Jon stood as the sole fighter. The Enforcer looked down at him with a menacing look, flexing its muscles and acting like it was completely unaffected by all their attacks.

Jon used his fear to channel his anger. Logan laid behind the beast, unmoving. Damn these invaders for hurting his best friend and fiancé!

Jon unclasped his cloak in defiance and let it slide off his shoulders onto the ground. He shouted, "Come and get it, asshole!"

The Enforcer reached out towards Jon, who hacked downwards at the beast's wrist, cutting deeply. He ran off to the side as the Enforcer brought its other arm down at him. Jon deflected the blow with his woodcutter's axe, which splintered from the blow and sent him to the ground.

Eve ran up to help Jon to his feet, but she was knocked away with a backhanded strike from the creature. She tumbled towards third base, shouting in pain.

Seeing his fiancé get hit sent Jon into a berserker rage. He picked up the bladed part of the axe and charged at the Enforcer. He shouted, "DIE!" as he struck the Enforcer's knees over and over.

The beast scooped up the enraged man with both hands and held him out. Jon dropped the axe blade but hammered his fists into the Enforcer's claws. The thing seemed to chuckle as it began to slowly squeeze. Jon felt ribs break, pissing him off more than hurting him. Even so, he wasn't able to do anything but shout a barbaric yelp at his opponent.

The Enforcer's humored look on its face changed to pain as it gasped.

Jon looked down and seen Logan was on his feet and attacking the creature.

Logan's leg was useless, but he managed to leap up on his good foot and stabbed the bolo through skin and muscle. He stabbed higher with his hunting knife and began stabbing his way up the Enforcer's body.

Jon grabbed the Enforcer's wrists with both arms and squeezed them against his side as tight as he could. The Enforcer let go of Jon, but the man's grip was too tight to get its arms free. It pulled and tugged as Logan made his way up its torso.

The Enforcer dropped to its knees as black blood rushed down each of Logan's stab wounds. Jon felt his arm pop out from his shoulder socket as the Enforcer finally managed to rip one of its hands away.

It tugged at Logan's cloak, flinging it off him. Jon dropped down to the ground. His strength had run out as he tried to set his arm back into its socket.

Logan was face to face with the Enforcer, holding himself in place by the hunting knife that was plunged into its collar. The Enforcer narrowed its uninjured eye before Logan stabbed the bolo longknife into it. Like he was sawing into a log, Logan stabbed again and again. The blade ripped through the Enforcer's brain and scraped the inside of its skull.

The Enforcer fell down onto its back, not moving. The fall sent Logan rolling away into the grass.

All fell silent as the cheering creatures had just watched their champion fall to humans. Humans who were so easily killed and taken before.

The only creature that looked pleased was the Queen. The cloaked ones had passed her test.

Chapter 38 - Home

The adrenaline had faded, giving way to pain. Logan sat up in center field clutching his fractured knee. He looked around the stadium, looking at the creatures as they watched the three.

Jon's arm was limp at his side as Logan watched him stumble over to Eve. She was lying face first in the grass and Logan feared she was dead. Jon turned her over and she looked up at him.

"Did...we win?" she asked.

"Yeah, babe, I think we did," he said before kissing her.

One by one, the creatures departed. There were no more cheers, no more hollering. In an unprecedented, reverent respect for the cloaked ones, they left them alone. The only sound was the chilled wind rushing over the top of the stadium.

When they were all gone, only the Queen remained, who had locked eyes with Logan. She bowed to him and a smile formed on her hardened face. Logan would never know what that truly meant, but in that moment, he had an idea. They were free to go.

The Queen turned and left, leaving the survivors alone on the field.

Logan stood as best he could and limped his way over to the dugout that Ironson had been thrown to. As he approached he seen the pilot sitting on the bench, his arms splayed out as if he were dropped there.

Logan carefully climbed down the few stairs into the lowered area and said, "Joseph?"

The marine slowly turned his head towards Logan and said, "Dunno...how we...did it."

"Me neither, but I think they're going to let us go," said Logan, who sat down next to the pilot on the bench.

"Don't think...I'll be going anywhere," Ironson said, each word sounding more and more painful.

"I'll get-"

"Nah, its ok," said Ironson, waving off whatever Logan was going to say, "Just...sit with me a moment..."

Across the field, they heard Jon yelp in pain as Eve helped him reset his dislocated arm.

Logan said, "The difference between these burrowers and others we've faced is night and day. These ones seem...human."

"Yeah..."

"I'm glad we've made it this far."

"Logan?"

"Yeah?"

"What do you think is after this?"

Logan took a long breath, not expecting that kind of question. He said, "I really don't know. I was never the religious-type, but who is to say?"

Ironson looked out to the sky, moving his head was about the only thing his broken body was capable of. He said, "I really want to...see my wife and kid again."

Logan looked over at the Marine Corps pilot who had become a good friend on their trek. He looked up at the sky as well before saying, "You will. What's great about life is the journey, not the end. It's about the adventure. At least that's how I've always seen things.

"Why I think that is because everyone dies the same. Sure, some might die of unnatural causes before they're old, but we all die. Death is the most natural part of life because it's the one thing we all have in common, no matter who we are.

"After that is just another adventure. On that spiritual path set before you, you'll find your loved ones. We'll all find each other in what comes after. Whether we're ghosts or balls of energy, we all come back together in some form."

There was no response, so Logan looked back over to the pilot. His head was slumped down onto his chest and he was no longer breathing.

Logan stood up on his good leg and saluted Ironson. He said, "Goodbye, Lieutenant."

Eve and Jon had found their way to the dugout, using each other as support to help walk. Eve was crying and Jon looked as sad as his rough face could.

Jon said, "We had our differences, but I respected him."

402

"He was a good man," Eve said.

"Yeah, he was," said Logan, "He deserves a proper burial."

"Agreed, but don't think any of us have the energy," said Jon, "And who knows if those bastards will come back."

Logan didn't like it, but he knew they had to leave him. He laid the pilot down onto the bench and folded his arms on his chest. He then took his cloak and laid it over the body.

The three said a final farewell to the man who had helped them fight and survive through the whole ordeal before leaving Busch Stadium.

When the survivors made their way to the street outside of the stadium, they were met by silence and trash fluttering in the wind. Across the street was the large parking lot that would have been filled during games.

Eve did her best to patch up Logan's broken knee. She made a splint out of the broken woodcutter's axe to straighten his leg. He used a metal pole as a crutch to help him walk.

Jon had retrieved his Winchester and their modified shotguns from the SUV wreck. They had no more ammo, but these weapons were part of them now. They kept them slung on their backs over their cloaks, which were dirty and ripped all over.

They made their way up the ramp back onto I-64. They emerged onto the elevated road on the opposite side of where the Queen had broken it. Exhausted and broken, they limped towards the river.

On their left they could see the Arch and the holes underneath it that led down to the Queen's nest. To their right was MacArthur Bridge, a long truss bridge connecting the east side of the river to the west. Ahead of them was the Poplar Street Bridge.

For some reason, Logan's mind went back to his brother and the secret he had been keeping for so long. He had been through so much with Eve and Jon that now seemed as good a time as any to reveal his dark past to them.

As they began crossing the bridge between rows of abandoned vehicles, Logan said, "I want to tell you guys something I've long kept secret."

Jon and Eve looked over at him as he said, "My brother never went to prison like I said he did. I... killed him."

Jon said, "Yeah, I kinda knew that already."

"You did?"

"Well, not for sure, but I had an idea. There was a line of people that would have done the same, man. I know he was your brother, but he was a piece of shit."

Eve said, "If you would have told us before all this, I would have been shocked, maybe even called the cops on you. But everything is different now. With everything we've seen and been through, it doesn't surprise me that you killed him. I just hope you can keep that darkness suppressed going forward."

"I think I've found a balance. I'm sorry I kept it a secret, but the only person I ever told was that priest," said Logan.

Eve said, "You can trust us, Logan. We have to stick together and I'm here for anything you need."

Jon said, "Well, I hope not *anything*..."

"Oh shut up," said Eve with a grin.

Logan couldn't help but grin too, even after what they had just been through. He said, "Thanks, guys."

They finished the walk over the bridge, leaving Missouri behind. As they entered Illinois, there was a reinvigorated sense that their home was near. East St. Louis was still ahead of them and Logan had no idea if the Queen's nest extended in this direction, but they kept walking nonetheless.

Habrok flew above them. Logan was starting to get used to having her around. It made him feel safe.

The abandoned vehicles began to thin out as they approached a major junction where multiple major roads came together. Like spaghetti the roads merge into one another.

The three heard a voice say, "Hey!"

Up ahead they could see Brent's semi-truck. It was dented and slashed, but he somehow made it to where the Marauder's were rendezvousing on the Illinois side of the Mississippi River. There were a few other vehicles there, spray painted with skulls with spikes welded into the fenders. Dead creatures and a few dead Marauders laid all around the convoy.

They could see people waving at them. A man with a

trucker's ball cap stood on top of a SUV. As the three limped

towards him, he said, "Where's Mann?"

Logan said, "He didn't make it."

Most of the Marauders had their faces hidden by hockey or

other such masks, but Logan could tell the news hit them hard. They

bowed their heads as the man on the semi said, "Did he go out like a

badass?"

"He did," said Logan, "Are you Bert?"

"I am. Looks like you three could do with some patching

up."

"Got any food?" asked Jon, "I'm starving."

"Heh, yeah, come to the back of the truck," said Bert, "We

lost a lot of people in the city, why don't you join us?"

Logan, Eve and Jon made their way to the back of the semi.

Logan said, "Thanks, but we have our own road."

A female Marauder was in the back of the semi-trailer,

taking inventory of their food and weapon stocks. As the three

approached, she said, "Dunno what ya'll did, but one minute we're

being swarmed and the next they all just gon' up and left."

Logan said, "I think we're safe, for the moment anyways."

The Marauders were surprisingly well stocked in medical

supplies. They were even more surprisingly generous in letting the

three use them. They told Logan how word had gotten around about

how he had let Mann live, so they considered it an honor to help him out.

While Eve handed out pain meds and re-bandaged everyone, Logan filled the Marauders in as to what transpired at Busch Stadium and about the Queen. None of them had ever seen her and were shocked that such a creature existed.

They all ate together, canned meat and vegetables mainly, but they heated it with a fire. It felt like a feast as the three were near starving. As they all ate, Bert told them about their plan to go to Fort Bragg in North Carolina and how they had enough fuel reserves to make it there.

After a few hours, the three were able to manage their pain well enough to be able to go on their way. Bert once again asked them to join them, but they declined as they wanted to go to Arborsville.

Bert said, "Well, the least I can do is give you some food and a car."

"Why are you so keen on helping us?" Logan asked.

Bert said, "Our original leader was a real sum'bitch. He looted, raped and murdered. When Mann took over, he said we needed to band together. It's us versus those creatures, now. So even though you won't join us, I'll carry on his legacy by helping you out."

"Thank you for everything," said Eve, "We're pretty banged up."

Bert shook all their hands and said, "Hey, don't mention it.

Make sure to take a walkie talkie with you, never know when it'll come in handy. If you want, you can take the Camaro. It's a real gas guzzler and we need vehicles that'll hold more people. Tom, gimme the keys to the Camaro!"

A skinny Marauder walked up and said, "The Camaro? But I like that car..."

"Bah, you don't even know how to drive stick, gimme the keys," said Bert as the Marauder begrudgingly gave him the keys, "Well, it's about time we were on our way. Don't want to stay in one place for very long."

"Be safe on the road," said Jon, who took the keys.

"You too," said Bert before going back to his semi.

As the Marauders rolled out one by one, only one vehicle was left. A black, 1969 Camaro Z28. A white skull was painted on its hood and spikes were welded into its front bumper.

"Hell yeah," Jon said before he hopped into the driver seat.

Eve looked at Logan but didn't say anything.

Logan said, "Let me guess, you have automatic shotgun."

"Yup!" she said.

"Well, it's a two-door, so let me get in first," said Logan.

When they were all in, Jon started up the engine. With a raging roar, the engine came to life. It was a sound that only an old muscle car could make. Jon turned the car around eastbound and started driving.

The afternoon sun shone down with a warm glow as the three made the drive eastwards. They passed through East St. Louis and Collinsville, then Troy. Habrok followed them in the sky. As they were passing by Highland, they all became anxious.

Logan had been fiddling with the walkie talkie, switching between different channels. He was met with static on every channel, however, so he set it aside.

"What're we going to do when we get home?" asked Eve.

"First we're going to my house to see if my parents are there, then to Logan's parents," said Jon.

"I hope they're there," said Eve, who set her hand on her fiancé's, which was on the stick shift.

"Me too," said Jon.

Logan said nothing, but he hoped the same.

After another twenty minutes, they seen the exit for Arborsville. Jon drove the muscle car up the ramp onto Route 127. A sign on the side of the road said WELCOME TO ARBORSVILLE.

They instinctively kept their hoods up, as they had no idea about the creatures that prowled there, or if there even were creatures there. They passed by fast food restaurants and gas stations before driving into Arborsville's city limits.

"We're home," said Jon, "Can't believe I'm actually saying that."

Arborsville was a small, quiet town, but the lack of any traffic or people was unsettling. Even though they had grown used to it in other places, seeing it where they lived was a bummer.

Both Jon's and Logan's parents lived on the east side of town. They drove through residential areas before pulling up to a quaint, but by no means small, brick house. A mailbox sat in the yard in front of it, fallen over. It said KILROY RESIDENCE.

They exited the Camaro and limped up to the door, which was wide open. Jon said, "I'll go in alone."

"We'll be right here if you need us, babe," said Eve.

Jon disappeared inside the house. While he searched, Eve turned to Logan and said, "Can you believe that we made it?"

Logan thought back on everything that had happened and said, "I honestly can't. It feels like a year, but it's only been what, a few months?"

"Something like that."

"You seen any of the burrowers?" Logan asked, keeping his eyes on places that they could potentially be watched from.

"None," Eve said, shaking her head, "Think there are some here?"

"Probably," said Logan, "If they're like the normal ones, they're not as active during the day."

Jon came back out of his childhood home with a relieved look and said, "I didn't see anything in there. Maybe they got away?"

"That's good news," said Eve, hugging Jon, "I'm sure they got somewhere safe."

"Time to check on Logan's," said Jon.

410

They all got back into the muscle car and drove through more residential areas until they found the Foster residence. It was a two-story house with yellow siding and black window shutters. It sat atop a steep hill. Logan's grandfather had built it in the '50s and it had stayed in the family ever since.

Jon drove them up the gravel driveway and they parked behind the house. As they exited, he said, "You want to go in alone?"

Logan said, "No, I'd like you to come with me."

"Ok, man, we're with ya," said Jon.

They entered the house and searched all the rooms, upstairs and downstairs. The decor and furniture were still mainly left over from when it was Logan's grandparents who lived there. The home seemed untouched by time.

There were no signs of his parents, alive or otherwise. On the kitchen table was a note. Logan picked it up and read it:

Logan,

There's no way to tell if you'll ever be able to read this, but your mother insisted. A lot of us packed up and left for Michigan. We have friends up there, and they said they knew of somewhere safe before the phones crapped out on us.

Anyways, your mother and I love you. If you ever read this and get the chance, come find us at Port Austin.

- Your Father

"They're alive," said Eve, hugging Logan.

"I hope they made it," said Logan, who was glad he didn't find them no longer amongst the living.

"Well, let's get to the car and figure out what we do from here," said Jon.

They left the house and got back into the Camaro. Jon and Eve started talking about what to do next while Logan played with the walkie talkie again.

He turned it between channels, but stopped when he heard a voice. Eve and Jon stopped talking as they heard it too, turning around to look at Logan.

"*-bunker just outside of town. If you are able to contact me, my name is William Sauk. I send out calls once every few hours, so if you hear me, please answer. We're safe here and have food and water.*"

The three looked stunned at hearing the voice. Eve said, "What do you want to do?"

Jon said, "Well answer back. If there's survivors here we should meet up with them."

Logan held in the receiver and said, "We hear you."

"*Holy Hell, I actually got an answer! Hey Ed, there's people out there! What's your name, stranger?*"

Logan thought for a moment before saying, "Call me Omega."

Made in the USA
Monee, IL
28 July 2021